THE SECRET OF THE TWIN PARCHMENTS

THE GOLDEN ONE

B.A. Knight

Michael Terence Publishing

First published in paperback by
Michael Terence Publishing in 2019
www.mtp.agency

ISBN 9781913289638

*Dedicated to my sister, Raluca, who pushed the
right button to make me start writing…*

Contents

Chapter One

THE BEGINNING OF THE END

"Enough!" snapped Alia, slamming her book shut. She was tired of being a silent bystander as opposed to living the life of the heroes in her books. Books, those wonderful, wonderful gates to worlds that had ceased to exist, or never did, where she could encounter people long lost between the pages of history, visit times that once were real. Her sister was so different, she didn't mind not being a part of the adventure, of the extraordinary life she could live if she was somebody else, roaming a different world. Alia would have given anything to be able to take a journey in the magical world of books, her desert island, where everything was possible.

Alia was an orphan teenager living with her grandmother and her twin sister in a small village in the English countryside. They didn't have much, but Alia knew that it could have been much worse if they hadn't had their grandmother to look after them. Her twin sister, Deanna, was more pragmatic, but they were both very grateful to Nanna for keeping them out of foster homes.

As a child, Alia used to imagine their big old house as a fortress that protected them from dragons and witches and other mythical creatures, which haunted her book-nourished imagination. And in spite of that wonderful imagination, which would help her in many dangerous and extraordinary situations, she was incapable of remembering the faces of her parents or indeed any of the moments they spent together. It was as if all her memories had been wiped from her heart and mind, something which caused her great pain and many sleepless nights.

Alia and Deanna had lost their parents in a car accident, when they were only four. Thanks to Nanna they always felt that they were part of a loving family. They didn't remember much, but somehow they knew how to speak French fluently. Nanna didn't like to talk about it and the girls never tried to find out more, not because they weren't curious but they loved their grandmother too much to cause her the pain she obviously felt at the very mention of her daughter and her son-in-law.

All Alia knew was that at some stage in their lives, they had lived in France. Her grandmother wouldn't tell her any more than that, maybe because she wanted to protect the girls from some awful past. They were identical twins, but with such different personalities. Deanna, always so busy with her friends and fencing competitions, didn't have time to dream about all that. How could she not care? How could she go on with her life not knowing what had happened to their parents? However, Alia was unaware of the storm that was ravaging Deanna's heart. Deanna had a different character, stronger and more practical. She didn't like to waste hours with a book in her hands.

Alia always remembered a conversation she once had with her grandmother. It was the first and last time Nanna ever agreed to tell them something about their parents. With tears in her eyes, she told them how much they were wanted and loved, how gentle their mother was, how protective and fun their father used to be. She even sang them the lullaby their mother used to sing, when they were babies. It was about a hummingbird named Rainbow. Then their big brown eyes filled with tears and Nanna stopped. It was obviously too painful, for all three of them.

"What's enough?" asked Deanna, when she heard Alia talking to herself.

"Nothing, just day dreaming, as usual when I'm reading a good book," said Alia sighing.

"Yes, as usual," said Deanna, rolling her eyes. "Do you want to come with me? Some of my friends and I are going out on our rollerblades. Look, it's stopped raining."

"No, I don't feel like it. I want to finish my book," she said, reopening her book where she had left off.

"As you wish! You will grow roots on this bed," said her sister, leaving the room with her rollerblades slung over one shoulder.

Alia could never understand her sister's lack of interest in their past. There had to be more than Nanna was willing to admit. For instance, why didn't she, their grandmother, ever take them to see their parent's graves? It was as if she couldn't accept they were gone. She decided it was time to do some research on her own. In the age of information, when nobody could keep a secret, it was impossible not to find something. But where to start? She knew she had a better chance of finding something in France, because they had moved to England with their grandmother after the death of their parents. They must have been about four years old when it happened. She began searching for car accidents that had happened ten years ago. She found 4,275 deadly accidents but not one linked to her parent's name. They never knew why, but their grandmother had made them take her last name, Hammersmith. When her parents got married, her mother had changed her name to Brecourt. Realising she didn't have enough information to go on, Alia decided to try to steal some from Nanna.

Chapter Two

PANDORA'S BOX

Nanna was not at home but Alia knew it wouldn't be long before she got back, so she waited, trying to think of some strategy to get her grandmother into a sharing mood. Her waiting was interrupted by the doorbell. She looked out of the window to see the postman. He was a skinny old man, who could have retired many years ago but he loved his job and the human contact it brought him too much. Also, nobody in this little village had the heart to tell him he was too old. Everybody enjoyed his company and his stories and somehow, they all knew that if they forced him to retire, it would kill him. So Alia let him in without hesitation. She had all the time in the world to listen to his endless stories, of how his parents had escaped the Nazis when he was just a baby.

"Hello Mr Reynolds," shouted Alia, knowing that he was a little deaf.

"Hello my dear! How are you?" shouted Mr Reynolds in reply. Alia found it amazing that deaf people had to shout themselves, just because they couldn't hear others.

"I'm fine," she answered, politely. "Just waiting for my grandmother to come home."

"Oh, so she's not in?"

"I'm afraid not. Do you want to leave a message for her, or is it just to deliver our mail? I can give it to her if you want."

"I do have some mail for her, but I came mostly to tell her that the contract she had with the French post has expired," said the old man.

"What contract?" she asked.

"When you want your mail to be transferred automatically from one address to another, you need to pay the postal service to do that for you and also you must sign a contract, but you have to renew it every year."

"And where is this address in France?" she said, her interest suddenly firing up. She so wanted to find out something, anything, that she was afraid to ask the wrong questions.

"In Paris, of course! The apartment that your parents owned when they had you and your sister," he said without a moment's hesitation. Poor Mr Reynolds had no idea he was giving away information that Nanna had tried so hard to keep secret. By now it was too late and he didn't seem to mind talking to Alia, in fact he was ready to talk to anybody who was willing to have a conversation with him.

"You could just leave the contract here. I'll make sure my grandmother signs it and returns it to you as soon as possible," she said innocently.

"Sure, thank you, Alia! You are just as nice and thoughtful as your mother was, God rest her soul!"

"Thank you… wait! What? You knew my mother?"

She couldn't believe what she had just heard. But of course, how stupid of her not to realise – the postman would know everybody in such a small village. She always thought that her grandmother had started a new life here, in this tiny place in the back of beyond, but now it made sense, her grandmother had simply returned to her own home, after the tragic accident that took her daughter. Still, she found it hard to believe that her grandmother would want to live all her life in such a remote place. She was too active, too sophisticated, too fascinating to bury herself here. She was not like other grandmothers, she never knitted, she wouldn't sit by the fireside, telling them endless stories about how she met their grandfather. She was the one who taught them to fight back if a boy dared touch them. She insisted they took fencing lessons rather than classical ballet. She encouraged them to learn German and Italian. With her for a grandmother, the girls didn't know the meaning of boredom. So it came as something of a shock, to find that Nanna had a past in this village.

"Of course I knew your mother, she was my daughter's best friend," said Mr Reynolds smiling awkwardly, as if he had opened an uncomfortable subject. "Well, you could say so, but your mother was very shy. She didn't really bond with anybody here. It was as if she didn't feel part of the community, like she didn't quite belong here. My daughter Angela made friends easily and she managed to get inside Samantha's world, your mother."

"So she didn't have any other friends?"

"No, she was always looking for the next book to read. Just like you, actually. I can't even imagine what she found to write about in her diary, she never did anything exciting. She would just leave her house, go to school and come back again.

"She kept a diary?"

"Yes, I saw it when she came to our house, to do some homework with Angela. It fell out of her backpack and she panicked as if she had dropped a raw egg on the floor, as if she was afraid it might get hurt. But a piece of paper can't feel pain, can it? She never showed it to anybody, Angela told me once, not even to her."

"So how did she meet my father, if she was so solitary?"

"I don't know. She met him in London. I never saw her after that."

"She never came to visit Nanna?"

"No, but your grandmother also left soon after that."

"Where did she go?"

"I don't know, but we didn't see her again for almost ten years. We even thought she had abandoned the house. There were some estate agents once, who came looking for the owner."

"And what happened?"

"Nothing! Nobody dared touch the house, it was as if it was haunted or something. People came, they took pictures, looked around and left. One day I tried talking to a couple, as they were leaving."

"And?"

"They wouldn't even stop to talk to me. They looked as if they'd seen a ghost."

"What? But that's ridiculous! There's nothing wrong with our house!"

"I know! I never understood what happened. But I'm glad the house was left untouched. Because the day your grandmother came back with you, she certainly looked like she couldn't handle any more problems."

"I don't remember that day, I was too young."

"I remember it very well. I remember it as if it was yesterday. I was just leaving the Pattisons' house, when I saw your grandmother getting out of a taxi with two small girls in her arms. She looked very tired, I thought she was sick or something. You didn't even leave the house for a few days. Poor Gloria, I guess she was mourning her daughter."

"What happened after?"

"A few days later, I saw you at the market. Your grandmother looked better, but she wouldn't let go of your hands, as if she was afraid that you would disappear into thin air. This is a small village, everybody knows everybody. Children can run around freely. She was so strict with you two at the beginning! But then you started school and everything went back to normal."

"Didn't she ever tell you where she had been all those years?"

"Nooo, she never told anyone, even her closest friends, if you could call them that. After she came back, I don't remember ever seeing her laugh. Her only moments of happiness were when she was with you."

"Do you know what happened to my parents?"

"No, sorry, all I heard was that there was a car crash. I always found that a bit strange, because your mother was an excellent driver. I always trusted her when she was going out with Angela."

"Do you know where my mother went to school after she left home?"

"Of course, she used to write to your grandmother twice a week, well she did for a while and then she stopped. I thought with all the modern means of communication she had abandoned letters, like everybody else. And then, one day I found a letter, but it was a letter like no other she had ever sent…"

He didn't have time to finish the sentence because Nanna walked in and slammed the door so loudly, that both Alia and Mr Reynolds jumped off their chairs. They had been so caught up in their story, that had forgotten why they were there.

"Oh, hello Mr Reynolds," said Nanna, smiling politely. "And how are you today?"

"I'm fine, Mrs Hammersmith, and you?"

"Excellent, thank you! Everything looks much better when the sun is shining after all that rain."

"Quite right! I'm always grateful when I don't have to run from house to house to deliver the mail, just to dodge the rain!"

"Did Alia at least offer you any tea? Coffee?"

"No, but I wouldn't mind an Earl Grey, thank you. I was just telling her how much she looked like her mother."

"Yes, she does. Would you like a biscuit with your tea, Mr Reynolds?" she said swiftly changing the subject. "I saw your granddaughter in town. She is getting more beautiful every day."

"I know and the boys are beginning to knock at her door. But she's far too young to be interested in them."

"So you think, but they grow up so fast… anyway, what did you bring me today?"

"I have a letter and the contract with the French post for next year," he said pointing to the envelopes on the table.

"Thank you. Alia, darling, do you mind getting my reading glasses from my room?" said Nanna quickly, as if eager to send Alia out of the room.

"Sure Nanna, right away," she said, knowing her grandmother wanted her out of the way, while she signed the contract, which Alia was not supposed to know about.

As she came back downstairs with the glasses, she could hear the postman leaving and saying goodbye to Nanna. She realised that her grandmother hadn't required the glasses in order to sign the contract, but she took them to her anyway. When she got down, Nanna was no longer in the living room but in the kitchen, unpacking the shopping bags. Alia couldn't help noticing that Nanna had not opened her letter. She had put it in her pocket as if waiting for a better moment, when she could be alone.

"I got you your glasses. Where did Mr Reynolds go? I thought he was staying for tea?"

"Oh, he had to leave, he still had some mail to deliver and he didn't want to be too late. Thanks for the glasses, I'll need them later to read a new recipe that Ms Anderson gave me."

"Ok. So, unless you need me for anything else, is it alright if I go and look for Deanna in the park?"

"Be my guest! But don't be too late, I'm cooking something new tonight."

"I can't wait! I promise we'll be home in time for dinner."

Alia looked at her watch. She realised she had no idea what the time was. She had been so focused on what Mr Reynolds was telling her, she completely lost track. But this felt like a big step forward, now Alia knew she could turn to him, when she found another opportunity. There was just one thing she needed to do before leaving the house, to write down the address she had seen on the contract: 248 Rue de Rivoli. Now she had something to go on! It was obviously the address of where she used to call home, back in the days when her parents were still alive. Then she put on her shoes and went in search of sister. At least she had somebody to talk to about all she had learned today.

Chapter Three

I WANT THE TRUTH!

Deanna left the house a little disappointed after her conversation with Alia. If her sister didn't understand her need to socialize, to be with girls and boys of their own age, then she was better off at home with her books! She was so much happier and more fun to be with than her sister. Everybody wanted to be with her, to be like her. She was tall, strong, athletic, she knew how to dress, even if their grandmother never let them become fashion victims.

Deanna was the kind of girl that was naturally beautiful whatever she did.

The twins were identical but still when they were together everybody's attention was on Deanna. She didn't mind, she liked it. It made her feel important. During fencing competitions, when she had her mask on, it didn't feel right. She couldn't wait to win so she could reveal her face and smile at the public. Her dark brown hair would fall on her shoulders and she would wave at all the people cheering her on. Still just a teenager, she was a natural born diva.

Alia didn't mind the shadow that her sister cast on her. She never wanted to be in the spotlight. At least she could be herself, and not worry about fitting in with the crowd.

As different as they were from each other, the two girls shared an unshakable bond as sisters. They were passionate about fencing, even though Deanna won every competition. Alia was more attracted to books and she could learn a foreign language more easily. Deanna had a lot of friends but also a lot of 'so-called friends', girls that only wanted to be seen in her company. She called them her satellites. Thanks to her sister, who was more realistic, she could tell the difference between who was genuine and who was not. Deep down, both of them found it hard to trust. They had each other and that was enough. Deanna knew she could always turn to her sister for help no matter what. Whereas Alia was the silent type, Deanna talked for both of them. So thanks to her sister, Alia had some friends when she was in the mood to socialize.

Deanna had been the last one to arrive at the park. The others, a group of six 13-14 year olds hung around, showing off and making a lot of noise. They were loud and confident and they all thought they were superstars, until Deanna showed up, then they fell into line, as if their leader had arrived.

"Hey, Deanna," said a skinny boy, who looked like a model. "Where's your sister then? Didn't she want to join us? Or are books more fun!" and he screamed with laughter.

"They're certainly more interesting than you," snapped Deanna.

"Don't mind him. He's jealous of anybody who can read," said another boy, so big and strong he looked about 30.

"I know," sighed Deanna putting on her rollerblades. "Leave my sister out of it. Come on, let's have some fun!"

They all rushed to get close to her, with their blades on.

"OK, everybody, let's go!" she shouted, as they all cheered and set off together, singing and laughing.

They were so busy rollerblading, none of them noticed a girl spying on them, from behind one of the nearby trees. She was blonde, thin, and small and although she looked as if she hated the other kids, secretly she wished she could be part of their group. She never understood all the fascination with Deanna, she wasn't even that beautiful. The spy was Lydia, the postman's granddaughter and daughter of Angela, the closest friend to Alia and Deanna's mother growing up. Lydia knew that everybody would like to be told the secret of the twins' past. What she wasn't aware of though, was she probably knew more than the girls themselves.

When she saw Deanna coming, with her face glowing from the fun and the exercise, all her jealousy resurfaced. Without knowing why, she just wanted to hurt Deanna, she wanted to see her cry.

Deanna stopped at a bench and took a bottle of water out of her backpack. She emptied it and was about to return to her friends when she saw Lydia.

"Hello, Lydia," she said, smiling.

"Hi," she replied, her face expressionless.

"Would you like to join us?"

"No, I didn't bring my rollers."

"Bummer," said Deanna sympathetically. "Next time. But if you like, when we finish, we'll get an ice cream at the truck. You can join us there?"

"Maybe later. I don't think your friends want me there. At least you've got friends."

"What do you mean by that? What are you talking about?"

"I was just saying, your sister, like your mother, she doesn't have any friends. Lucky for her she has you."

"Why are you talking about my mother, all of a sudden? What do you have to say about my mother? You never even met her!"

"No, but my mother did. And she told me that she was the only friend your mother ever had. Pathetic!"

"Not as pathetic as you, hiding behind trees, watching everybody else having fun."

"This is what you call fun! I call fun going to a concert or on holiday to an exotic beach. But your grandmother could never afford anything like that, could she? Ever since your parents were kidnapped and she tried to buy their freedom, you've been poor! And that's all you'll ever be! Poor!" Lydia kept throwing that word at Deanna with such vehemence, that she finally ran out of breath.

At that moment, Alia was just approaching along the path and she heard Lydia's last words. She stopped dead in her tracks. Her parents kidnapped? Not dead in a car accident? This day was getting more and more bizarre, really strange. She could have hidden somewhere out of sight and learned even more, but she decided it was time to stop this aggression.

"Hi, Lydia," said Alia, forcing herself to smile, as a shocked Lydia spun round to face her. "I'm surprised to hear all these mean things coming out of your mouth. If your mother won our mother's trust, she must be quite a nice person."

"She is," said Lydia. "So?"

"So I thought you would be too, but I see that jealousy is stronger than reason."

"Jealous? Me? What would I be jealous of?"

"Deanna, of course, she's everything you'll never be."

"It's alright Alia, leave her," said Deanna. "It's not worth it, we have better things to do than argue with her. Let's go."

"That's right, run, run, run like your mother did," Lydia sneered. "She turned her back on your grandmother, when she needed her most, when she was ill! All that she cared about was her stupid diary…"

And then, all of a sudden, she stopped, the twins had disappeared and she realised she was talking to herself. However, they hadn't gone far. They were doing a Lydia trick and hiding, hoping to hear her say anything else, but without giving her the satisfaction of seeing they were interested.

In the end, they watched her leave. Almost immediately the other kids turned up and Deanna was grateful they hadn't witnessed Lydia's insults. Poor Lydia, she wasn't the most popular girl in their school, and she would have become the main subject of mockery for a week after this. She had always known that Lydia was not her biggest fan, but she never thought that she hated her that much. Deanna lived in a world, where everybody loved her, well… everybody was supposed to love her. She wasn't spoiled or arrogant, Nanna wouldn't have allowed that, she was just innocent and very friendly. In the end, that was the force which drew people to her. Alia was less charismatic, but she was sweet and kind and helpful. She couldn't understand either, what had they done to make Lydia so aggressive. Oh well, one more mystery to solve. But now at least they had a lead.

"Let's go! I have so much to tell you," she whispered in Deanna's ear.

"All right, me too," said Deanna. "Just let me say goodbye to my friends. Otherwise they will start asking questions about why I left like a thief!"

"I'll see you back at home, as soon as you can," said Alia. "Nanna is waiting for us for dinner."

"You go ahead, I'll be right there."

"Don't forget your backpack!"

"I won't," said Deanna leaving.

Alia got back home alone, but very excited. She wondered if Nanna might agree to answer a few of her questions. She felt that this was her lucky day and it was now or never. When she entered the house, Nanna was in the kitchen. Alia thought she was still cooking, but that couldn't have been further from the truth.

Chapter Four

A GHOST FROM THE PAST

Nanna had started the cooking earlier, but as soon as she heard Alia leave the house, she washed her hands, took out the letter she had received that morning and sat down at the kitchen table. The second she opened the envelope, her face turned whiter than the paper and her hands trembled. She read the letter twice, not even realising she had left the tap running at the sink. The contents of the letter troubled her very much. It took a lot to get under Nanna's skin, but this had shaken her to the core.

Nanna, real name Gloria, was 61 years old but she looked 50. People who didn't know their situation, couldn't tell if she was the grandmother or the mother. She was very active, energetic and extremely strict with the girls. She could speak 8 languages and started to teach the girls all of them. She had realised very early on, she couldn't afford to act like a normal grandmother, she would never know the luxury of spoiling her granddaughters. She acted as if she had to train them for something, as if she expected an attack at any moment and they had to be ready for war. Life in their small, quiet village didn't seem to warrant that kind of education, but still nobody asked questions, they somehow knew that the girls had lived a very different life before turning up here at their grandmother's house.

Gloria's sole aim in life was to keep the girls safe. She knew nobody would be able to find them in such a remote place, but she could never fully relax. She never enjoyed a picnic with the girls in a public park, or going to the cinema. Now that they were older and she knew she had taught them well, she realised she had to give them some freedom to live their adolescence. But she was not happy about it. The last thing she wanted was for the girls to start asking questions, so she tried to provide some semblance of a normal life.

When she had returned to the village with the girls, she knew she was burying herself. But she had no choice, it was the best place to hide them. Nobody knew who she was hiding them from. And now this letter had come to shatter their calm little universe. Gloria knew that their happiness couldn't last forever, but there was still so much she wanted to teach the girls, to prepare them for what was coming. She started reading the letter for a third time, as if somehow that could change its message. Again her hands shook as she held the letter and started to read out loud:

"Dear madame Gloria,

As we agreed so many years ago, me and my wife were in charge of keeping the apartment in Rue de Rivoli as you left it. Everything went well for almost ten years, that's why I never bothered you with anything. You always redirected the mail so there was nothing other than taxes to take care of. We never encountered money problems, you were always very careful about that and I thank you.

But as you asked me to, I wish to inform you that a man came and asked for the Count de Brecourt. It was quite strange, because when I told him that Vincent de Brecourt was dead, he wouldn't believe me. He tried to enter the apartment to check if I was lying. My wife didn't want to let him in, but he left us no choice.

He went straight to your daughter's bedroom as if he had been there before. We tried to stop him but he started to look under the bed, trying to move the carpet. I had to threaten him with the police, to get him out of the apartment. Just before he left, he told me to pass a message to Mr and Mme de Brecourt, as if he hadn't heard they were dead.

He said, and I quote: "Not even time can protect you from my master's will and punishment!" I will never be able to get those words out of my head.

After he left, we went to the bedroom to see if he had stolen anything. I don't think he had the time to take anything. But we were a little shaken by the incident. I thought it was important to tell you as soon as possible. And as we agreed, we are only using the old-fashioned post to communicate, because the modern electronic ways are so easily hacked and also because nobody would expect that somebody was still using the old postman as messenger.

We will go on with our lives and our duties. If something should change, let me know as soon as possible and we will act accordingly. My wife continues to go to your daughter's grave to change the flowers, only roses, as you asked.

Your faithful servant, Gilles Lacroix."

Gloria put the letter down. Her mind was racing, searching for answers. Who was the man who had come to her apartment in Paris? She had an idea who sent him but she had hoped that "the master" the intruder referred to was dead. Apparently not. That changed everything. She had an important decision to make, a life changing one. But for now, she had to focus on the girls. The letter must be kept secret, they should know nothing. It became even more important to keep them hidden. And most important, she had to… cook!

With no enthusiasm for the task, she started preparing their evening meal. She had tried very hard to become part of that small community, and not to attract the attention of some of the more vicious housewives in the neighbourhood. It was torture for her to bake cookies and sell pancakes for the girls at school. She would have preferred to fight ten Trojan wars than to have a conversation with any of the dull, small-minded, characterless mums. But at least one of them helped her out with a recipe she could just about manage to cook. As soon as she put on her apron, Alia appeared.

"What happened?" asked Gloria, looking at her flushed face. "Were you running?"

"Oh, hi Nanna! Yes, I hurried home, I didn't want to be late for dinner. Deanna and I lost track of time in the park."

"By the way, where is she? I haven't seen her all day."

"She was right behind me. She just wanted to say goodbye to her friends. And what are you cooking?"

"Oh, nothing complicated, you know me."

"Yes, I know you are better in the library than in the kitchen," joked Alia. "Do you need any help?"

"No, it's Ok, thank you. You can go to your room. I'll call when it's ready."

"If you say so. Please tell Deanna when she gets home that I'm in my room waiting for her."

"All right," said Nanna, grateful to be left alone with her thoughts.

If only she could find out who the intruder was, if only she knew his name or his face! She was afraid that the same person would find them, and take what he was searching for in Paris.

Chapter Five

BEYOND THE SEA

Two days earlier in Paris, two men took a stroll in the Luxembourg Park, Mr d'Harcourt and Mr Landemare. It was the month of May and all the gardens of Paris bloomed with a magical display of flowers, brilliant with colour and scenting the air with their perfume. The garden of the Luxembourg Palace outshone all the rest, and people thronged there to jog, practise yoga, or karate, or play tennis or soccer or just stroll in the sunshine or take their kids to the playground there. On any sunny day in May, the sheer volume of people enjoying the park, made it impossible to have a normal conversation without shouting.

Harcourt and Landemare needed that kind of anonymity afforded by the crowds. They felt sure they blended in and nobody would look twice at them in this setting. They were dressed for tennis and each carried his racket, as if he played regularly. Despite the noise surrounding them in the park, they spoke in low voices and moved their hands a lot as if they were afraid somebody could lip read what they were saying.

"Are you sure the girl is 14 now?" said Harcourt.

"Yes," said Landemare emphatically. "Maybe not exactly but her birthday should be soon. I think it's May 18th. But don't worry, Mr d'Harcourt, thanks to Facebook, we'll find out everything there is to know."

"I thought the old witch didn't let her have a Facebook account?"

"Yes, but all kids of her age do. So when her birthday comes they'll post birthday wishes on their own pages and we'll be notified automatically if her name, or the grandmother's, appears anywhere."

"Genius! I love technology! I wish I could use it in another time, I would be God!" said Harcourt, rather too loudly, causing Landemare to hiss in alarm.

"Don't be ridiculous! Such dreams are dangerous. Let's try to change our future and not our past."

"You're right, we must focus on the most urgent matter, finding the girl and the diary. Are you sure she's got it?"

"Who else could have it? Unless…"

"Unless what?" said Harcourt, stopping in his tracks.

"Unless she was so smart as to leave it here in Paris, so that if somebody found her and the girl…"

"Of course, so we could never have the girl and the diary in the same place at the same time. The old witch, devious as ever."

"But now the question is, did she keep the apartment her daughter owns, or did she sell it?" said Landemare, encouraging Harcourt to move on, as people were bunching up behind them.

"There is only one way to find out. You must go there and see for yourself. But be careful, you mustn't be recognised or it will all fall apart."

"Who could recognise me? I haven't been seen in Paris for 10 years, well at least since the incident."

"You're right. The only person who could know you is Gloria Hammersmith and she is God knows where, believing that we're dead."

"Ok, that's settled. Now, tell me what do you intend to do with the girl once we find her?" asked Landemare, a look of concern crossing his face.

"Kill her, of course! The diary can only have one owner and that should be me, not her. While she's alive I can never have full power over it."

"And do you think that Gloria knows where the other one is?"

"No, I don't, because if she did, she would try to get her greedy hands on it."

"Why?" said Landemare, pausing himself in the middle of the path. "She already has the first one, why would she need the other?"

"Because the one we are looking for is strong, very strong, but is incomplete without its twin. Never in the past have they been together. There are no recollections about the second one."

"Why do you think that is?"

"Because nobody lived long enough to tell the story."

"Aren't you afraid that if you find it, something bad could happen to us?"

"I think it was never properly mastered," said Harcourt. "I think in good hands, it is capable of great things."

"Or horrific things!"

"Absolute power may frighten you, but not me. I can see all the possibilities that will open up in front of my eyes."

"Samantha never looked for absolute power. She never used the diary for that," said Landemare, urging them both forward again.

"Samantha was stupid!" said Harcourt. "A silly girl that dreamed of a knight in shining armour, galloping up on a white horse to rescue her from her boring life. For her the diary was just a ticket out of the rat hole her wicked mother had trapped her in. She used it to get to Paris and meet that weird husband of hers. She never looked back."

"How well did you know Samantha?"

"I followed her every step, I watched her every move waiting for the moment to kill her. But then she had the girl. I didn't see that coming so soon. She was very young when she had her. And then, everything changed. The diary had found its new owner. Now killing Samantha is not enough, the baby must die too."

"So why didn't you do it at the same time?"

"That, my friend is a very long story."

"We have all the time in the world. I have to wait until it's dark to check if the apartment is occupied or not," said Landemare.

The two men continued their walk in the crowded park. They looked for all the world like two old friends catching up. Nobody could have guessed the terrible acts they were planning, nor the unimaginable story that Mr d'Harcourt was disclosing to Landemare.

As the sun set behind the Palace of Luxembourg, Mr d'Harcourt went on his way and left Gilbert Landemare free do his job.

Rue de Rivoli was a very noisy street, full of souvenir shops and café bars. You could distinguish the tourists from the locals, because the tourists dawdled and all the locals were in a hurry. Gilbert Landemare behaved just like any other tourist, hanging around, admiring the beautiful architecture. Then he stayed waiting in the shadows for about two hours, keeping a certain door in his sights.

Finally, he saw a man and a woman going in and a minute later a light appeared at the window. He thought they must be the new owners, but when he saw the name printed by the doorbell, he realised he knew exactly who they were. So he decided to go up and we know what happened then.

Ten minutes later he came out. He was a little angry but mostly he felt disappointed. He couldn't find what he was looking for. He had wasted an entire evening. At least he knew the diary was no longer in Paris, at least not in this apartment. So his mission remained the same, whatever it took, find it.

He arrived back at Harcourt's house, knowing the man was impatient for news and the problem was he didn't have any. Once inside, he went straight to the dining room, where Harcourt was having dinner.

"So, what do you have for me?" asked Maxime d'Harcourt immediately.

"Nothing! The old witch has a couple looking after the apartment. They didn't let me search. I just had time to look under the bed, but it was so clean, I don't think anything could have stayed there untouched for ten years."

"Well, at least we know it's not there and, most importantly, we know that she must be planning to come back one day."

"You're taking this quite well," said Gilbert in disbelief.

"Do I have a choice?"

"You could have those two disappear and search the apartment for clues?"

"You're starting to think like me! But no, we can't do that. It would make Gloria suspicious and she would know it was me. And just for now at least, I don't want to make her angry."

"Don't tell me you're afraid of her!"

"She is capable of many things that would give you nightmares, but she's less dangerous than she used to be. Now that her daughter is out of the picture, she might be easier to get to."

"What do you mean 'out of the picture'? You mean dead, don't you?"

"Not really, but close enough. Let's just say she won't be bothering us for a long, long time," said Harcourt with such an evil laugh, it made even Landemare shiver.

"So what's the next step?"

"We wait to have some information about the girl's birthday. We have nowhere else to go. That will give us her location."

"And then?"

"Then," said Harcourt raising his glass of wine. "We'll make sure that the diary belongs to me, and me alone!"

Chapter Six

LIKE TWO PEAS IN A POD

What the two men had failed to discover, was that Samantha didn't have one girl, but two. It was a vital detail, which would one day afford them an element of surprise.

Alia couldn't wait to talk to her sister. Deanna showed up soon enough and they started to share what they had found out. They exchanged questions and conclusions for more than ten minutes.

"Why do you think Lydia doesn't like me?" asked Deanna.

"Do you really care?"

"No, but I think it has something to do with her mother and ours."

"Maybe, but they were best friends," said Alia.

"At the beginning they were, or at least that's what everybody thinks. We don't know what really happened between them. Maybe they fell out over a boy or something?"

"I don't think so," said Alia, shaking her head. "The postman said that Mum didn't go out much, in fact hardly at all."

"Well, I can't think of anything else."

"Maybe we would know more if only we could find our Mum's diary, that seemed so important for her?"

"I never remember a diary, do you?" said Deanna, frowning.

"No, but maybe Nanna knows something. She could tell us?"

"You know she never tells us anything."

"Why would she hide something so unimportant as a diary? I'm sure it's up there, lying somewhere in the attic with tons of spiderwebs on it. I hope she didn't throw it away."

"Let's go ask her!" said Deanna, jumping to her feet.

"Wait!" yelled Alia. "Are we going to ask about the address in Paris too?"

"That's another story. I don't think she's going to discuss that one with us."

"You may be right, but we can try anyway."

"It might make her angry, and we don't want that, do we?"

"Nooo, we don't," agreed Alia, pulling a face.

Just then they heard their grandmother calling them for dinner.

It didn't take them long to polish off the food. They were both pretty hungry from their exertions in the park. Finally, they put down their knives and forks at the end of the meal.

"Oh Nanna, that was amazing. It was delicious!" said Alia, beaming at her grandmother.

"Go easy on me, you know I can sense irony!" laughed Nanna as they started clearing the table.

"I'm serious, you really nailed that one," said Alia trying to look serious. She needed her grandmother in a good mood.

"Thank you. So girls, what did you do today? Alia, I know you were here at home most of the day. What about you, Deanna?"

"Well, we went rollerblading. And we want to tell you what happened to us afterwards."

"What? Is everything all right?" Nanna looked panicked and almost dropped the plates she was holding.

"Yes, we're fine, but we wanted to ask you something," said Deanna.

"Go ahead, what is it?"

"When I was at the park, I caught Lydia spying on me."

"Lydia? The postman's granddaughter?"

"Yes, do you know her?"

"Not really. What did she want?"

"That's where it becomes interesting. She waited for me to be alone to attack me."

"Attack you?"

"Insult me, call me names. The worst was when she started insulting our mother."

"Your mother? What did she have to say about your mother?"

"That she didn't have any friends and that she was just a lonely freak, who carried her diary everywhere she went. Is any of that true?"

"She was a little bit shy, but your mother was not a freak!" said Nanna angrily.

"And what about the diary? Is that true?" asked Deanna.

Nanna hesitated. The conversation was taking a turn she didn't like. But now the dice had been rolled, she needed to get out of this as fast as she could.

"She did have a diary, but only for a little while. It was just a phase, like with a lot of teenagers, I guess. As far as I remember, she burned it one day, after discovering that Angela had tried to read it and she had written there about a boy in their class. She didn't want her classmates to know about her crush, and make fun of her, so she put the old notebook in the fire."

"In that case, Lydia is just mean!" said Deanna disappointed.

"And jealous!" added Alia.

"That, I can understand, said Nanna. Look at you girls, you have everything that all the other girls only dream of. Now, have you got any more questions? If not get yourselves off to bed. Sounds like you've had a long day. And about Lydia, let her say whatever she wants, you don't care, agreed?"

"All right, Nanna, good night."

"Good night girls."

The girls left the kitchen together. As soon as they were alone in their room they started talking.

"Ok, that went well," said Alia.

"Very. At least she confirmed that Mum had a diary."

"Yes, but apparently she burned it."

"Alia, did you really buy that? She told us that to stop us asking questions and put us off looking for it."

"How can you be so sure that Mum didn't burn her diary as Nanna said?"

"If you had a diary, which you put all your life, all your soul and all your thoughts into, wouldn't you like to keep it, so that when you're old, you can remember all your childhood and teenage years? Mum was a dreamer, she knew the value of memories. No, I'm sure the diary still exists, we just have to know where to look for it."

"What about that address in Paris?" asked Alia. "What if she left it there? Mum must have taken it with her, when she moved out."

"No, I think Nanna cleaned the apartment in Paris before we left. Do you realise, this apartment has been empty for a decade. Nanna must have known she wouldn't be back soon."

"Deanna, do you think the diary is still here in this house?"

"Yes, but where on earth is it hidden?"

"No idea. But let's sleep on it. We won't go looking for it tonight," said Alia who was already half asleep.

"You're right," said Deanna turning off the light.

After a few moments, Deanna couldn't resist breaking the silence.

"Do you realise how crazy Lydia must be, to attack me like that for no good reason? Do you think she likes some boy, who doesn't like her back and she's blaming me?"

"Maybe, but who could she like?"

"I don't know, but she sure was aggressive today."

"We'll keep on the look out at school. Maybe we'll see something we missed before, simply because we weren't looking for it."

"Maybe, well, good night."

"Good night… again."

It was a very long night, for all three of them. Nanna was looking for a strategy, Alia started to dream about what it would be like to live in Paris and Deanna was trying to remember if at any occasion she had been mean enough to Lydia, to give her a reason to hate her that much. And on top of everything, all three of them remembered that the girls' birthday was coming soon.

Alia and Deanna were used to the rules, no party at home, no friends invited over, just a simple party at the bowling alley. Ten friends max and nothing after. Even their friends knew the tradition. But this year it was going to be different. They wanted more, Nanna wanted less. The girls had no idea what their grandmother was planning for their future and certainly not that it would involve changing their lives forever.

Chapter Seven

THE BIRTHDAY PARTY

Just a few days before their birthday, the girls were desperate to tell their grandmother what they wanted - a party, a real, full-on party. It had to be here at home. The house was big enough to host at least 50 people. They wanted to invite everybody, especially Deanna, who had a lot of friends who would have been disappointed if they weren't invited. Alia was easier to satisfy. She had a few friends of her own, but mostly she knew people because Deanna knew people. But every time they saw their grandmother, they couldn't find the courage to ask. Somehow, they felt she wouldn't be happy about their idea.

It was a huge house, too big for just the three of them. They didn't even use half of the rooms. The girls remembered that one day, when they were younger, they played a game. They started to explore the house. They were on holiday from school and it was raining. They were so bored that they started to play Sherlock Holmes and Dr Watson. One thing led to another, they left their room, crept past their grandmother's bedroom and decided to look upstairs. The trouble was, they had never ventured up there before.

They got a little scared but even more curious. Their room was on the first floor with Nanna's bedroom. The kitchen and the dining room was on the ground floor. That is all they knew. But the house had another floor, an attic and a basement. Nanna never went upstairs, so they thought there must be nothing of interest there. But today, it seemed that the secret part of the house was hiding a treasure. A treasure just waiting to be found by two curious little girls.

When they placed one foot on the stairs, it creaked so loudly, it frightened them. But they soon realised that Nanna's punishment would be far more scary than whatever lurked upstairs. Nanna had never forbidden them to walk in the house, but she had organized their living space so well, that they had never felt the need to use an extra room. Step by step they arrived at the top and they found themselves faced with five doors.

"Alia," whispered Deanna.

"What? You startled me," answered Alia, slightly louder than she meant to.

"Where do we go now?"

"I don't know, what do you think?"

"Well, let's start on the left and look in each room."

"I don't think we are supposed to be here," said Alia, unsure of accepting Deanna's suggestion.

"It's too late now, isn't it? If you're too scared you can go back downstairs whenever you want."

"I don't want to, don't be silly."

"All right then. Let's go."

Slowly, Deanna opened the first door on their left. They were little, so they were very surprised to find a room covered in a thick layer of dust. They saw a bed, a closet and a table. Nothing unusual. But on the table lay a big map, that seemed very old. They tried to look at it but they didn't want to disturb the dust, in case Nanna could see they had been there. In their innocence, they never thought about their footprints.

They gently closed the door. The second room wasn't very different, except there was no bed, just a couch. In the closet the girls saw some dusty clothes, but well ironed and put on their hangers. They had never seen clothes like that, at least not in their village.

The third room turned out to be a bathroom, so they closed the door without going in. They never got to the fifth, because when they opened the fourth door they stopped and gasped in amazement. It was a huge room, with walls full of mirrors, but not like IKEA mirrors. Everything in the room smelled of old, scented candles. They could almost smell the smoke. In the centre stood a big sculpture of Diana, the goddess of hunting, while at the sides there were chairs, that looked like thrones. But what surprised them the most was a large staircase, which led upstairs. They always thought that attic stairs should be narrow and the door small. But not here.

"WOW!" said Alia in disbelief. "Where are we?"

"I don't know, but it's amazing! It's like in a fairy tale!"

"It looks like a ballroom!"

"I know, but can you imagine Nanna throwing balls?"

"She did teach us how to dance, didn't she?"

"So we should see what's in the attic, don't you think?"

"Sure!"

"Girls!" shouted Nanna, right behind them. "What are you doing here?"

Both girls screamed in shock.

"Nothing, Nanna, we were just playing hide and seek," Alia lied, not very convincingly.

"You can play downstairs, there's no reason for you to come up here! It's not a playground!"

"We know, Nanna, but we have never been here before. It's so beautiful," said Deanna.

"It is, but you are not allowed here, understand?"

"Yes Nanna, we understand," said Deanna, looking down at her feet.

"Now, downstairs, both of you and get ready for dinner."

So the three of them returned to reality. But the girls never forgot that day. They accepted the fact that it was forbidden, but now that their 14th birthday was just around the corner, they dreamed that Nanna would open up the ballroom for them. They never imagined just how determined Nanna was to keep that door closed. So when they finally found the courage to ask her, all hell broke loose.

"But why not? Why not? Why can't we have a birthday like our friends?" pleaded Deanna. "It would be the first time we could feel like everyone else. And you wouldn't even have to spend much money on us."

"What do you mean? I hope you don't think that I would let a bunch of uncivilized teenagers break everything in my house!" answered Nanna sensing the conflict.

"We don't need the whole house! Just the ballroom!" chipped in Alia, who could see that arguing with Nanna was futile. "We never use it anyway. When was the last time you went in there?"

"It doesn't matter! This house in not for parties!"

"I bet our mother would have let us organize our birthday!" whined Deanna without thinking. As soon as she heard the words come out of her mouth, she regretted it.

"Well, your mother is not here," sighed Nanna, taking the girls by surprise as they expected anger, not sadness. "I wish she was, then we wouldn't need to hide all our lives."

"Why are we hiding, Nanna? Did our mother do something wrong? Is that why our parents are dead?" asked Alia, seizing the opportunity to learn some new information.

"Your mother did nothing wrong! You must know that! But unfortunately, I don't know more. So there's no point in asking me questions!"

With that, Nanna ended the conversation. She wondered if she'd been too harsh on them, but she didn't want to take chances, not now that things had started to happen.

As for the twins, of course they wanted some explanation, some answers to their questions, but they were used to not getting any. So, on the morning of their birthday, as usual, they went to school and invited their friends to go bowling. Alia hid in the shadows and Deanna was saluted like a star. In the evening, their grandmother prepared them their favourite food, pizza, they had their cake and then they went to their room.

"For once Nanna could have made an exception from her stupid rules!" said Deanna, who couldn't help expressing her disappointment.

"Shut up, she might hear you," whispered Alia, closing the door behind them.

"I don't care! What can she do to me, ground me? I feel punished enough already."

"I think she can do worse than that. At least we could get out today. Do you remember, one year, for our birthday we had to go to church with her?"

"Yes, it was awful. We got so bored that we started eating peanuts that I found in my pocket."

"And after that we got so sick, we didn't go to school for a week."

"Worst birthday ever!" said Deanna. "You're right, it could be worse. But still, that doesn't mean what she's doing is right."

"Maybe when we get older…"

"Never, I tell you! She will never let us go upstairs and have a party there."

"It was such a long time ago. If we hadn't witnessed it together, I would have mistaken it for a dream, not a real memory."

"It was not a dream, it was all very real! A dream would be to see it again."

"Maybe one day, when she's not at home we could sneak in?" suggested Alia.

"No, it's impossible, she's blocked off the door."

"What? How do you know?"

"One day," confessed Deanna. "When you were at the library with Nanna, knowing how we can't get you out in less than an hour, I decided to go upstairs, just to take a look."

"And?"

"Well, she had closed all the doors, a long time ago, maybe just after our indiscretion."

"So you couldn't see anything?"

"Nothing, it was like it never existed."

"Why do you think she does that?"

"What?"

"Keeps everything a secret. I mean, do you realise she's never told us anything about our parents, about their death or even their life?" said Alia. "All grandparents, when the parents die young, tell stories to their grandchildren, so they can imagine how their parents used to be. Do you realise that we know nothing about our parents? We didn't even know that we used to live in an apartment in Paris."

"I admit, that is weird, but you do realise that our grandmother is no ordinary grandmother. And our life isn't an ordinary one?"

"Sometimes I wish I were normal, ordinary… or at least find out why we are not."

"I like being special," beamed Deanna. "The mystery keeps everybody talking about me at school. If I can't have a special birthday party, at least I can have the fame."

"You and your fame, did anybody write on Facebook for your birthday?"

"Yes, but as you know Sammy's older brother made the account on a fake name so Nanna couldn't find it."

"So did you get a lot of posts?" asked Alia.

"Yes, about 200!"

"Nanna would kill you if she found out."

"What she doesn't know won't hurt her. And she can't find out because it doesn't have my name on it."

And so the girls kept talking until Deanna finally fell asleep from all the excitement of the day. They believed tomorrow would be just like any normal day. They had no idea of events unfolding in France, nor that something had happened that would remove the word normal from their lives forever.

Chapter Eight

WHAT HAPPENS IN PARIS...

Maxime Harcourt and Gilbert Landemare spent the whole month of May waiting for birthday news on Facebook, with absolutely no success. Now they were starting to worry. Maybe the plan wasn't so clever after all. But they had no other lead. It still never occurred to them that Gloria would communicate with that couple in Paris, in the old fashioned way, by post.

They searched every email account in her name or her daughter's name with a hacker and found nothing. They even began to think she may have sold the apartment Rue de Rivoli and the couple had nothing to do with any of it. They were very afraid that Gloria had cut all the ties with her old life.

"Still no news on Facebook?" asked Maxime impatiently.

"No! It's as if they never existed! In this day and age, if you're not on Facebook, you don't exist! Or you do, but on some desert island with no signal, no smartphone and no access to the internet. How is that even possible?"

"With Gloria, anything is possible," said Maxime, with a sigh of exhaustion. "That was what I was afraid of."

"There must be a way to find her. Or, can't we just look for the other diary? It must be easier to find."

"It's impossible to find the Silver One without the Golden One. Because even if we find it, we can never use it."

"Why not?"

"Only the person who has the Golden One can put his hands on the Silver One."

"But you can still use the Golden One on its own?"

"Yes, because it was the original. The second one is like the younger sister. It was created just after but it was never a perfect copy. It had flaws, it couldn't be controlled. Some even said it had its own will."

"That sounds pretty unbelievable to me," said Gilbert.

"I never got my hands on the second. I can only repeat what I heard."

"Let's just try to find the first one, then we will search for the unruly one," said Gilbert, trying to be ironic.

"I just had an idea," said Maxime. "Where did Gloria live before she followed her daughter to Paris?"

"The last time she was seen was in England, in a small village, somewhere out of London. Why, you don't think she would be that stupid to stay there? It's so near, you'd think she would have gone halfway round the world."

"You say stupid, I say brilliant," said Maxime, his mood lifting. "We never thought of looking right under our noses."

"Alright, we can look, but it's such a long shot."

"Search under the name of Hammersmith, or Brecourt."

"Maybe she changed her name. That would have been smart."

"She could have changed hers yes, but not the girl's. So they are probably somewhere using the same last name."

"I'll get onto it and let you know."

"Try to be more discreet than the last time. Don't break down any doors and don't involve the police. There are a lot of things you can't explain about yourself."

"I'll be invisible, I promise."

"If you have news in England, you have to come back immediately, do you understand? Let me handle Gloria," said Maxime.

"Yes, but can I search the house? If I find the diary, I can steal it?"

"No! You will do no such thing! Gloria would know if somebody so much as touched the diary."

"How could she know if she's not at home?" said Gilbert, sounding increasingly curious about this woman's powers.

"She just knows. You think her daughter told her from the beginning that she had found it? No, because she didn't think it was important. But Gloria found out. But by then it was too late, Samantha and the diary had become inseparable."

"Inseparable?"

"The diary can only have one master," said Maxime, raising Gilbert's interest even further.

"So anybody can write in it, but not when another is present?"

"No, that would be too easy. You must write something in particular to become the master. And you must prove yourself worthy."

"You have to pass a test to earn the right?"

"Not just one, many tests, and the first one is to prove that you come from a noble family."

"Really?" scoffed Gilbert. "And how do you do that, take a blood test?"

"If I were you, my friend," said Maxime coming close to Gilbert, his voice hardening. "I would take your task more seriously. Many have tried before you."

"And?"

"And they were destroyed," said Maxime, casually turning away to glance out of the window.

"Destroyed by whom? Don't tell me it was the diary, how can a diary destroy somebody?" said Gilbert sounding a little less confident.

"Oh, in many ways," said Maxime, smiling. "But that's not your problem. Your job is to find out if Gloria is really hiding in England."

"Ok, if she's there I'll find her. I won't contact you again until my return. We'll meet in Paris one week from today. I think one week is enough to find the old witch and her granddaughter."

"It would be a mistake to underestimate Gloria. Don't do anything that encroaches on their life. Just locate her."

"Trust me," said Gilbert. "As soon as I see her, I'll run, run like the wind."

They said their goodbyes and Gilbert left to prepare for his trip.

Reaching London was easy, getting to a small hamlet in the middle of the countryside, was not. He booked all his tickets online. In the village he found only one hotel, so it wasn't a difficult choice. The next day he left Paris. He was proud of the fact he spoke English, however, in reality it was more like Shakespeare's English, with a French accent. He arrived in London by train to King's Cross and then took a long-distance coach. He knew the brief was just to find out if Gloria was there, but he wished it was more. He preferred action over spying every time.

It hadn't occurred to him that by the time he got there, Gloria would have already left. He thought he had the element of surprise so he didn't expect to be surprised himself. Maxime did warn him, anyone who underestimated Gloria paid a high price and would regret it. But he thought he was one step ahead of her. He just couldn't understand why he didn't have the right to take the diary if he found it. His boss was too secretive and he didn't like it. He felt as if he didn't trust him completely. And he was sure that Maxime himself didn't know everything. There had to be a higher command somewhere. He knew Harcourt pretty well and he felt that his boss was obeying orders from somebody else, someone even more frightening than Gloria. Harcourt was not the kind of person to bow to anyone, but this time he seemed absolutely terrified at the prospect of failing.

Gilbert shrugged his shoulders, he wasn't there to ask questions. As long as he got paid, he'd do the job, even if sometimes he didn't like it. He knew, as always, if a better offer arose, he would have no problem betraying the lot of them. It was all down to who paid the most. He had no friends, no family, just a thirst for money. He liked good food, expensive clothes and luxury cars. He followed money, not people, his so-called loyalty was always up for sale. He had worked for Harcourt longer than anybody else, simply because he paid him more. Behind that shallow appearance though, he harboured a sad and complicated past, a past he had succeeded in burying so deeply, no-one knew who he really was.

Following the coach ride, he had to wait forever, for a lone, small bus to arrive at the bus stop and take him to the village. When he got off, he had no idea where to go from there. So he entered the first and only pub the village possessed. He asked for a beer and he found a place at the bar. Everybody was staring at him. In such a small village where everyone knew each other, a stranger on his own was a rarity and definitely the subject of gossip and speculation. Of course, nobody dared speak out loud in front of him, so the bartender decided to take up the challenge and start a conversation.

"Hi there, is it still raining outside?" he said, feeling a bit stupid, as he knew it wasn't.

"No, it stopped a while ago," said Gilbert, who was just as keen to get some information out of the bartender, as the man was from him.

"Do you come from London?" said the barman.

"No, no. I'm not English."

"Yes, I can tell by your accent."

"Can you tell me where can I find Gloria Hammersmith?" said Gilbert, launching straight in.

"What do you want with her?" asked the barman, rather surprised.

"Oh, nothing much, but we were good friends in school and I was in the neighbourhood and I thought I should maybe stop and pay her a visit," lied Gilbert.

"Well, I haven't seen her in a while," lied the bartender in return, sensing something not quite right about this stranger.

"But she does still live here?"

"She used to, but now I don't know. Where did you say you met her?"

"I didn't. Never mind, I shall go and book a room in a hotel and I'll be on my way first thing in the morning."

"As you wish. But if I do see her again, who should I say was looking for her?" said the bartender keen to get a name.

"It doesn't matter. If I can't surprise her now, I'll try another time."

"Ok, you should get to the hotel soon, before Hadley goes to sleep. If he snores you can fire a canon near him, and he won't wake up."

"Thanks for that," said Gilbert finishing off his drink in a hurry. He was disappointed not to find out more about Gloria. It seemed these people were not as stupid as he thought.

However, there was still hope, because Gloria was obviously no stranger to them. The question was when did she leave and where did she go? He arrived at the hotel, not a moment too soon. Hadley was already half asleep. Gilbert took his key and trudged upstairs to a small room overlooking the empty street. He was sure the next day he would find answers to all of his questions and with that thought, he went to bed and was very quickly asleep.

Chapter Nine

THE CALM BEFORE THE STORM

After the girls' birthday Gloria made a decision. The letter from Paris came as a sign that their quiet days were over. If she didn't feel safe anymore, there was no reason to stay. She thought that now her enemies had searched the Paris apartment, it wouldn't be long before they made their way here, to her old house in England. They had to get away as soon as possible. Telling the girls was the difficult part. They had a life, a life they considered normal. If they left, how could she offer them that once again? They would have to start all over, in a different country, with different people. But there was no choice, she had to get them away from that evil man, who would not spare them if he found them.

The next day, she called the girls together and told them they weren't going to school.

"Why?" asked Alia surprised.

"I have to tell you something. But I need you to listen and to cooperate. There is nothing that will change my mind."

"Should we be worried, Nanna?" said Deanna.

"You won't like it, but we have no choice. And right now, I cannot explain anything to you."

"Just tell us, don't keep us waiting," said Alia, impatient to hear what on earth was going on with Nanna.

"We must move to Paris," said their grandmother.

"What?" both girls cried in disbelief. "Paris?"

"Yes, and we can't wait any longer. You have to go and pack. Don't bring everything you own, just a few things. We can buy everything we need in Paris. I need you to travel light, so we can leave as fast as possible."

"What are we running away from Nanna?" said Alia, sensing the danger in her grandmother's words.

"We are not running, don't be silly!" said Gloria, with an unconvincing smile.

"Then why are we leaving so suddenly?" asked Deanna. "We're happy here."

"I told you, no questions!" said Nanna desperately trying not to lose patience. "Now just go and pack!"

"Alright, Nanna," said Alia trying to calm her down. "So when do we actually leave?"

"First thing in the morning. I'll meet you tonight for dinner. I must go and put some things in order before leaving."

"Ok, we'll see you tonight. Let's go, Deanna."

The girls left Gloria alone in the kitchen. She grabbed her handbag and left. At least she didn't have to explain anything. It had gone better than she thought, at least that's what she believed.

In reality, Deanna was outraged. She wasn't ready to leave the life she had worked so hard to create. To lose all her friends overnight? She would have to start all over again, in a place where she was nobody. Whereas Alia found the idea of moving to Paris amazing. She saw the endless opportunities to live the life she dreamed of. To have the adventures she never thought possible. Finally, she could escape confines of her world in this boring village.

"Can you believe Nanna?" said Deanna angrily.

"What?"

"Don't tell me you're happy with her decision?" she said, even more angrily. She had hoped to find an ally in her sister.

"Well, I'm not happy, but I'm not surprised either," said Alia calmly.

"You saw that coming?"

"Don't you remember what I told you about the letter Nanna got about a week ago?"

"Sure, but what does that have to do with anything?"

"It's no coincidence that the letter was from Paris. And let's not forget about the apartment that Nanna kept Rue de Rivoli."

"Do you think we'll move there?"

"No doubt. Where else can we go?"

"Oh, you can never know with Nanna. She'll say we're going to Paris and we'll end up in Beijing."

"If she says we're going to Paris, it means we're going to Paris," said Alia trying to convince herself.

"Where shall we start packing?" asked Deanna.

"I have an idea!"

"What?"

"Do you remember our little adventure upstairs?"

"Yes…"

"Well, don't you feel like trying to find out the truth about that place before we leave? It's killing me not knowing. I always thought I had time to explore, but leaving this house without finding out what is up there would be unbearable."

"You're right, I never thought of that. And Nanna won't be home for a couple of hours."

"Let's go," said Alia, taking her phone in case they needed extra light.

The girls left their bedroom, found the stairs that creaked even louder than they remembered, and went up to the next floor of the house, which they had lived in for ten years. It was amazing they had taken so long to try to discover what was hiding upstairs. After all these years, they weren't even sure that what they saw would still be there. Also, they didn't know if they could open the doors.

Deanna turned the first door knob, they held their breath. The door opened easily. As they remembered there was the table with the map. Without knowing why she was doing that, Alia took the map, and slid it into the cylinder especially for that purpose, near the table. Next they tried the second door knob. The door opened as easily as the first. They saw the same clothes full of dust. But when they tried to open the door of the ballroom, they found it locked. It was useless to try to break in, their grandmother would have known.

They turned to door number five, fully believing that too would be locked against them, but surprisingly, the door swung open. Apparently, Nanna was only trying to keep the ballroom secret, or at least something in it.

They were a little disappointed by the last room. They only found a wooden desk, but not like the one they saw in the first room. This one looked like somebody used to draw on it a lot and belonged in the office of an old architect. The armchair was even older. And a lot of papers and pencils lay on the desktop and in all that mess, Alia found a music sheet for a piano, which she put in her pocket, together with a small key. She had never seen a key like it and she couldn't imagine what kind of door it was for.

"Deanna, look what I've just found. What do you think it is?"

"It's a key."

"I know it's a key, but have you ever seen one like this before?"

"No, but maybe it's not for a door, but a drawer."

"Yes, from that desk!"

Alia tried the key in every drawer she saw. But it didn't work. She had the idea of also trying the drawers of the desk in the other room. It didn't work there either, but she discovered one that wasn't locked. In it she found a white quill. She took it, planning to figure out its purpose later. There was also a ring, not made of gold, but maybe silver and it had a big seal on it. She determined to Google that later. It also went into a pocket and she left the room, to find out what her sister was up to.

In the meantime, Deanna had been searching the other room. She was curious about the clothes they had seen in the wardrobe. She didn't dare take them out, but when she took a step back, she lost her balance and nudged the wardrobe with her shoulder. For a large piece of furniture, it moved surprisingly easily. And then she saw the mark on the floor, where the wardrobe had stood. There was no dust on the floorboards and she noticed a little hole in the wood.

"Alia, come quickly!" she shouted excitedly.

"I'm coming, what's wrong?"

"I think I've found the lock for our key."

"What?? Where?"

"Come, I'll show you!"

Alia arrived in a hurry, waving the key in her hand. She gave it to Deanna, who was already on her knees. She twisted the key and a small piece of wood moved. Deanna put her hand inside and pulled out a little box.

"What is that?" asked Alia.

"I don't know, it looks like a little jewellery box. Let's open it?"

"Wait!" said Alia. "Let's just wait till later. Now let's continue our search."

"You're right, we don't know how much time we have before Nanna gets back."

"Deanna, how long have we been up here?"

"About an hour, an hour and a half."

"Let's hurry. We still have packing to do after this."

"The ballroom is closed, the desks are closed, the wardrobe is full of old clothes," said Deanna, recounting everything she'd found.

"Wait, what's that?" asked Alia, pulling out some fabric from behind an ugly old dress in the wardrobe.

"Looks like a bag. Or a backpack. But really, really old," said Deanna, wrinkling her nose.

"Let's just take it and leave. We'll have time to study everything later."

Fortunately, they had just made it to their room, when they heard their grandmother opening the front door.

"Girls, I'm home," she called out. "Do you need any help with your packing?"

"No, Nanna, we're almost done," lied Alia pulling her suitcase out from under her bed.

"Perfect!" said Nanna, coming to the foot of the stairs. "As soon as you've finished, we're out of here. We have a bus in two hours."

"Two hours?" wailed Deanna, looking down at her from the landing. "I thought we were leaving tomorrow. I don't even have time to call my friends to say goodbye."

"You will do no such thing!" said Nanna. Nobody must know we left.
"Why?"

"Because we need to leave fast and silently. Is your luggage ready?"

"No," said Alia, joining Deanna on the landing. "Give us another hour?"

"Ok," said Nanna, seeming satisfied with that answer and disappeared into the living room downstairs.

Now, the girls really started to pack. Alia was wondering where she could put the map, so Nanna wouldn't see it. She decided to take it out, fold it in four and put it in a book, along with the white quill. She put the little box inside a real jewellery box. The bag they had found upstairs was small enough to fit in her suitcase.

Deanna just couldn't decide which clothes to pack. In the end she realised that the less she took with her, the more her grandmother would have to buy for her in Paris. She didn't mind the idea of shopping in Paris at all.

An hour later, they both went downstairs with their small suitcases. Their grandmother was happy they'd been so efficient. The three of them came out of the house, walked swiftly to the bus stop, stepped onto the bus and left without ever looking back.

Chapter Ten

THE STORM

If they had delayed their departure until the next morning, they would have seen a weird man going round in circles in the village. First, he went to the pub for breakfast, then he started looking for anybody who might be able willing to answer a few questions. He ended up trying the library, and there he found none other than Angela, the postman's daughter.

"Hello!" said Angela. "Can I help you?"

"I don't know," said Gilbert, then decided to get straight to the point. "Do you know Gloria Hammersmith?"

"Who's asking?"

"An old friend. I wanted to surprise her, she's not expecting me."

"Does this old friend have a name?"

"Ah - yes… of course… I'm François."

"So François, you want to know where Gloria is?"

"Yes, to surprise her, as I said." Gilbert was starting to lose patience with this irritating woman.

"Ok, she lives just down the street, in the biggest house on the left. You can't miss it. It has a little carriage for children on the front lawn. I always found that carriage creepy and not at all decorative. Do you want to know anything else?"

"Yes, actually. Can you tell me if there is a moment in the day when she is not at home?"

"She goes out a lot, but she doesn't have a schedule and no routine. She always goes to do her shopping or running errands at variable times. As if somebody is studying her habits and she doesn't want to become too predictable."

"Right, so I don't know when is the best time to call on her?"

"You could go right now, the girls are at home, apparently they are sick, they didn't go to school yesterday."

"The girls? What girls?" asked Gilbert sensing he wouldn't like the answer.

"Her granddaughters, of course."

"I only knew about one of them."

"They are twins. Is there a problem?"

"No, of course not. Why would there be a problem? I only wanted to know, so I could bring them a gift. Lucky that I found out. Now I can go and search for a second present. How old are the girls, as far as I can remember they must be 12 or 13?"

"They're 14, in the same class as my daughter at school. They didn't even invite her to their party, they are so mean and jealous!"

"When was their birthday?"

"On Thursday."

"Ok, thank you. It was nice to meet you!"

"Me too, François."

"Just one last thing, did you know Gloria's daughter?"

"Samantha?" said Angela. "I was her best friend for a while."

"What happened?" asked Gilbert.

"She had a diary that became more important than our friendship."

"How is that possible? How can a diary ruin a friendship?" asked Gilbert with fake innocence.

"I don't know. She got so absorbed in that thing, it was as if the diary ran her life. She kept it in her bag all the time, but she never wrote in it in front of people."

"Weird," said Gilbert happy to have started this conversation.

"Yes, she became weird. And her mother too. She used to work and then all of the sudden she stopped."

"Gloria was never ordinary," said Gilbert trying to give the impression he knew her.

"No, but at least she is not isolated. She knows the people in the village but she doesn't have any friends."

"Then she'll be happy to see me," said Gilbert.

"I'm sure."

Gilbert left the library, thrilled with all the information he had gathered. It was enough to let him go back home to his master. He could confirm that Gloria was living there. He had no idea of the implications of two girls, rather than one, and that they were twins. But he didn't want to stop there. He went to check the house out with his own eyes, hoping also to see Gloria. He couldn't imagine why his master didn't want him to look for the diary. She couldn't be that scary. How could an old lady stop him from searching her house?

When he arrived outside the house, he realised something was not quite right. It certainly was the biggest house in the village, more like a manor, which had been modified over the years. It had lost most of its land and its imperious appearance. But the stone used to build it, and the size of the windows revealed its history. Gilbert felt as if he had stepped back in time to another era. He was not a man who scared easily, but he felt intimidated, as if at any moment an archer would let fly an arrow from the remaining tower and bring him down.

According to that woman in the library, the girls should have been at home, sick, but there was no sign of them, not a window open, no lights on. And the gate hung open. The temptation was strong. What could happen if he just went and knocked and the door? He could just be a stranger, lost in a village, asking for help.

He walked through the gate and approached the house. The size of it impressed him. He had never thought of Gloria as rich. But apparently she was. Nobody came out to stop him, so he ventured further, right up to the front door. He knocked and waited and when he was sure nobody would answer, he set about opening the door. Even though it was locked, it was no contest for his skills at breaking in. Nobody stopped him. He got into the house and tried to find out if someone was inside. All was silence, so he found the courage to start searching the house, step by step.

He found absolutely nothing, which gave him any clues about who lived there, but more importantly he realised the birds had flown the nest. Clothes were missing from the opened cupboards and the house was deserted. He resisted the urge to start looking for the diary, his boss had been very clear about that. So, it would be more profitable if he just gave his boss all the news. Harcourt would know better, how to proceed from here.

The next day, Gilbert retraced his journey back to London and took the Eurostar to Paris. When he arrived at Gare du Nord, he called his boss to warn him, they needed to meet sooner than planned. Harcourt was very happy not to have to wait for a week.

Chapter Eleven

EVERYBODY IS IN PARIS

Gloria and the girls took a taxi from Gare du Nord. Rue de Rivoli was blocked because of the traffic, as usual. Alia and Deanna were amazed by everything around them. They had left Paris when they were little, they had no memories, not even of their parents. It was as if their brains had been reset, when they left France. As soon as they arrived at the flat, Gloria took her phone and tapped in a number. She whispered something to whoever answered and the door opened. The apartment was on the second floor. When they got upstairs, Gloria opened the door and the girls saw the couple that looked after their home.

"Hello," said Gilles Lacroix.

"Hello," said Gloria. "How are you Gilles?"

"I'm better now that I see you travelled safely. We were a little worried."

"And you, Béa, how are you?" said Gloria to Gilles' wife.

"Very well, happy to see you and the girls again," said the woman politely.

"Hello," said the girls in unison. Both of them wondered why they didn't recognise her.

"Let's get you in and settled," said Gilles.

The girls were very anxious to see their new room. So they took their luggage and followed Gilles. The apartment was bigger than they imagined. The hallway was narrow but the rooms were large and the ceilings beautifully decorated. They couldn't believe this was their new home, it was more like visiting a palace. They were sharing the same room, but they wouldn't have had it otherwise. Gilles showed them where the bathroom was, then left them to themselves.

"Can you believe it?" squeaked Alia.

"It's incredible. Two days ago we were going to school in the middle of nowhere and now we have our own room in Paris!" answered Deanna. "Lucky for us Nanna taught us French."

"Well, I don't know about you, I remember learning fencing, Spanish and German, but not French. I don't think Nanna taught us French. I think we spoke French when we were small. Nanna improved on it."

"I think you're right," said Deanna and started unpacking her case.

"What are you doing?" said Alia surprised.

"Unpacking, why?"

"We can do that later. Let's go and see if Nanna will allow us out to explore. We're in Paris!"

They ran to find their grandmother. She agreed to let them go out, but only in the neighbourhood. For them it was more than enough, they lived in front of the Louvre, with the Champs Élysée at their feet.

The very next day they started at their new school. At first they were nervous, but soon discovered it wasn't so difficult and the teachers were very helpful to foreign students. They spoke French fluently, their spelling was correct, so school was easy. Deanna started to make friends straight away, while Alia was still getting to know her environment. She discovered an English bookstore just on the ground floor of their building. She visited it at every opportunity. The girls didn't feel the same pressure as they used to. They started their fencing lessons. They had an amazing teacher who saw their talent straight away. They continued to study foreign languages with their grandmother. The nice couple who took care of the apartment moved out, but Gloria didn't abandon them and Béa came once a week to help with the cooking and cleaning. What they were not aware of, was that someone was watching their every move. Every time they entered or left the apartment, Gilbert was there, spying on them from the shadows.

As soon as he returned from England, he went to see his master. They both realised that Gloria had outsmarted them. They had no idea where she had gone. They tried searching where they knew she had relatives, but it all led to a dead end. She could have been anywhere. It took them quite a while to realise that Gloria was actually hiding under their very noses. So Gilbert started to watch the apartment Rue de Rivoli again. Soon enough he saw the twins coming out of the building. They were dressed for horse riding lessons. He followed them. He started to learn their schedule. But he couldn't see Gloria. He wondered if she ever ventured out of the house.

One day he saw the three of them leaving for the Opera Garnier, at least he knew Gloria was still alive. He wondered what his master had planned for the girls. He would never dare to ask directly, he feared him too much, but he started to understand that Harcourt needed more information before taking action. So Gilbert kept a journal, noting the girls' routine. Crucially, he never once saw them with the diary. Either the girls didn't have it, or they kept it very well hidden. But their lives seemed so boring, he doubted they kept any diary, never mind that one.

One day everything changed. School broke up for the summer and Alia and Deanna were on holiday. No more lessons till autumn. They went out for longer periods of time, but they were easy to follow. Gloria on the other hand was impossible. All his efforts to find her were frustrated and most of the time, he had no idea where she was. But Harcourt assured him that Gloria could not keep the diary without the girls. As far as Gilbert could tell, just knowing where they were all the time didn't help much. All this time spent with no action, he felt was wasting his time. Then one day it dawned on him, what the purpose of all this boring activity was.

Chapter Twelve

TWO WEEKS EARLIER...

After unpacking everything and getting comfortable in their new home, Gloria took the girls shopping. They never knew all these years, that Nanna had money. They always led a very modest life, not realising their grandmother had chosen that for them. They didn't complain, in the village there was nothing to spend money on anyway. But now Deanna was living her dream, choosing her wardrobe from the pages of the latest fashion magazines. At the same time, Alia was living her own dream, of exploring, visiting museum, gardens. She realised it would take her years to get to know Paris and an eternity to get bored of it. Finally, the girls could say they were genuinely happy.

There was just one thing that didn't go their way. The items they had found in their old house seemed to be useless. They had put so much hope in them, believing these things would lead to finding their mother's diary. But the jewellery box was impossible to open, the map led nowhere, the quill was made of a goose feather, but nothing interesting.

Then one Sunday afternoon, when Alia went to her grandmother's bedroom, she saw a little jewellery box. She had never seen Gloria wearing jewellery so she was puzzled. When she opened it, she found just a solitary ring. It was simple, with just a 'fleur de lys' emblem, like a golden seal. The seal looked familiar. She had seen it somewhere before. She knew it was the symbol of French royalty, but she couldn't remember where she had last seen it. Alia decided to take it, maybe Nanna wouldn't notice, at least for a day or two.

"Deanna, look what I found!" said Alia running into their room.

"What?" asked Deanna.

"I found this ring!" said Alia waving it in front of her sister.

"I saw that somewhere," said Deanna, studying the design.

"Yes, me too, but where?"

"I think I know, let me check something," said Deanna leaving Alia bursting with curiosity.

Deanna came back with the little box they had found in their old house, the box they had never opened. It was the size of an octagonal earring box. One side was completely different from the others and it had a 'fleur de lys' engraved on it, exactly like the one on the seal. Deanna put the ring on the box and to their surprise it matched. At the touch of the ring, the silver box opened with a little click, and resembled the petals of a flower. The girls looked at it in amazement.

"That's incredible," said Alia in awe.

"It looks like a compass," said Deanna studying every detail.

"Yes, but it is a little different, it doesn't seem to show north."

"How did you figure that out?"

"I'm not sure. Let's go and find another compass and compare it"

"Where can we find a compass near here?" said Deanna.

"It's easy. They sell them at the bookshop downstairs."

"What?" said Deanna, surprised at her sister's knowledge of the place so soon.

"Just let me put the ring back, we don't need it anymore," said Alia.

"Exactly, we don't want Nanna to find out about our little misdemeanour" whispered Deanna.

Alia returned to Nanna's room. She wasn't afraid of finding her there, because now Gloria had to open two doors before entering her room, so she had time to leave if she heard something. But she was afraid she might touch or move something and Nanna would know somebody had been there. And she was so protective of her stuff. She was careful to leave everything in its place.

When she got back to their room, Deanna was dressed and ready, with the opened box in her hand.

"Ok, let's go," said Alia.

They ran down the stairs and out into the street. Deanna realised it was the first time she'd entered the English bookstore. Deanna was no 'nerd', as she often called her sister, but she had to admit that the place was amazing, its shelves packed with wonderful books. As they entered, they came across the children's section, with titles that could attract the curiosity of any child, or even adult for that matter. She found herself thinking that if she ever wrote a book, which was rather improbable, this is where she would like to find her masterpiece. She understood now why Alia spent so much time here. Even the smell was enough to welcome the readers inside. The shop was two storeys high and it sold things you would never have imagined to find in such a place, for instance compasses. They chose one, paid for it and hurried back to their room.

"Now, let's see," said Alia her curiosity at fever pitch. "Let's see if the compass we found really is different."

"It is!" shouted Deanna. "Look, when you put it in the same position, it should show the same direction. A compass always shows-"

"North!" said Alia.

"Exactly, and assuming the compass we just bought is right, that means our compass shows… well, not north. But…"

"South-east, this one shows south-east," said Alia studying their broken compass. She was very disappointed. She couldn't understand why Nanna had been so secretive about those rooms upstairs, when all they had found was a map that led nowhere, an empty bag and now a broken compass. She had great hopes when she opened the box, but now all hope for something interesting was gone.

"Why do you think Nanna kept it so well hidden all this time? It is just a broken compass," said Deanna.

"You read my mind. Nanna would never do anything without a logical reason," said Alia.

"And everything we found is useless."

"Also, nothing was in the same place. Did you notice the rooms upstairs were in a total mess? Have you ever seen Nanna's room other than spotless?" asked Alia.

"No, you're right. It's not like her to leave the house like that. Unless…"

"Unless what?"

"Unless she left it like that on purpose," said Deanna feeling she was getting close to something. Something important.

"But why would she?" asked Alia.

"I think the mess was her way of hiding something in plain sight. It's very clever if you think about it. Even if you found something, you wouldn't necessarily take any notice of it."

"And the compass was well hidden, we found it by accident," said Alia starting to understand where Deanna was going.

"So it means that the objects we found had a value. But why were they spread in different places?"

"Maybe because they are important only if they are together!" said Alia, with rising excitement.

"If you're right, then what is the link between a quill, a map, a backpack and a compass?" asked Deanna.

"Maybe we can find a link between the map and the compass?" said Alia.

"We could if the compass wasn't broken," said Deanna starting to show her frustration with the situation. They had spent so many hours trying to fathom the whole thing out.

"Maybe we're looking in the wrong direction?" said Alia.

"What? What did you just say?" asked Deanna, excited.

"I said, maybe we are looking in the wrong direction," repeated Alia, not understanding Deanna's excitement.

"What does the compass show?"

"The wrong direction. But we've already looked at the map. It's just a very old map of Paris and the surrounding area."

"Yes, and we looked north, because there was a marking of the north on the map."

"Yes, and there are a lot of places, where you could hide something like a diary. We looked for every castle, every church. But it would be impossible for us to go and ask in all of them."

"But what if we were looking at the wrong north?"

"What do you mean?" asked Alia.

"What if the compass is there just to show us the north for this map?"

"Then we really were looking in the wrong direction," said Alia finally understanding Deanna's logic.

They took the map and the compass, turned the map to match the north of the compass and looked where that led them. According to the compass, north was showing as south-west.

"Ok, we changed the direction, but it doesn't get us closer to a specific point," complained Alia.

"At least now we know there is something to look for. What else do we have on the map that can give us a clue?" asked Deanna.

"There's the year it was printed, I guess. 1944."

"That doesn't help us much. Maybe we should look for a building from that year?"

"Good idea, let's search," said Alia taking out her smartphone. The royal chapel of Dreux, construction started in1816. Close enough."

"I don't think so. It must be something more precise to help us. If we take every building before 1944 we'll go nowhere," said Deanna. "What else?"

"Well, not much, just the printer's name."

"What is it?"

"Rochefoucauld and Co. I told you, nothing important," said Alia.

"It might be…" said Deanna, searching something on her phone.

"What?"

"Rochefoucauld and Co doesn't exist. At least not in printing. It never did."

"That's strange," said Alia.

"I think it's a clue."

"A clue for what?" asked Nanna, standing in the open doorway, scaring the girls half to death, they had been so absorbed in their recent discoveries.

"Nanna!" gasped Alia. "When did you get home?"

"Five minutes ago. What are you doing girls?"

"Just talking," answered Deanna.

"What do you say we go out and do some shopping? I just realised, it's summer and we have nothing to wear… the three of us."

"Great!" said Deanna. "Let's go."

"Do I have to come?" groaned Alia.

"Yes, you need clothes too. I won't take no for an answer."

"Ok Nanna. You're right. I'd never go shopping on my own."

The three of them left the apartment. The girls would have much preferred to stay and try to figure things out. It would have to wait until tomorrow. However, with tomorrow came even more surprises.

Chapter Thirteen

THE OTHER TWINS

Neuilly sur Seine is one of the richest and most expensive suburbs of Paris. To buy an apartment there, you had to be fabulously wealthy, or have inherited it from your family. Its residents paid the price of being close to Paris, while still enjoying life near a park, and the added luxury of a little garden behind their block. Parents drop their children off at school in the morning, then hurry to get to work. In the afternoon, they take the subway and collect their children from school. The routine is repeated every day, except on weekends when the children take lessons in horse riding and tennis. Sundays they go to church, because people in the rich suburbs are very catholic, they like to be seen all dressed alike, with three or more children. After church, they go to buy their baguette, then all go home and have lunch together. When it's sunny they take a walk in the park or ride their bike. Nobody dares be different.

However, one family seemed to be breaking the tradition. They didn't possess anything like the money the others enjoyed, but they did have a very nice apartment. Everybody wondered how they could afford a place like that, because it's not enough just to own it, you have to have the money to keep it. The couple were about forty, very nice but kept themselves separate from the rest of the community. The mother didn't go to the same hairdresser as the other wives, she probably couldn't afford it. The father didn't join the other men, smoking cigars and drinking cognac in the back rooms of bistros.

The couple had two boys, twins, and they enjoyed all the same activities as their friends. They took riding lessons, played tennis and went out with their mates. The parents made sacrifices so that their children could have a normal life, normal according to their standards, of course!

The twins were not hard to notice. Every girl in school wanted to be with one of them, and they didn't mind which one. Not only they were very handsome but they had an air of mystery. They were very close, and they were identical. They had dark hair and dark eyes and they didn't smile very often, but when they did, their eyes smiled too. That was enough to melt every girl's heart. And they had a very nice voice that made them impossible to refuse. Even their parents were incapable of saying no to them. They were tall for their age, just fifteen years old. They seemed rather fragile but in every sporting competition they came in first.

Even the teachers who knew them well couldn't tell them apart. They were doing very well at school, and they made everything look effortless. But they had one weak point. They were shy with the girls. They were aware that they could have any girl in their school, but they didn't seem to be interested. At first everybody thought that they couldn't find a girl good enough for them. But in fact they weren't looking. They tried dating once or twice, but they were searching for the same deep connection they had together. And that was simply impossible. Girls seemed shallow to them. So they decided to leave it to fate. When the right girl came along, they'd know. Their parents were ambitious like all parents that sacrifice their life for their children, but the boys didn't feel any pressure and they were happy.

"What do you want to do today?" asked Marc as they were getting out of bed.

"I was thinking of going to Jardin du Luxembourg and playing tennis," said Victor.

"Wouldn't you prefer going to Jardin de Tuileries? I heard they have a new attraction."

"Ok. And when we get bored, we can go and play tennis."

The boys had breakfast and got dressed. When they left their home that day, they had no idea that their routine lives were about to be changed forever.

Chapter Fourteen

GLORIA

As the girls were getting ready to go to the Jardin des Tuileries, Gloria asked Gilles and Béa to come by. She welcomed them with coffee and cookies.

"How are the girls doing?" asked Béa, taking a cookie from the plate.

"They are starting to feel at home here," replied Gloria.

"They are at home here… at least they used to be."

"It's much more difficult now, they're older and harder to influence."

"Maybe you should start by telling them the truth?" said Gilles.

"I know," sighed Gloria. "But I'm not ready to spoil their childhood just yet."

"Maybe you would spoil their childhood but at the same time, you would give them a past, answer questions they never dare to ask," said Béa.

"If I tell them the truth, they will want more and they will start searching. What do I do when they find out all of the truth?"

"Maybe they need to know all of the truth so they can protect themselves from Harcourt and his so-called friends" answered Gilles.

"Do you really think they are in danger?"

"You didn't see the guy that came here. He was very determined to take what he had been looking for so long. And I am sure that he isn't the most dangerous of the group."

"Perhaps they don't know you're here," said Béa.

"Oh, they know!" said Gloria. "I'm not fooling myself. When I came here, it was not to hide from them, but try to protect the girls. I succeeded to hide them for ten years. Now that they are fourteen, Harcourt is in more trouble than the girls."

"What do you mean?"

"Harcourt can't have the diary. Without the girls the diary is useless. It is one of the girls who must hand it to him."

"Where is the diary now?" asked Gilles.

"Safe," answered Gloria, the question unsettling her. "Why?"

"Don't forget I was there the last time someone handled it. I don't like the idea that Harcourt could get his dirty hands on it."

"It was terrible, but I won't make the same mistake twice," said Gloria.

"You can't. You can't lose your daughter twice," said Gilles. "At least you learned the real power of the diary."

"Samantha tried to warn me, but I didn't listen. She had seen everything. Her husband was a dreamer. He couldn't protect them. I should have," said Gloria.

"You can't blame yourself for everything," said Gilles.

"Not for everything, but for my daughter's life I can."

"What's done is done, Gloria. Let's concentrate on keeping the diary where it is hidden for as long as possible."

"Béa, try to get close to the girls, become their friend. So I'll know when it is the right time to tell them the truth," asked Gloria. She wasn't very happy to involve the Lacroix in the girls' lives, but she didn't have any choice. She tried not to get too close to them, she was afraid of the questions.

"Ok, it shouldn't be too hard," said Béa.

"You would be surprised. Alia talks only to Deanna and Deanna has enough friends."

"I'll do my best," said Béa. "I really like those girls."

"Then let's keep them safe… and innocent if possible," said Gloria.

"As long as the girls are safe, we are all safe," said Gilles.

"Where are they now?" asked Béa.

"They went to Jardin des Tuileries. Apparently, there are new attractions in the park," said Gloria. We'll let them have their freedom. As long they are busy, they won't have time to look around."

She had no idea that the girls were already onto something and they were only trying to go about normal activities, so Nanna wouldn't get suspicious. But behind her back, they had bought a map of Paris and its surroundings, a modern one, to compare with the old. They were also searching for information about that quill.

Gloria had every reason to be worried. But she wanted so much to be able to prepare the girls correctly for the inevitable confrontation with Harcourt. They had to become stronger, and wiser, more like warriors than teenagers. They were up against an enemy who had neither morals nor conscience. They had to crush him or to be crushed.

On the other hand, it wasn't fair to ask them to give up their innocence just because of a mistake she made 25 years ago, when she let Samantha use the diary for the first time. Now she was facing almost the same decision, but this time the girls will not give her the choice. She thought she was in control, but she wasn't. But, as long as she was alive, the girls would always have a confidante and a protector. She went to the window, to see if she could spot the girls in the crowd. But there were too many people, it was hopeless.

Chapter Fifteen

HAVING FUN

In the winter, the gardens of the Louvre museum are quiet, except for some hardy tourists, attracted to the park which has so much history to offer. But as soon as the sunny days arrive, Parisians come out of hibernation. Entire families go out for walks and tourists start to eat their sandwiches outside, on the grass.

For residents of the neighbourhood, it's the best time of the year. Because starting in June, the gardens become an amusement park, and with that, the noise, the excitement of the children riding the roller coaster, the smell of food and cotton candy. Deanna and Alia left the apartment and two minutes later they were in the park. Alia was wearing blue shorts with a blue t-shirt. It was all she knew about fashion, not to mix too many colours. Deanna had on a yellow dress, with shorts underneath, because in an amusement park it's not a good idea to wear dresses, which could reveal too much. Although the boys didn't seem to mind. They had chosen to go early to avoid the crowd. But still they had to wait in line for the main attractions.

"Do you want to try "la boule"?" asked Deanna.

"Are you crazy? Do you see me riding in that ball from hell?"

"Why not? It should be fun," said Deanna laughing.

"Let's split here. The lines are too long, we can't wait for each attraction," suggested Alia.

"Ok, I'll meet you here as soon as I am done with mine," agreed Deanna.

Alia went right and Deanna went left. Deanna stood in line for almost half an hour, before realising she needed somebody to accompany her because the attraction had two seats. Everybody in line came in pairs, except for one guy, who didn't seem to realise he was missing a partner. Deanna knew she couldn't count on her sister, and even if she did, she didn't want to get out of that long line to go and find her. She had waited too long. So she took the courage to talk to the lonely boy. She didn't even know which language to speak to him in. What if he was a polish tourist and he didn't speak English or French, or Spanish, or any other language she had learned with Nanna? How to start? While she was asking herself all those questions, help came.

"Hi, do you speak English? Or French?" asked the boy, startling her.

"Both. Pick which is more comfortable for you," she answered, blushing. If somebody from her old life had seen her now, she thought, they would have said she was definitely Alia, the shy one. Nobody had seen Deanna blush since she was five.

"Ok," said the boy in French. "Do you mind sharing this ride with me? I need a partner and you…"

"Need one too. I noticed."

"Ok, then it's settled. We're in this together," he said smiling.

Deanna was completely enchanted. When he smiled, when he showed his amazing white teeth, when his bright eyes glowed even brighter, her world turned upside down. She had never felt love before. She couldn't put a name on her feelings but she had lost all sense of time and space. She was used to having the world at her feet, but now all she wanted was for this moment to go on forever. But it was brought to an abrupt halt, when the guy responsible for their safety, came to put them in the 'boule'. She realised then that she didn't even know his name.

"What's your name?" he asked as if he had read her mind.

"Deanna, and yours?" She felt relieved to be doing small talk, to disguise her embarrassment.

"I'm Victor. Nice meeting you Deanna."

Please, stop smiling, stop smiling, Deanna screamed inside her head.

"Have you done this before?" she asked, making a supreme effort to make her voice sound normal.

"No, never. You?"

"It's my first time, too. When I'm frightened I tend to talk nonsense. Don't mind me if I say too much."

"Then this will be fun, since we will have everything recorded on a memory card," he said.

"I won't let you have it," said Deanna smiling for the first time.

"I have my rights, you cannot stop me."

"I'll find a way. But now it's time to get killed."

"If you want you can take my hand. I won't let you fall."

I think I already did! Thought Deanna to herself.

"Ok, thank you," she managed to say out loud.

The moment Deanna touched Victor's hand, he felt a shiver down his spine that he couldn't explain. He had never felt anything like that before. It was as if they were connected. He felt like he had known her before, as if they had already been friends, for an eternity. Other girls he had met, never gave him that feeling, only awkwardness. When they started jumping with that ball, he wasn't looking at the view, he turned his head to see her looking at him too. They both looked away, feeling the same pleasure that the other one was interested.

As the security guy was guiding them towards the exit, they realised that they hadn't let go of their hands. So they went together to see the video and both asked for a copy, in case they never saw each other again. At least, they thought, they would have a souvenir.

"See, I have my copy. This way I'll never forget this moment," grinned Victor.

"I couldn't forget it, it was too intense," said Deanna hoping he wouldn't read between the lines.

"I liked it, but I don't think I could do it again, could you?" asked Victor.

"I prefer other rides, but I had to see for myself. It's not such a big deal."

"You are so brave now, but you should have seen yourself up there," he said.

They both started laughing. For a moment she forgot everything, the adrenaline gave her the courage to look in her purse for a pen, she took his hand and she wrote her phone number on the back of it.

His hands started to sweat, he was afraid that the ink might wear off, so he took the pen from her hand and he wrote his phone number for her, just to be sure they didn't lose contact. Everything was so surprisingly natural. He wasn't a dreamer, but it was almost as if this couldn't be real.

She was just about to tell him something, when a group of Chinese teenagers passed by and they got separated. One moment later she felt her sister at her side.

"Was it as terrifying as it looks from the ground?" asked Alia.

"No, I don't understand all the screaming we can hear from our room."

"Would you like to do something else?" asked Alia.

"I wouldn't mind an ice-cream," said Deanna still dreaming about Victor, about his amazing smile, his warm hands, and his eyes, oh, those eyes!

"Let's go. Then we can go home and see what we can make of that map," said Alia.

"Agreed," said Deanna. She had no hope of finding Victor again, it was way too crowded. But she had his number. She wrote it down fast so she couldn't lose it."

The girls left the park and went straight home. Their search didn't go very well, because Deanna had her head in the clouds. Alia noticed something was wrong with her sister, but as long as Deanna didn't want to talk about it, she didn't want to force her. She knew that when her sister was ready, she would open up. Alia wondered if something had happened in the park while they were separated, so she decided to leave Deanna alone with her thoughts. She left the apartment and went downstairs to the bookshop, hoping they had something new.

Chapter Sixteen

THE SPIES

While the four teenagers were having fun in the park, Gilbert Landemare and Maxime d'Harcourt were looking down at them from another apartment in Rue de Rivoli, they had rented purely to keep their eyes on the girls. Gloria couldn't have been more wrong, when she thought that they were far away from them. They were like two predators watching their prey. The girls had no idea they were being watched all the time. However, the two men were not totally happy with the apartment, because it wasn't close enough to hear anything. But they had no choice. Being able to spy on them constantly should be enough. But when they saw Deanna with Victor, they became suspicious.

"Who is that boy?" asked Harcourt. "Does she know him?"

"I have no idea. I have never seen him before. Maybe he is just asking the time?" suggested Gilbert.

"In that case why are they going together on that ride?"

"Oh, ok, so they must know each other," said Gilbert trying to read the situation.

"They seem to be quite close," said Maxime.

"Where did he disappear?" asked Gilbert, not seeing how they split up.

"I don't know, but the boy looks familiar. I've seen those eyes before."

"Where?" asked Gilbert. He couldn't understand how somebody could recognise someone else by their eyes and especially from that distance. But he didn't want to disturb his master, and put him in a worse mood.

"I don't remember. It feels like a very long time ago… when I was young."

"When you were young?" said Gilbert. "Were you as lonely then as you are now?"

"Me, lonely? I was never alone," said Maxime, almost about to reveal something of his past. "I had many friends and too many girlfriends."

"Then, what happened?"

"A girl happened!" snapped Maxime, irritated by Gilbert's tone of voice. "You don't have to feel pity for me, you fool!"

"I don't, I just wanted to know you a little better," said Gilbert, trying to calm him down. Seeing his boss like that scared him. He knew that he was dangerous when he got angry.

"You know more than enough about me. My past isn't any of your business."

"It's not, you're right. Let's go down and grab a cup of coffee. We've been here for too long."

"Ok, the girls have left anyway. I saw them going into the building."

The two men left just as Alia was going downstairs, to the bookshop. They would soon realise that they were in the right place at the right time. But for now they were almost alone in the coffee house, everybody else chose to sit outside. They preferred inside because they had more privacy. They had to speak louder because of the noise around them, but they were careful about what they said.

"What if Gloria realises that we've found her and the girls, and she takes them away again?" said Gilbert, drinking his coffee.

"We shall follow them. They can't get away from us this time. We found them again after ten years. I won't let her escape me now, not ever," said Harcourt. "This time she won't leave Paris alive, I promise you that."

"You hate her that much?"

"She took everything from me, so in the end, when I've finished with the girls, I shall leave her with nothing, exactly as she did to me." Harcourt spoke so calmly, it was as if he was discussing the weather.

"And who will kill them? You?" asked Gilbert, feeling anxious. He really didn't want to kill the girls. The old witch, no problem, but the innocent girls…

"Don't worry, we won't get our hands dirty. The diary will do his job," answered Maxime, making Gilbert's anxiety climb.

"What do you mean?"

"It's not yet time to talk to you about this diary. When the moment comes you will know everything that you need to know about it. And about the other one. Hopefully we won't need it."

"Why?"

"Well let's say that if we are in a situation that requires the second diary, we will be in a lot of trouble," said Maxime coolly before ordering another coffee.

"Look!" Gilbert interrupted. "Isn't that Alia with the same boy, who spoke to Deanna earlier?"

"So it is. I don't know how you tell the girls apart. They are identical."

"Alia was in blue, Deanna in yellow. Unless she changed her clothes, but I don't think so. What's strange, is the guy has changed his."

"Ok, if you say so. Let's see what happens next. Then you will follow Alia and I will follow the boy."

"Why? Is he important?" asked Gilbert. "You wouldn't want to kill him too, just because he is talking to the girls?"

"His face looks familiar. I already had that feeling when I first saw him in the park. I need to know more about him."

So when Alia and the boy separated, the two spies split up to follow them. Alia went directly home and the boy took the subway and then the bus to Neuilly. He entered a building and Maxime was left alone to investigate. He had no idea what he was looking for, but he thought that if he could set eyes on the boy's parents, maybe he would understand the feeling that he was having about that boy. But he discovered nothing, and returned home disappointed.

Chapter Seventeen

THE WH SMITH BOOKSHOP

Alia left Deanna at home. She had never seen her so out of this world. She had always been her rock, her anchor in the real world. Now she barely breathed, she didn't eat and she wouldn't tell her what's going on. This frustrated Alia and since she had never seen Deanna in love, she had no idea what was wrong. When she arrived at the book shop, she was still thinking about her sister, and not really paying attention at what was going on around her. She collided with a boy, knocked him flying and with him a whole shelf full of books.

"I'm so sorry, I'm sorry," she said trying to help him up.

"It's Ok, no harm done," he said smiling. "But your boss won't be too happy about those books."

"Whose boss?" asked Alia, upset. "What are you talking about?" She didn't mind being mistaken for an employee, but the fact he thought she looked old enough to work there, was what rankled with her.

"I'm sorry, I assumed you were working here!" he said adding salt to the wound.

"And what gave you that impression?"

"I've seen you here, more than once, and you seem so familiar with the place."

"Yes, because I like reading and it is the only place where I can find books in English."

"You can always buy on the internet," suggested the boy, trying to get her to forget his mistake.

"I don't like buying on the internet, I like to touch the books, I like…"

"Their smell, the sound they make when you turn the pages to see what it's about."

"Exactly, it's not the same."

"I feel the same way. And I can't stand e-books," said the boy smiling again. He knew he was on the right track and she had got over their unfortunate start.

"So did you find something interesting today?" asked Alia when she saw all the books in his arms.

"Obviously, and you?"

"I've just arrived. I was too busy injuring you and making all this mess," said Alia blushing.

"Let's take a look together, maybe I missed something."

So they started looking around, sharing opinions about the books they had both read, asking for opinions, giving opinions. At least two or three hours went by and they were still among the shelves discussing books. Everybody else had left the shop. Reality kicked in when they started to feel thirsty, but neither of them wanted to break the spell.

"Aren't you thirsty after all this talking?" he asked shyly.

"If you want to leave, don't let me keep you," said Alia worried that he was getting bored. She had finally found somebody to share her passion for books with.

"No, I don't want to leave," he tried to reassure her. "I just want to have a drink with you."

"Oh, Ok," said Alia, blushing again with embarrassment.

So they took their books, paid for them and then went to the coffeehouse nearby. They chose a table far from the noisy tourists and continued their conversation.

"So, which will be the first book you'll read?" said the boy, whose name she had discovered, was Marc.

"I think the one about the French castles. I like reading about French history from a stranger's point of view," she replied. not even noticing that the waiter had brought their sodas.

"Me too. It doesn't sound like a history lesson at school."

"Exactly, it's not boring."

"I have a history teacher, who managed to send himself to sleep, during one of his lessons."

"No, he fell asleep?

"While talking."

"And what did you do?" asked Alia laughing.

"We let him sleep, and when the bell rang, we acted as if he had just dozed off for a couple of seconds and we hadn't noticed."

"You are nice. If he had been in our class, he would have woken up with a fake moustache, and fingers in a glass of water."

"We are not nice, but we are afraid of him," said Marc, happy to see her laugh at his jokes.

"Do you want to look have a look at my book together?"

"Sure, let's take a peek."

"Do you travel much, with your parents?" she asked.

"We used to, Alia, especially in France. My parents don't like to go out of the country."

"Why?"

"I don't know. They say there are so many beautiful places here, that we don't need to go further," said Marc, shrugging his shoulders.

"They're right, there are lots of wonderful places to visit in France but that doesn't mean that you can't go elsewhere. I lived in England and it's very beautiful. London is amazing."

"I'm sure. I dream about going backpacking through England, Scotland and Ireland. If my parents won't take me, I'll go as soon as I'm 18, I'll go and live my dream."

Alia was looking at him with so much admiration, for his independence, for his determination. She wondered if, for the first time in her life she had found somebody worthy to be her friend. Not that she felt so highly about herself, but because she was aware that she was very boring for most of the people her age. For the first time she felt that talking to somebody was not an effort. Usually, all conversation bored her and gave her the feeling she would rather be at home with a good book. Some would say she was shy, but in fact she lived better in the world of books than in the real world.

"I would like to be able to do the same. Go, live the adventure," said Alia.

"Who's stopping you?" asked Marc. "You have to wait a little longer than me, but it's not impossible."

"Nanna. If you knew her, you would soon realise that nothing happens without her agreement."

"Yes, but when you're 18 she couldn't stop you. You can do what you want."

"I owe everything to my grandmother. If it weren't for her, I would be in foster home. I couldn't do that to her."

"You have to live your life. You can't wait for your grandmother's approval for every decision you make."

"I know, but for now, I'm stuck," said Alia with a sigh.

"So let's take a virtual trip round a castle. You choose which one," said Marc, smiling.

"Ok, let's try Chambord," she suggested.

"Oh, the Loire valley. It is my favourite in that region."

"It looks like the palace of a princess," said Alia.

"Would you like to be a princess?" he asked.

"Who wouldn't like to be a prince or a princess?"

"Me. All the traditions, all the fuss about how to eat, when to keep your legs crossed, and not crossed, how to wave your hand, how to tilt your head. Do you realise, all that effort is just for appearances."

"You're right. But can't I have the castle without the disadvantages?"

"You can't have it all. It is very dangerous to think that you can have all that you want."

"I know… I realised a long time ago that you can't have the brain and the looks at the same time," said Alia ironically.

"Oh, do you think I'm stupid or ugly?" he asked, laughing.

"Neither. I wasn't talking about you."

"I hope that you weren't talking about you either. Because it's not true."

Alia wasn't sure if that was a compliment or he was just polite. But she was having fun and she didn't feel like analysing every word. She thought it best to change the subject.

"How about this castle, have you been to that one?"

"Of course, it's not that far. It belonged to the Rochefoucauld family. It is a 16th century castle. It is also a hotel and a restaurant. But we never slept or ate there. It's too expensive."

"Wait! Go back! What family did you say it belonged to?" Alia almost screamed.

"Rochefoucauld. You scared me," he said wondering what was wrong with her.

"Sorry, I have to go," she said leaping up. "But it was nice meeting you, really nice!" She searched for some coins to pay for her soda.

"No, don't go. Did I say something wrong?"

"No, everything was perfect. Almost too good to be true. But I have to go now."

"At least let me buy you this drink?"

"Ok, but the next one is on me," said Alia with a smile. She was trying to impress on him that it wasn't his fault she was dashing off so rudely.

"There will be a next one?"

"I hope so, that's what friends do, isn't it? They get together from time to time."

"Friends? Ok, friends. Can you give me your phone number?" asked Marc with a hint of disappointment in his voice.

Alia wrote her number on a napkin for him, thanked him for a wonderful afternoon and left running. Marc paid for the drinks and left. Neither of them noticed the two men, leaving the café at the same time and following each of them home.

Marc took the subway. He was so absorbed in his thoughts that he didn't see the crowd around him. He tried to understand what had just happened. Where everything went wrong. He had spent a wonderful afternoon with a girl, who wasn't trying to be with him. He didn't feel like a trophy, he didn't feel the effort he usually suffered, just to have a normal conversation. Everything went so naturally. He had finally found a girl to laugh at his jokes and not get offended. Or at least to forgive his mistakes. He had never met a girl so funny and smart and beautiful and… not aware that she was all that. That was her most adorable quality, that she was completely unaware of her charm.

He checked his pocket, afraid that he might lose the napkin with her number on. But at least he knew he could always find her in their bookshop. He could never go there again without thinking of her, or remembering how they met. From now on, it seemed he couldn't do anything without thinking of her.

There was just one thing that cast a shadow on his happiness. She had called him "a friend". That's what he always called the girls he wouldn't like to go out with. If she saw him as a friend, did it mean she could never see him as a boyfriend? And he wasn't sure that he could stand to be around her, touch her, breathe her perfume, knowing that she could never love him. Because even if he had only just become aware of her existence, one thing he was sure of, he had fallen hopelessly in love with Alia.

Chapter Eighteen

A BIG DISCOVERY

Alia didn't stop running until she arrived at home. Unfortunately, Nanna was there and she wasn't busy. Gloria started to ask questions about their day, how did they spend it? How was the park and why did they leave so early? Where did she go after that? Alia was under the impression that Nanna would never stop with all the boring questions. And she didn't feel like telling her about Marc. She had a feeling Nanna wouldn't agree with him. She wouldn't understand her need to have a friend, especially if it was a boy. If Marc had been a girl it wouldn't have been a problem. But Nanna was too narrow minded to accept the idea of a friendship between a boy and a girl. So Alia gave her the answers she thought Nanna would want to hear.

It felt like an eternity until the moment Gloria let her go to her room. She had about an hour until dinnertime, to tell her sister about the momentous discovery, which had sadly brought her wonderful afternoon with Marc to an abrupt end. She decided not to tell Deanna about him, afraid that she might want to meet him and take him away from her. From her experience with her sister, if she wanted something, she had to keep it secret. Deanna was not mean, or selfish but she attracted everyone and everything naturally. So for now they would only talk about what interested them most, the castle.

"Hello," said Alia entering the room. "Feeling better?"

"I'm fine. Earlier I was just a little tired from the park," said Deanna, defending herself. She realised that her behaviour was difficult to explain and she was grateful to Alia that she didn't ask her any questions, which she didn't want to answer. Deanna was not aware of what was happening to Alia.

"I'm glad to see that you are able to exchange some words with me. Earlier I was talking to myself. Now, are you ready to hear something amazing?" asked Alia. She wanted to have Deanna's full attention.

"Always," said Deanna, suddenly interested.

"I think I've found the place we're looking for on the map," said Alia, pausing for a moment to let the information sink in.

"What? How come?"

"It doesn't matter. The important thing is that I know where to search. But the problem is how to get there," said Alia, aware she had captured her sister's complete attention.

"So where is it? Tell me! Don't be mean, leaving me hanging on like that."

"It's called Chateau d'Esclimont, in the department of Eure et Loire, not far from here."

"Ok, but how can you be so sure that this is our place?"

"I checked. It's in the right direction and guess the name of its former owner?"

"I don't know! You're being cruel!"

"The family of Rochefoucauld." Alia dropped the bomb.

"Oh, as in Rochefoucauld and co? You think this was the clue we were missing?"

"What else could it be? They had to leave something to be more precise about the map. And you said it yourself, a printer with that name doesn't exist."

"Ok, but how do we get there?"

"I have an idea. We ask Nanna to take us. We say it's for some homework assignment and we want to do this as soon as possible."

"Genius!"

"Let's mention it at dinner tonight."

"Good idea," agreed Deanna.

They took out the map to make sure the castle was on it. It was all very well talking about it, but if they were wrong, it meant, back to square one. The print on the map was a little faded, so they had difficulties finding the castle. Then, after a few moments of adrenaline rush, they saw it: Chateau d'Esclimont. It felt like such a massive breakthrough. They started to feel hope again, and the rush that only a treasure hunt can give. Maybe there was something about that diary that was worth all this secrecy. If Nanna wasn't so mysterious about it all, they would have never tried to look for it. And now they were one step closer to solving the mystery. But they needed Nanna's help, without letting her realise that she was helping them. This would be the difficult part. As far as they knew, Gloria wasn't aware that they had found the map and the compass, not to mention the quill and the backpack. Just as they started discussing how to find a subtle way to get Nanna to take them to the castle, she called them in for dinner.

"So girls, are you hungry?" said Nanna putting the forks on the table.

"Starving," said Alia, trying butter Nanna up and put her in a good mood.

"Was it good in the park? Did you have fun?"

"Yes, but it was a little too crowded for my liking," said Alia.

"You prefer the crowd in the bookshop," said Deanna. "I don't know how you stand the heat and all those people touching each other in such a small place."

"I don't understand either how you were able to do the 'boule'!"

"It was fun, but I don't expect you to understand, you are afraid of everything," said Deanna and had a sudden flashback to Victor. She felt a shiver down her spine just thinking about him and his perfect eyes and his perfect smile.

"Ok girls, no need to argue. What do you want to do tomorrow?" asked Nanna, dropping herself neatly into the girls' trap.

"I want to visit Versailles," said Alia, starting to think about a strategy and hoping that Deanna would go along with it.

"Versailles? When it is so hot outside?" cried Deanna.

"Yes, we live so close by and it's a shame not to go and see it," persisted Alia.

"Why don't you think about the armies of tourists that invade Versailles every day? We will stay in line for hours to see three old paintings and an inappropriate display of what they like to call 'modern art'" wailed Deanna.

"So what do you propose?" asked Alia, hoping that Deanna would have the inspiration not to be too straightforward. Any deviation from their normal arguments would arouse suspicion and definitely kill off their plan.

"Nanna, have you ever been to the forest of Rambouillet?" asked Deanna, looking meaningfully at Alia.

Nanna interpreted that look as Deanna trying to impose her will on Alia. But Alia understood straight away where Deanna was going.

"Don't tell me you want to go biking in the forest?" said Alia, looking at Nanna rather than Deanna.

"Why not?" said Deanna. "What do you say? It could be fun. And we never get to use our bikes, because you're always saying the traffic is too dangerous in Paris."

"It is. But I see no harm in taking a walk in the great park of Rambouillet," said Nanna, unaware of the play the girls were performing in front of her.

"And my castle?" said Alia disappointed.

"There are a few castles in the neighbourhood. We can visit those," said Nanna coming up with the idea. At least she thought she had.

"Alright then, in that case I'm in," said Alia trying to hide her satisfaction.

"Thank you, Nanna! I'll go and prepare our bikes for tomorrow," said Deanna.

"Now let's eat. You can do that later."

The girls were so excited they could hardly bring themselves to eat. They forced themselves for a while, but it was too difficult, so after fifteen minutes they faked a headache each and left. It turned out to be a very long night, full of dreams, hopes and doubts. The next morning could bring them closer to that diary than ever before. What did they hope to find in it? The girls didn't know. Maybe some answers, some information about their parents, about what happened to them. And not the least, why the diary had to be so well hidden.

Chapter Nineteen

THE BOYS

When Marc got home, Victor didn't ask where he had been, because he saw all the books in his arms. It wasn't the first time his brother had left him alone, to go that special bookshop on Rue de Rivoli. But he had never seen Marc look quite the way he did now.

"What happened to you? Are you sick or something?" asked Victor, looking worried.

"Why do you ask me that? I'm fine," said Marc, not ready to share his little secret with his brother, just yet.

"You certainly don't look fine. But if you say there's nothing wrong, I believe you. I see you had a good time at the bookshop." said Victor, changing the conversation.

"Why do you say that?" asked Marc, panic-stricken.

"Look at all the books you got. Mum and Dad won't be very pleased to see that you spend all your allowance money on books."

"What they don't know can't hurt them. Can't we just say we spent all day together?" asked Marc.

"Why lie to them? Do you have something to hide? Even worse, are you hiding something from ME?"

"No, no. I just don't want them to know I don't have any money left," said Marc, struggling.

"Ok, ok, but I'm not lending you any money!" said Victor, laughing.

"Do you know when Mum and Dad are getting home?"

"In about an hour."

"But I'm hungry, now. Do you want to order pizza?" asked Marc.

"I don't feel like it. I'm still a little sick from that ride I went on today, the one you didn't go on with me," said Victor.

"I told you not to go there, I bet you're regretting it now," said Marc .

"Not at all, my friend. I met the most amazing girl. And I think she liked me too," sighed Victor, throwing himself on the bed.

"All girls like you," said Marc feeling a little guilty that he hadn't shared his experience. But he wasn't sure at all about Alia's feelings.

"Not like that. I can't explain why it was different, but it was."

"I guess you're completely and hopelessly in love with this girl," said Marc happy to see his brother happy. But on the other hand, it reminded him that the girl he met didn't share his feelings.

"And so what if I am? After all, she did say she wanted to see me again. I'll give her a few more days because I don't want to look desperate. And then I'll call her."

"You do that. Don't let her get away. She seems special if she got you to talk like that," Marc forced himself to smile to encourage his brother.

"She is special, and beautiful, and smart, and funny and… special."

"Ok, Romeo, I get it! She's special! Let's just decide what to do tomorrow to keep your thoughts off your Juliet."

"Thomas's parents are taking him to visit the Abbey de Vaux de Cernay," said Victor. "He asked me if we want to go with him. He's afraid he might get too bored. Or become a monk…"

"That would be great. Mum and Dad like Tom, they might let us join him. At least we won't stay at home doing nothing. We'll ask them tonight at dinner."

When their parents arrived back from work, they called Tom's parents to confirm. They were happy to see their boys going out during the holidays, while they had to work and couldn't share the days with them.

The next day Marc and Victor took their backpacks with their lunch and left to meet Thomas. The abbey they wanted to see was not very far, about one hour's drive from Paris, situated in the forest of Rambouillet. They were all charmed by the valley of Chevreuse, with its small villages, so different from Paris. It seemed so calm and clean, with everything in the right place, a good place to go biking, or walking or jogging.

As Victor looked out of the window, he saw a group of three women on bikes. One was tying her shoelaces. Victor was left breathless and he twisted his head round to see better, but the car was going too fast. He was sure he had just seen Deanna. On the other hand, he kept seeing Deanna everywhere. It would have been too strange to be in the same place, at the same time, two days in a row, that was enough to persuade a person that fate and destiny existed. But he didn't believe in either. He didn't believe in faith at all. So he tried to forget about her, at least for today. He didn't want to tell the others, in case they laughed at him.

They arrived at the abbey at about ten o'clock. The sun was shining through the ancient rose window. Marc, who was the romantic one, could smell the passage of time on the amazing building. He could almost hear the whisper of the monks, their prayers rising to a higher authority. The silence was only interrupted by the sound of the birds, nesting in the old trees surrounding the building.

The abbey had been turned into a hotel and restaurant, but even the other guests didn't dare to break the silence. They started the visit as all tourists do by taking pictures. At the entrance, Thomas's parents decided to take the guided tour. The guide was a young girl, Emilie, a history student working summers for extra money. She started to describe the history of the place. It all started in 1118, with Simon, Lord of Neauphle. It had a rather sad destiny, as it was reduced to ruins, during the Hundred Years' War, then restored by the Rothschild family. The abbey was the home of members of the great families in the history of France, the Marly, Yvelines, Montfort, Chevreuse and Montmorency.

"Now," said Emilie. "About the architecture of this magnificent place. As in any other Cistercian abbey, the monastic edifice and the church were built around the cloister, after a plan ordered by the 'Charte de Charité', the 'Us et Coutumes' and the fundamental rules of the order."

The tour moved on, following their enthusiastic guide.

"The cloister and the monastic edifice are situated at the north of the church. At the east, a long building that we can still see here," she said, pointing in that direction. "Extended the transept and included the sacristy, the chapter room and the passageway from the cloister to the garden."

Marc, Victor and Thomas found it hard to feel as enthralled by the history, as the adults in the group.

"As it was a very big community, they needed a big farm, a barn, a smithy, cellars and an icehouse. Can you guess why they needed an icehouse?" asked Emilie suddenly, in an attempt to regain the boys' attention.

"Because they didn't have a fridge?" asked Thomas shyly. "And there is nothing in the Bible against ice cream?" he added making all three of them start laughing behind the adults.

"You are half right. They didn't use the ice just for ice cream. They needed to keep their meat fresh. Let's not forget that at that time they didn't have the means to hunt as they wished all year long. And they could store ice for a few months if the icehouse was well isolated. But thank you for your attention," added the guide with a hint of irony. "At the west we have the lake and in the hill, we had the mill."

The adults smiled and nodded their appreciation, to their young guide, who certainly knew her stuff. But the teenagers were on the verge of falling asleep and could hardly stifle yawns as Emilie's voice persisted.

"The church still exists, at least pieces of it, a wall at the south from the altar and the Chapels, the western front with the two gates and the wonderful rose, which is considered a unique masterpiece from the 12th century."

The boys suddenly decided it would be more amusing to take selfies, as all teenagers do, when they get somewhere new. But when Victor tried to take one just near the fountain at the entrance, Marc backed into him accidently and knocked his brother into the water. Luckily it was warm outside, because Victor's pants and tee shirt were soaked. Tom went a few steps further and grabbed a picture of Victor in the fountain.

"It'll make an awesome post on Facebook," he grinned. Then his parents called him for a family photo, so he left the twins to handle the accident.

"Are you Ok?" said Marc, giving Victor his hand to help him out.

"I'm fine, but we have to stop Tom from posting my picture on Facebook," said Victor, standing there dripping from head to foot. "And one other thing... I think I've found something in there."

"A frog?" asked Marc starting to laugh.

"No, I think it's a bottle."

"Somebody chucked a bottle in the fountain, and you picked it up. Smart."

"The thing is, I don't think it's any kind of ordinary bottle," said Victor, leaning over the edge and taking it out of the water.

For sure, it was not like any other bottle they had ever seen.

"It looks really old," said Victor, studying it.

"How come it's still here?" said Marc. "They must clean the fountain regularly. They should have found it before now."

"Not necessarily. The bottle was under the edge. My hand slipped in a place impossible to find normally. It was well hidden."

"There seems to be something in it. Maybe it's a SOS message from a lady in distress."

"It should be in the sea for that, dumbo. Let's just open it?"

"I think we have to break it."

They managed to break it without making too much noise, because they didn't want to attract Tom's attention. Victor took out a little piece of parchment and a small key. Marc held the parchment gently and started to read. It was in Latin, but he understood enough to translate for his brother.

"So matters stood when our opponents ran out of water, for our soldiers had cut off the approaches to the castrum and they could not get out to draw water. Lack of water produced lack of courage and of the will to resist."

"What do you think it all means?" asked Victor when his brother finished the translation.

"We should see where this comes from. It looks like an old manuscript."

"It must have been written by a monk from here."

"It seems he is talking about a siege," said Marc, trying to work it out.

"You're right, but do you think it was a siege of the abbey?"

"Let's Google it. Was there a siege here anytime in history?"

Victor took his phone, which luckily had dropped out of his hand onto the ground, when he fell in the water.

"Hmm, apparently there was no siege, but there was a Cistercian monk in the 12th century, who witnessed the siege of the castle of Termes in 1210," Victor, scrolled the information on his phone and carried on. "His name was Peter de Vaux de Cernay and he wrote Historia Albigensis," he said looking over at his brother.

"So this bottle was really meant to be here. It obviously didn't get here by accident," said Marc, beginning to believe they had really come across something interesting.

"Ok, but why did he leave this here? Who was this parchment meant for?" asked Victor.

"I can't imagine. It is not a secret text, because it's part of a known book. The Albigensian Crusade is no mystery," said Marc.

"Don't tell me you know something about this crusade?"

"The Albigensian Crusade or the Cathar Crusade was initiated by Pope Innocent III to eliminate Catharism in Languedoc. It had a role in the creation and institutionalization of both the Dominican Order and the Medieval Inquisition. The Cistercian monks were used to convince the Cathars to give up their fate and come back to Catholicism," said Marc exactly as if he was reading from a history book. His brother was openly impressed.

"You really are a geek!"

"I like reading. It comes in handy sometimes."

"So it must hide something brought from the crusades that a monk shouldn't have. That explains the efforts to keep this object hidden."

"Let's read the text one more time," said Marc. "It talks about the siege and their strategy to leave the people without water."

"The siege of the castle of Termes? It was thirst that put an end to that. Do you think it's linked?"

"I don't know. It's too far. It has to be closer. Don't forget that in the 12th century they didn't have cars and roads, so they couldn't travel 300 or 400 Km as we do. I think that it is here, on this property."

"Wait," said Victor. "Tom's waving to us. I think it is time for lunch. Time always flies when we're having fun!"

"And we're not being very polite, it looks like we're ignoring them."

"I know, but I'd really like to find an answer to this before we leave," said Victor. "Who knows when we'll come back here again."

"Ok, but right now, we have to go and eat with them."

Marc hid the bottle by a fence, and carefully put the piece of parchment in his pocket. Then they joined Tom's family, just as the guided tour was finishing.

"Built in limestone and millstone, the facade is still untouched, the capital post from the main entrance is divided in three by four foothills aligned with the great arches. At the base it is pierced by a gothic arched door. Now let's move on to the fountain of Saint Thibaut."

And so the whole group started walking on the perfectly mowed lawn and the guide continued her speech.

"The archways in full arch rests on the pilasters decorated on their sides and capital with monsters, masks, music instruments, funerals, peasants or warriors. You can see a salamander, the emblem of Francois 1er, a Sainte Barbe and the coat of arms of the abbey, three fleur-de-lys and three silver croissants among all those decorations. In the corners of the archways you can see flower or fruit medallions that close up on women and men from antiquity. The archways are two meters high and the pillars are at one meter from one another…"

"Oh my God! Could she be more boring?" whispered Thomas to his parents, which made the boys very happy as they didn't dare say it out loud themselves. They didn't want to seem disrespectful, but they would have given anything to be able to explore this amazing place full of history and mystery by themselves. So the five of them left the group, feeling slightly guilty, but still mightily relieved.

They ate a quick picnic lunch, sitting on a blanket in the grounds of the abbey. When they'd all finished their sandwiches, they played a game of mime. The boys couldn't wait to return to their treasure hunt. They were convinced the parchment was hiding an amazing secret.

Chapter Twenty

THE GIRLS

The same morning, the girls left home with Nanna, all dressed up for a day in the forest. They attached their bikes to the car, two on the roof rack and Nanna's on the brace at the back. When they arrived at the forest of Rambouillet, they left the car and took to their bikes. The air was still fresh, the birds singing and the sun started to warm the surface of the road. After about half an hour, they began to feel tired because the road had become quite rough. So they decided to look for a place to get a drink.

The road was quite long through the forest, but they knew of lots of villages where they could stop. However, the first thing they came across was a large, imposing gate, with a plate Béaring the name of a castle. The girls couldn't believe their luck, it was the castle of Esclimont, the one the compass indicated on the map. They went through the gates, into some woodland and when they arrived at the edge of the forest, the sight left them breathless. They were standing on a high point, looking down at an had an amazing castle with a bridge, a great terrace and a lake. It was like something in a fairy tale. The only thing missing was the knight in shining armour.

The girls couldn't believe their eyes. But why would their mother hide the diary here? Why go to all this trouble to put it in a 16th century castle? And for the first time they thought that the diary could in some way be related to their parents' death. They felt they owed it to their parents to find it and that maybe by reading the contents, it would help them to understand.

"Ladies and gentlemen, I give you Chateau d'Esclimont!" said Alia, with a flourish. She had done her homework before coming. "The name comes from the Latin 'Eclusa montis' because at the beginning there was a dam here. You can still see a dungeon that replaced a wooden tower, a symbol of the lordly power. Later it served as an entry porch with three gates, a large one in the middle and two small ones on the sides. In 1543 the castle suffered an important transformation into an Italian Renaissance style residence. At the end of the 18th century the owner ordered the construction of the chapel which was still used in 1965."

They pushed their bikes down the hillside towards the castle. Nanna wanted to go inside to use the bathroom, so the girls found a table on the terrace, with an amazing view over the lake. Then the three of them ordered tea, mineral waters and other refreshments from the menu. When Nanna was settled, happily watching the swans gliding across the lake, the girls looked at each other and rose from the table at the same time.

"Where are you going?" asked Nanna.

"To the bathroom," they said in unison.

Alia and Deanna went in search of the bathroom, in case Nanna was watching. And then they went in search of clues. The castle was magnificent, but frankly a small book could be anywhere, at least that's how the girls imagined the diary. They went around the caste, and at the back they saw a wooden gate, the ancient porch entry, that was not in use. And above the gate, in a monumental alcove, there was a statue. And above the mullioned window, a portrait of François de la Rochefoucauld, carved in a medallion and with the initial F.

"Look Deanna!" said Alia.

"What?"

"Look up!"

"Ok, a statue," said Deanna.

"Yes, but look whose statue is it is: François de Rochefoucauld, god-father of François I 1494, a slight change from 1944."

"The year on the map!" said Deanna.

"So I think we are in the right place," said Alia.

Before Alia could stop her, Deanna was scaling the wall, until she reached the equestrian statue. She hoped to find something behind the flag, but she found nothing. She even risked falling by checking on the other side of the statue as well. Disappointed she jumped back down and landed with a thump next to Alia, who was speechless.

"Are you crazy?" whispered Alia, even though she already knew the answer. Deanna was fearless, not crazy. And she was very aware of her capabilities.

"I hoped I might find something there."

"How could Mum have hidden the diary there?" said Alia, in exasperation.

"I don't know but it was worth a shot," said Deanna, brushing the dust off her clothes. "But then why did the map send us here?"

"I don't know. Let's look a little longer, but then we'll have to go, Nanna will start to worry."

"Wait!" said Deanna, suddenly having an idea. "What if the sculpture shows the way?"

"What do you mean?"

"Look at the flag. It points to a room right above the gate. But how can we get there?"

"I think there are guests there. After all it is a hotel."

"It is now, but was it when Mum hid the diary?"

"We'll find out, but now we must go back to Nanna. We'll find a way to come back here soon."

So the girls abandoned the statue with regret and went back to the table, where Gloria had started to lose patience. They sat there for about an hour, the view was amazing, the atmosphere magical and Deanna was in her romantic mood. She could already see her marriage to Victor there. It was the perfect spot.

Alia on the other hand started to feel weak. She couldn't explain, but ever since they got there, she wasn't feeling herself. At first she had a feeling of deja-vu that became stronger with every minute. And when they got closer to the sculpture, her heart was pounding like crazy. At first she thought it was just fatigue, but then she realised she wasn't really tired. She felt sad. She didn't want to share that with Deanna because her sister didn't seem to have the same problem. And she didn't want to share it with Nanna either, because she would force her to go to the doctor's and it didn't seem to be a problem any doctor could fix.

Eventually, they returned to their car. Nanna was happy that everything had gone well, the girls were only half satisfied. They felt they had got closer, but now they had to find another way to go to the castle, and even more difficult, get into the room above the sculpture.

Chapter Twenty-One

THE PEACEMAKER

Harcourt and Gilbert went crazy when they saw the girls leave so early in the morning. They didn't know where the girls were going, or even if it was worthwhile following them. Then they watched the girls taking their bikes, so they assumed tracking them on foot wouldn't be so interesting after all. Harcourt decided to give Gilbert the day off. He was completely unaware of the turn that their day out was about to take.

Gilbert left Harcourt alone. As soon as he left, Harcourt took his phone and tapped in a number. He couldn't afford to keep it in the memory of his phone, in case somebody stole it. But he realised that ever since he had a smart phone, he had lost his ability to memorize phone numbers. But this particular one had to be remembered at all costs. It was the number of his boss.

"Yes, your servant left," said Harcourt. "And he knows nothing. At least nothing that matters. When are you coming to France? …I told you, they didn't find it yet. I don't even think the girls know anything about it …Gloria is still Gloria. She shows nothing but she doesn't know she's being followed. At least she doesn't act like it… Ok, I'll see you as soon as you get to Paris."

Without saying goodbye, he closed the phone and left. But he didn't go far. He decided that since the girls were out for the day, he might just get inside their apartment. He believed he could find something interesting. After all, he knew the code and he knew how to get inside. Once he was in Gloria's bedroom, he started to look around. But he found nothing, until he noticed a small music box, and a small key near it. He wanted to turn the key, but it didn't seem to match the lock, so he decided to leave it for now.

He went to the girls' room but they had been more careful, so he found nothing to show that either Deanna or Alia knew anything. He even searched under the bed, where he knew that there was a secret compartment under the floor, about the size of a shoe box. But it was empty and it seemed that nobody had touched it for a very long time. It didn't occur to him that the girls had become very adept at hiding things, because they had to, if they wanted to keep secrets from Gloria, who was smarter than anyone. So, unknown to him, he didn't stand a chance of finding anything. And besides that, Alia took the map, the quill and the compass everywhere with her. She had transformed an old book into a treasure box.

Disappointed, he left the apartment, and not a moment too soon, because as he was leaving the building, Béa was entering the code at the front door. He smiled at her as if he was just a visitor and said hello. Béa smiled back, but when she looked at him closer, she had the feeling she had seen him before.

Harcourt got back to his apartment and took out the key, the only object that hadn't seemed in its right place. But also, he had recognised the woman entering Gloria's apartment. He picked up his phone and called his boss back, the mysterious man he called The Peacemaker, and gave him the name of Gloria's friend. The Peacemaker in return, handed him some information that pleased Harcourt very much. Smiling, he opened his computer and started typing. Nobody but he knew his plan. When he'd finished typing, he printed out a letter and left.

When Béa finished cleaning the apartment, she left and headed for the bus. Harcourt followed her. When she got off and arrived at her apartment building, he waited till she'd gone upstairs. Then he found her mailbox and put the letter in. He felt pleased with himself. He'd acted alone because he didn't want Gilbert involved. Some things were better done by him, and him alone.

He was sure of the effect his letter would have. He didn't wait for Béa to find it, he knew she would come to him, he just had to be patient. And God knows he was patient. He had waited for this diary for an eternity. A few more weeks or months meant nothing to him. But this time he would let nobody get in his way. Not even The Peacemaker. But obviously he didn't know the man well enough, because he was unaware of how dangerous it was to double cross him. This diary seemed to drive everybody crazy, even while it remained hidden. Nobody knew what its exposure would bring. It was ready to come out... and express its will.

Chapter Twenty-Two

THE LETTER

Béa and Gilles had a long history with Gloria and unbeknownst to the girls, also with Gloria's daughter, their mother. They were in their forties, still very much in love and very discreet. That's what made them the perfect couple for Gloria. She trusted them with everything and she knew she owed them a lot. They didn't have any children, but they wanted one so badly. Béa was about the age of Samantha, Gloria's daughter. They were friends when Samantha got pregnant and had the twin girls. As hard as that was for Béa, she helped raise them. She was never jealous of Samantha for having two children when she wasn't able to have any.

She was almost like a second mother to the twins. When the girls' parents disappeared, Béa knew that she had to let them go with their grandmother. But it was so hard for her, Alia and Deanna had filled such a void in her heart. The girls left and she and her husband Gilles had to live in Samantha's apartment. That was challenging too, but they were trustworthy and faithful. So when Gloria let them know she was coming back with the girls, Béa realised she had to return to her old home. Still, she was thrilled to have the girls in her life again.

When it became too late for her to try to have a child, they applied to an adoption agency. In France it's not easy to adopt. And she didn't have the kind of job that looked good on paper. How could they explain that, with jobs which only paid the minimum wage, they could afford to live in a big apartment on Rue de Rivoli? Obviously, the agreement with Gloria was not official, so nobody could explain their generous income. But right now, they were happy to have the girls back in Paris, to be able to watch them grow up and hopefully to help them through their teenage years.

Gilles was the silent type, he didn't express his emotions much, but deep down he loved Deanna and Alia. Still he yearned for his own child, desperately and hopelessly. Now they were expecting news from the adoption agency and he was afraid that their file would be rejected, leaving them with no second chance. When the letter finally arrived, they were both excited and very worried at the same time. But when Béa opened it, she almost fell off her feet.

There was no address on the envelope. She started to read it out loud for Gilles.

"Mr and Mrs Lacroix,

You don't know who I am, not for now anyway. I need something that only you can give me and I would do anything to get it. I can be your best friend… or your worst nightmare. You choose. If you decide to work with me, I can guarantee you that your wish will come true sooner than you think. If you don't want to trust me, I can assure you will never become parents. As you can guess I have very powerful friends that could put you at the top of the adoption list. The same friends can make sure you will be on the blacklist of every agency in the country. If you are interested in what I have to ask you, simply put a note in your mailbox and I will contact you to arrange a meeting.

The Dream Maker."

Béa started shaking. She imagined all her dreams shattered in one moment. What could he want from them? What did they have to offer?

Without hesitation she took a pen and wrote down a few words: 'What do you want?' She folded the paper in four, went downstairs and put it in their mailbox.

Gilles suggested they stayed awake and watched, to see who came to take the note. But they agreed, probably nothing would happen that night. So they went to bed and endured a long sleepless night.

The next day they had a lot of work to do for Gloria, so when they returned home, it was already late. Béa rushed to the mailbox, her note was gone and in its place two tickets for the theatre. The play was tonight and they had to hurry if they wanted to make it. They were desperate to get there, terrified that this 'Dream Maker' would see it as a lack of interest if they didn't show up. They changed their clothes and raced from the flat.

They arrived just as the play was about to begin. They rushed in and searched for their seats. They were sure that their mystery man had to be there somewhere. They didn't even know the name of the play, all they cared about was to show this man they were doing what he asked. They started looking around, but on their left they had an old couple and on the right a family with two children. None of them looked like criminals. Privately Béa was terrified, but she wanted to do this. She would give anything she had, in fact she couldn't think of anything in her possession that she wouldn't give up, to secure a good place on an adoption list. However, she wasn't prepared to sacrifice what Harcourt was about to demand of her.

When Harcourt approached her in the bar during the interval, she found him vaguely attractive. He was tall, dark hair, brown eyes, a beautiful suit, expensive shoes, not at all what she expected.

"Hello Mrs Lacroix, are you enjoying the play?" he asked, leaning casually against the bar and helping himself to some peanuts.

"It's very interesting, but the actors don't seem very experienced," said Béa not knowing quite how to react.

"You can't have it all, at least not every time," said Harcourt, by way of small talk.

"It depends on what you want most," said Béa, fed up with this unbearable conversation.

"And what do you want the most, Mrs Lacroix?"

"I think you know. But what do you want from me?"

"I'll tell you in a moment. Before that, you must answer a couple of questions. And don't forget, I hold your dreams in my hand," he said, curling his fingers as if around a physical object.

"Go ahead," said Béa trying to appear brave.

"How well do you know Gloria Hammersmith?"

"Gloria?" she answered trying to conceal her surprise. "I wouldn't say well, I do her laundry and clean her apartment once a week." She began to fear this might be more complicated then she thought.

"Are you telling me that you didn't know her before? Don't forget who you are talking to."

"I knew her before, because she was paying us to stay and watch the apartment in her absence. But I had never met or seen her before that, I swear."

"What is your relationship with her now?"

"We became what you might call friends, but if you know Gloria a little, it's obvious that 'friends' is a big word."

"But she trusts you?"

"Yes, she does. With the apartment, but that's all."

"And the girls?" asked Harcourt, the question Béa feared the most.

"What about the girls?" asked Béa trying to look nonchalant.

"Do they trust you? Do you speak about more than the weather with them?"

"Not much. You know how they are at this age. Two years older than them and you are ancient. They don't tell me anything."

"But Gloria has asked you to keep an eye on them?"

"Yes, but I'm as discreet as possible."

"Why is Gloria so overprotective of these girls?" said Harcourt, going in closer for the kill.

"They are her only family, they are her responsibility. She has lost her daughter and she doesn't want anything to happen to the girls. That's understandable, isn't it?"

"Of course."

"Now let's talk about why we're here. The play is about to start, and my husband is waiting for me," said Béa with some force.

"I think you've already guessed. I need an inside man… or woman in Gloria's life. You have to become her friend. I want information about where she goes, what she does, what she eats. And not just Gloria, but the girls too. I need to know if they have friends, or boyfriends. When they go out, what are they reading. Everything."

"But that means spying on them. I'm not in the house all the time," said Béa horrified at what he was proposing. He was asking her to betray the one person who had helped her.

"You don't have to do that 24/7. That would be strange and Gloria would know something was wrong. Only when she asks you to go. And I need to know if there is something missing or new in their home. Every tiny little detail counts. I need you to tell me, even if one of the girls buys new underwear."

"Ok," said Béa. "For how long?"

"Until I tell you when to stop," said Harcourt smiling triumphantly.

"And how do I let you know when I have something for you?"

"You leave it in your mail. That is how we will communicate. Now off you go and enjoy the rest of the play!" and with that he was gone.

Béa got back to her seat and explained to her husband what had just happened. They stayed until the play was over, but all they could think about was how to get out of this situation. They came up with only one solution, it wasn't perfect, but they had no other ideas. So it had to work.

In the meantime, Harcourt was so pleased with himself that he called The Peacemaker right away to give him the good news. At least now he had somebody to provide them with inside information. The Peacemaker was satisfied but Harcourt knew there was a long way to go before his mission was complete. He could not rest until the diary was in the hands of his superior.

Chapter Twenty-Three

A VISIT FROM LYDIA REYNOLDS

While the girls pursued their treasure hunt in Paris, living Alia's dream of adventure, their old friends back in the English village, carried on with their lives. Obviously the girls were not missing their old boring life, but did the people from their past miss them? Deanna's friends spoke about her from time to time, but there was always a new diva ready to take her place, who they could all follow and imitate. Gloria's old neighbours mentioned Gloria a few times in conversation, but as she had never truly been part of their little world, her absence generally went unnoticed.

Only one person felt the disappearance of the girls at a deeper level and that was Deanna's old foe, Lydia. First, she thought they must be on vacation. But nobody had been warned, not even Deanna's closest friends. Then she started to dwell on the bad things she said to Deanna before they left and a deep sense of guilt crept in. She should never have criticised their dead mother.

Still, Lydia couldn't understand why the girls had left without telling anyone, and why weren't the police looking for them? Maybe they hadn't been abducted, but she was the only one who was genuinely worried, so she decided to investigate on her own. She took a book in case somebody questioned what she was doing snooping round their old house. She would say she had to return a book and that she wanted to leave it in the mail box. She had prepared her story.

When she reached the house, she stepped confidently through the gate and knocked on the front door. She waited to make sure nobody was inside, then tested the door handle, the door was not locked. After another wait, she crept inside and closed the door behind her. This was the first time she had ever set foot in this house, and she realised she had always wanted to see where Deanna lived. After all it was envy that had driven her to talk to her like that in the park.

Everything was untouched since the girls had left. The dust coated everything and it was quite creepy because Gloria hadn't bothered to cover the furniture or the carpets.

Lydia went into the girls' room, where she realised that they were a lot simpler than she thought. She arrived at Gloria's bedroom, where there was nothing left. Lydia was surprised to see that the girls had left a lot of useful stuff behind, Gloria had left nothing. As if she was afraid to leave a trace of her existence in the house. Her investigation took her further upstairs, where the girls had left all those rooms closed. But when Lydia arrived, all the doors stood open. The dust had covered all traces of Deanna's and Alia's intrusion. But Lydia couldn't have known that these rooms were forbidden territory for the girls.

When she came across the ballroom, just like the girls, she was left speechless. She started to look into the mirrors, to dance, to act as if there were people around her. She touched every frame, every statue trying to make sure she wasn't dreaming. But everything was real, she was in a ballroom in an abandoned mansion. If only she had friends to share this discovery with. But as always, she was alone. Nobody was interested in what she had to say. So she decided to stay a little longer, to enjoy her fairy tale. She imagined a handsome count or a prince, inviting her to dance, and falling in love with her at first sight.

But her dream was short lived, as soon as she saw herself reflected back from the many mirrors covering the walls, she knew she was not princess material. She would never meet a Prince Charming and she would never get out of her village. Suddenly all the jealousy of Deanna came crashing back. Even if she had been abducted, she would definitely be experiencing a better and more exciting life. She didn't need somebody like Lydia to rescue her. She realised she had been silly to worry about Deanna and Alia.

Then she noticed something that the girls didn't have time to see, when they came here the first time. All the mirrors were symmetrical except the last one on the left, that didn't have a twin. This one was unique and Lydia couldn't help going over and examining it. She peered at the decoration on the frame. All the other mirrors were identical, why was this one different? Then she realised, instead of angels holding hands on this mirror, there were two girls dancing with flowers in their hands.

Lydia stopped and ran her hand over the frame to see if it was real. She almost touched the figurines with her nose, in her desire to take a better look at those girls dancing. The weirdest thing, those girls looked exactly like Deanna and Alia. But it was impossible, the mirror had to be a lot older than them. But how could you explain the decoration on the mirror? She had no idea, so she studied it a little more and even took pictures with her phone, to prove to herself later that she hadn't been dreaming. After that, she had no idea who else to show it to, but she needed proof, if there had been some sort of abduction. On the other hand, there was the small matter of her breaking into someone else's house.

Just near the mirror stood a chair. She felt the need to sit down for a few minutes to admire the view, and that was the only chair that didn't look like a throne. But when she sat down, something unusual happened. It made her think she was hallucinating. While she was sitting on the chair, she looked at herself in the mirror. Her reflection wasn't wearing the same clothes as she did. Her image was wearing a dress from the 17th century. It had a wig, make up and shoes as in a film. She leapt up in fear, whereupon the image changed back to a normal reflection of herself. Now she was convinced that it was just a trick of her imagination and sat back down again. But the image changed again. Apparently the chair was changing the image. She had no other logical explanation.

So she sat down again, but this time she tried to keep calm and see what happened next. But nothing happened. She got up only to see that on the frame of the mirror there were a few words engraved in Latin: *'Et nunc ex parte nos non potest.'* She was good enough at school to understand something of Latin. It meant 'Not even time can part us. She thought it was so romantic, that she wanted to remember the phrase. She had an idea she had seen it once before, in a photo, but she couldn't remember where. So she started writing it in the dust on the mirror. As soon as the last word was written the image in the mirror became blurry and Lydia disappeared.

Chapter Twenty-Four

LOVE IS IN THE AIR

In the morning Victor decided that it was too sunny to stay inside, so he persuaded Marc to go horse riding. At Neuilly they had a club where only the rich children went, so he didn't like to go alone because he had nothing to talk about with them. But today Marc wasn't in the mood for outdoor activities. He wanted to stay and read one of the books he and Alia had chosen. He would have liked the opportunity to exchange ideas with her about it. While Marc was building a strategy about his relationship with Alia, Victor collected his riding gear and left.

It was only 10 o'clock when he arrived. He chose his favourite horse, who luckily was available, but when he lifted the saddle up to put it on, he saw a face on the other side of the horse.

"Deanna! What are you doing here?" asked Victor surprised.

"I could ask you the same question!" said Deanna blushing.

"I come here every week and I always take Windy," said Victor.

"Me too. Windy is my horse every Thursday morning."

"I never come on Thursday, that's why I've never seen you here."

"And that's why we are able to share Windy," said Deanna.

"So, what now? I guess I could take another horse," said Victor hoping Deanna would appreciate the gesture.

"Thanks! Let's go outside together and warm up."

As soon as they were outside on their horses, they both started showing off. There was no way of telling which was the better rider, but Victor couldn't help observing her grace and elegance. Her brown hair was bouncing, her skin was like a fresh peach. Her lips were red from the excitement and she never showed a sign of tiredness.

Victor realised that she was a worthy opponent and he had no reason to go easy on her. He appreciated the fact that she was not some kind of princess, who waited for the boy to do everything. She had to be difficult to tame, but he didn't want a puppet. He wanted her. Watching her challenging him, he thought that was the girl for him. But was she interested in him? A girl like her must have a hundred boys fawning around her. What he didn't know was that all the boys were intimidated by a girl like Deanna, who knew what she wanted, and who wouldn't settle for anything but the best. And Deanna wanted a boy who would challenge her back, that would make her be the best.

So when Victor started showing what he was capable of, Deanna was so impressed that she forgot that she was also on a horse. Windy got scared and threw her off. Victor stopped to help Deanna up. She felt embarrassed, so she blushed, which Victor found even more adorable. He took her by the waist afraid that she might have broken something. But luckily, she was alright and able to get back on the horse. They decided to go easy and to take a walk in the park. Their horses were a little tired so they were happy with that idea.

"Where did you learn to ride like that?" asked Victor.

"In England, at home, we had a small club where everybody could ride."

"You call England home, but you speak French like a… well French."

"Thank you, but it's understandable, I was born in France and raised in England."

"So you are neither English nor French!" said Victor laughing.

"Or both! Depends on how you look at it," said Deanna satisfied with her answer.

"So which one do you prefer?" said Victor, hoping she would say French.

"I've lived longer in England than in France, but here I feel more at home. And in England we lived in a small village that could never compare to Paris."

They continued walking, their morning turned into noon, but they didn't feel hungry , then the horses started to look tired, so they went back to the club. They still didn't have the heart to split up, so they went to grab a bite together.

They were talking as if they had known each other for ever. Everything was so natural and easy. Deanna showed him her favourite spot near the Seine, he showed her his favourite boat on the docks.

They avoided the touristy areas. Victor knew a garden where they could be all alone. Deanna appreciated the fact that he didn't try to kiss her, when they got close to smell a flower. She didn't want to rush things, she was aware that they were living the best part at the beginning of a relationship.

Victor wasn't so sure about Deanna's feelings. Boys aren't capable of reading the signs. Victor was no different. For him, if she hadn't kissed him in the first two minutes, it meant that she was not interested. So he got a little down and disappointed. When Deanna saw that, she thought that he must be getting bored, so she took her backpack and decided to go home. Victor tried to stop her but he was too proud to beg. If she didn't want to be with him, fine!

Deanna left him and took the bus home. It was not until then that she realised the time. Nanna would be furious. And Alia would be worried. She wasn't used to taking an entire day away from her twin. How would she explain a whole day alone? She had no intention of talking about Victor. She used the time on the bus to think of an explanation. When she got home, Gloria wasn't there and neither was Alia. Now it was Deanna's turn to worry.

Chapter Twenty-Five

THE AGE OF INNOCENCE

Alia waited for Deanna to leave so she could do what she wanted. She didn't feel like going to the park with her, so she said she would stay at home. After an hour or two she decided to go out. She was a little hungry, Gloria had left them something to eat but she was in the mood for something more cheerful, like pizza for instance. Not far from their home there was a pizza place she liked, so picked up a book and went for a walk.

The waiter at the pizza place recognised her immediately, because they went there at least once a week. He gave her a table in a corner so that nobody would bother her. So she started reading while she waited.

"Excuse me, Miss, is it your lunch break or can you can wait on me?" said a voice that Alia only recognised, when she raised her eyes from her book.

"What makes you think I'm a waitress here?" she said, then stopped, realising it was only a joke.

Marc stood close to her, and she remembered that when they first met he had mistaken her for an employee in the bookshop. She was surprised to see that he recognised her.

"Marc, what are you doing here?"

"I came here to eat. I love their pizzas," said Marc not knowing if he could sit with her.

"Are you alone?" asked Alia.

"Yes, I wanted to be alone today," said Marc, regretting it, as soon as the words had come out of his mouth.

"Enjoy your pizza then," said Alia a little too abruptly and went back to her book.

"Thank you, but you see, usually this is my table," lied Marc looking for an excuse to sit with her.

"Then you can join me, I don't mind."

"I'd love to. What are you reading?" said Marc satisfied his little trick had worked.

"Little Women. Have you read it?"

"It's a classic but no. I guess it's more like a girl's book," he said.

And so they went on, discussing their favourite subject, books. They finished their pizza but not the conversation. Somehow the conversation came round to talking about girls and boys at their schools.

"At my school, there's a group of girls who won't even talk to you if you don't have the latest smartphone," said Alia.

"Even worse, in my school there are two boys who will steal your phone, if it's more expensive than theirs."

"That's incredible," said Alia in disbelief. "And nobody tries to stop them?"

"I tried once but I don't want to fight."

"I love to fight, not on the street but as a sport."

"What kind of sport?" asked Marc, incapable of imagining Alia good at sports.

"Fencing."

"Well, that is a nice sport," said Marc with admiration. "Very elegant! And you don't risk breaking anything."

Deep down inside he was hoping to discover a girl that he didn't like. But as time went on, and he got to know Alia better, his feelings for her became stronger. He realised that they could never be together in the way he wanted them to be, because obviously she didn't look at him that way. Everything she said was amazing, when she laughed his heart was laughing too. He had never met a girl so passionate about books and life. He had been on dates but every time they were too long, the girls only liked to talk about themselves and fashion and cinema. So even if he had tried to forget about her he realised that it was hopeless. He was attracted like a moth to a flame. It hurt to see her near him and not be able to touch her beautiful brown hair. It hurt to see her red lips smile and not be able to kiss them. It hurt so badly and there was no medicine that could take that pain away.

"On the other hand I still haven't found any boy at school, who isn't a show off and a clown," said Alia interrupting his thoughts.

"We are so boring…"

"Not all boys are boring," said Alia quickly, trying to undo her mistake. "You are anything but boring."

"So what am I?" asked Marc.

"You are my friend," she said spontaneously.

He never thought he could get more hurt, but Alia's words shot like an arrow, with perfect precision into his heart.

"You are my friend too. It's a pity we don't go to the same school. We could see each other more often."

"You wouldn't want to be seen with me. I'm just a geek with three books in her bag," said Alia, smiling sadly.

"So what? I always have a book in my bag too. In case I have a few moments to spare," he said.

"But you could have any girl in school."

"Not any girl. And I want only one, and that one I can't have."

He would have liked to be able to tell Alia that it was her he wanted the most, but he didn't want to ruin what he was building with her, even if it wasn't the ideal relationship. At least that way he got to be around her.

"I think you didn't try hard enough. Only a stupid girl could be so blind not to see what an amazing guy you are."

"I think she is simply not interested," said Marc with a sigh.

This conversation was a torture for him. He even thought he was being punished for all the girls he had rejected because he hadn't been interested. He had got to see what it felt like to face someone who says "Let's just be friends!" But for now it was all that he could get. They went on about their schools, and then they started talking about their parents. Marc quickly changed the subject because he saw that Alia didn't want to talk about it. Marc avoided talking about his brother and Alia said nothing about her sister. They had no logical reason for this and before too long, they would regret having hidden the existence of their twins.

As the day wore on, they left the restaurant and went for a walk. It was amazing how the hours were short around Alia. Marc was under a spell. He could have listened to Alia for hours. At one moment he tried to catch her by her shoulders, just "as a friend", but one second later Alia saw a small dog and got on her knees to pet it. She didn't even seem to notice his hand.

He wanted to share the discovery they had made at Vaux-de-Cernay with her. He was sure she would have liked a treasure hunt, but he wasn't sure his brother would have liked it. He promised himself that as soon as they had something more he would talk to her about it. Alia, on the other hand, would have liked to talk to him about the lead they had on her mother's diary. But with Deanna on her mind, she said nothing. Maybe if, at that exact moment one of them had said something, anything, it would have spared them a lot of tears and sorrow later. But they both kept the secret and they went on with trivial conversation. They weren't even aware that they had been followed all afternoon.

95

Chapter Twenty-Six

SPYING ISN'T WHAT IT USED TO BE

Gilbert never thought following a teenager could be so boring. All that Alia did was read, or walk. And that same boy again. How could he listen to her all day long? He must be as boring as her. As the day went by, Gilbert decided to leave them alone, guessing that at one point they would split up and each of them would go home.

Meanwhile, on the other side of the town, Harcourt was following Deanna. He had more luck, as the horse riding turned out to be more interesting. He was wondering when Béa would start spying on the girls, he hated this job. In the morning he saw Gloria leaving the apartment but no sign of Béa. What he didn't know was that he had chosen the wrong person to follow, because Gloria had gone to meet Béa.

Gloria had no idea what was going on with Béa, but she knew her well enough to see that something was wrong. When they finally met on a hidden bench in a park, Béa was ready to put her plan into action.

"Hello Béa," said Gloria sitting down.

"Hello, Gloria, thank you for meeting me here, as weird as it seems."

"You can never be too cautious. But what are you scared of?"

"I'll get straight to the point," said Béa, taking a deep breath. "How well do you know a guy named Maxime Le Guy?"

"I don't know anybody called that, but I do have a Maxime d'Harcourt, in the past."

"Maybe he changed his name. Or he just gave me a fake one. He is taller than Gilles, dark hair and…"

"A scar on the left cheek," continued Gloria.

"Exactly! So it is the same person."

"But why do you know Harcourt?"

"Because he came to me. And what I'm about to say can cost me the only thing I really want in this world, a baby," said Béa.

"What does a baby have to do with Harcourt?" asked Gloria trying to understand.

"That's how he got me to listen, he threatened us. If I didn't do what he asked, he would make sure we could never adopt."

"Listen, he is very dangerous, but he doesn't have the influence to do something like that," said Gloria.

"Maybe not him, but he talked to me about his powerful friend," said Béa.

Gloria had turned as white as a sheet. Béa was sure that Gloria would fall if she hadn't already been sitting down. Harcourt didn't seem to frighten Gloria, but his friend… well that was another story.

"And what does Harcourt want?" said Gloria, trying to hide her emotions.

"Basically, he wants me to spy on you for him. I don't know what he's looking for, but he wants it badly. Do you have any idea what it is about?" asked Béa.

"No, I have nothing in my possession that would push someone to this kind of crime."

"Couldn't it be the diary?"

"Don't talk nonsense, Béa. That diary disappeared ten years ago. It will stay hidden as long as I can have anything to do with it. I don't want to bring it back into the world, and especially not into the hands of Harcourt."

"Alright, we can stop that. It is enough to give him the impression that I am spying on you, but actually we will be giving him the information we want him to have."

"That is a very good idea," said Gloria smiling. She was lucky to have such a faithful friend on her side.

"But it does mean I have to come more often and spend more time with the girls. What do we tell them?"

"You're right. They mustn't know that somebody is watching them," said Gloria. "I was hoping that Harcourt would leave us alone for a few more years. But all we have to do is not give him any reason to think that we know something."

"Maybe one day you will tell me the truth about that diary and why everybody wants it so badly," .said Béa looking around as if she was afraid someone was listening.

"I hope you realise that is not a trust issue, but designed to keep you safe. Don't you see, everybody who comes into contact with it, is in danger, if not dead, like Samantha."

"Ok, but for now let's see, what do I say to him the next time he summons me?" asked Béa.

"You tell him that we don't plan to travel, that the girls are going through a nasty adolescence and our relationship is not how it should be. And that it will take a while for you to get closer to them. They grew up without a mother and at the age of 14, it's not likely they'll start searching for one. But you will inform him of every step that they take."

"Fine, and if you really want to go somewhere that you don't want him to find, I'll say that you are sick and I am with you, to take care of you or the girls. That way you can move without someone chasing you."

"Perfect, wonderful idea!" said Gloria.

"I'll leave first, in case we are being followed," said Béa, standing up and walking casually away.

Gloria sat for another five minutes before leaving. She looked around to see if there was anybody nearby whom she recognised.

Chapter Twenty-Seven

THE NIGHT IS LONG FOR THE GIRLS

When Gloria got home both girls were in their room waiting for her to have dinner. Neither was ready to tell what they had been doing all day long.

Each of them had prepared a story, and they told it at dinner with a lot of conviction. Then they all went to bed to think about what had happened that day.

Deanna had her head in the clouds, her heart was tired from all the excitement but there was no way she could sleep. She kept remembering every word Victor said, trying to read between the lines, to guess what his feelings were. She was sure that he was interested, but she was afraid to put her hopes too high. She knew that she was in a place where Victor could easily hurt her. She hated the fact that he had this power over her. She was used to being in control, she had never experienced such feelings and she didn't like it. She felt that her brain has abandoned her, telling her to be careful but her heart was in complete control. When she was with Victor she felt naked, all her shields down. And she couldn't talk to Alia because she knew that her sister wouldn't understand. Alia was the dreamer and now she needed somebody more pragmatic to tell her to forget about Victor, he was too dreamy, he was out of her league. They hadn't even set a date and she was sure that he wouldn't call her. After all, their meetings had both been accidental, so maybe he was just polite, too nice to reject her. She wasn't sure if she wanted to know what his feelings were. But she was not ready to wait for him to call. She made a resolution. Tomorrow she would talk to Alia to work harder on the diary project. She had left it aside in at a time when they had made some progress. With this she found a little peace of mind to fall asleep.

Alia was less tormented because she didn't have the same intense feelings. She had spent a very enjoyable day with somebody who had entertained her. When Deanna left she thought she would be alone, but the day turned out to be a lot more fun. She liked Marc's company and she hoped she had not been too boring for him. But she didn't analyse the situation too deeply. They were good friends, very much alike, but nothing more.

Gloria was very worried. She knew from Harcourt's involvement that The Peacemaker must be nearby and in her experience, that couldn't be good. It meant that she had to get out of the nest to protect the girls sooner than she would have liked. She wondered if the girls were ready to find out the truth. Suddenly, Gloria felt old and tired. She had fought enough. But the girls needed her to prepare them for what lay ahead. She decided to leave the girls another week and then to tell them all about the diary. Unfortunately, The Peacemaker had other plans.

Chapter Twenty-Eight

BACK TO THE PEACEMAKER

The next day Alia was in the mood to go shopping. It was so exceptional that Deanna didn't want to waste such a rare opportunity to go to the malls with her sister. So they left Gloria at home and with Gilbert stalking them, they took the subway to the mall. Paris is surrounded by a million shopping paradises, where people can waste a whole day spending money, they only had to choose one.

After a few hours of trying on clothes, laughing at each other and eating junk food, Alia and Deanna decided to split up for a while, because Alia wanted to see a movie and Deanna had a few more shops to visit.

When Alia arrived at the cinema she saw none other than Marc in the queue for popcorn. She sneaked up beside him and asked:

"I would like some salted popcorn and a large soda, please. And ASAP because the movie is about to start."

Marc, without even turning his head recognised her voice. And he got so excited to meet her that he spun round and threw popcorn all over her.

"I'm not sure that your boss will be too happy about all the popcorn you're wasting," said Alia and started laughing.

"You owe me a movie, because you scared me!" said Marc trying to remove the popcorn from her hair and clothes.

Alia took a few steps back to stop Marc from touching her. He was so clumsy she had never seen him like that before.

"Ok," she said. "I think we are here for the same movie, so let's go."

They went into the cinema together and for the third time, they were together without noticing Gilbert, who was on a mission.

When the lights went out Marc and Alia stopped talking. Meanwhile Gilbert took some time finding Alia in the dark. He sat down right behind her and slipped a little piece of paper in her pocket. Then he left to find Deanna, and did the same with her while she was searching the skirt racks.

The notes he left in the girls' pockets, was actually one note cut into two pieces, one for Alia and one for Deanna. It was meant to be put together. The Peacemaker had a message for the girls but he had no idea that something would come up between them and they would never get to read it together. He had delivered the message in this way, so that if Gloria found one, she couldn't see what it meant, nor where it came from. He hoped that he could infiltrate the girls' thoughts and make them see what kind of woman Gloria was.

Chapter Twenty-Nine

LOVE IS COMPLICATED

When the movie was over, Alia and Marc left the cinema, so at ease with each other that they were almost holding hands. And then something important happened. Deanna came out of a shop and saw them together. Marc said something and she saw Alia laugh and put her head on his shoulder. And worst of all, she saw him touch Alia's hair gently to brush a strand of it out of her eyes. This wouldn't have been a problem had Deanna known that Marc had an identical twin, and that she was in fact in love with a totally different boy. All she saw was the one boy she had ever been in love with, completely and madly in love with her sister. And her sister was indulging him. She was so outraged that she didn't even stop to remember that she had never told Alia about her crush, so technically she was not stealing her boyfriend, who technically was not her boyfriend.

Alia and Marc didn't see her so she left without a word, not caring that her sister would worry about her. She went home determined never to speak to her sister again. It didn't even cross her mind that it was her fault that she didn't tell Alia about the boy she had met. And what kind of person meets a girl and five seconds later is caressing her twin's face. Obviously, Victor had a fetish on twins and he didn't deserve one tear from her.

Then, on her way home she met Victor who was off to join his brother. She was so upset that she didn't even notice that he was dressed differently, and if he had been with Alia, he would never have had the time to be where he was now. Sadly all reasoning had gone out the window, and she was blinded with jealousy. At that moment she realised how much she loved Victor. She was crying and she was angry with herself for letting herself cry like that over a boy. So she cried even more.

When Victor saw her, he had no idea why she was so upset and why she didn't want to talk to him. He didn't dare force her. He could never have imagined the complicated situation they had all fallen into. And that the whole mess could easily have been avoided if one of the four had talked about it. But the problem was created by secrets and none of them seemed capable of untangling it. So Victor allowed Deanna to run away from him, believing she must have a problem that she didn't want to share with him. He still couldn't stop himself from noticing how beautiful she looked, even when she was crying.

Luckily, Gloria was not at home when Deanna got there, so she was free to express her frustration and anger as she felt it. She wanted to confront her sister, to tell her that the boy she was with wasn't a good person, but after that she realised that Victor had never declared his love, that she had never encouraged that. The mental picture of her sister and the boy she loved together was torturing her. Even if they were in love she could never accept this relationship. It hurt too much.

She fell on the bed and was so exhausted that she fell asleep. When Gloria came home and saw Deanna in bed, it didn't even cross her mind that the twins were involved in such high drama of love and jealousy.

When Alia came out of the cinema with Marc, they said goodbye and she started searching for Deanna in the mall. She tried her cell phone but there was no answer. She started to worry but she thought that Deanna must have lost patience and gone home. She didn't like the idea that her sister had left her there, but she had to make a decision. So she went home hoping to find her sister there. She was even a little angry that Deanna hadn't at least sent her a message, or answered the phone. She wanted to question Deanna about why she had been so selfish and careless.

When she arrived home and saw her sister, she realised that it was war. She couldn't understand why Deanna was so upset. From her point of view she had done nothing wrong. But Deanna was not ready to talk about it.

Dinner was silent and awkward, full of negative energy. Gloria had nothing to say. She had learned a long time ago that she had no place between the girls. When they had a problem she had to let them solve it together. All she could do was to put out the fire if she saw sparks.

Chapter Thirty

FINALLY SOMEBODY TALKS

Victor let Deanna leave and then regretted it a second later. He wanted to know what was going on with her, he wanted to take care of her if she was hurt. He had no idea that she was hurt because of him; he would have never forgiven himself if he thought he was the reason for her tears. But how could he know? He just felt he would have liked to take her in his arms, dry her tears and tell her that he would protect her. But, silly him, he let her go and he didn't even see which direction she'd gone in. So he decided to go and look for his brother.

He knew Marc had wanted to see a movie, so when he arrived at the mall he called his brother, who told him that the movie was over and that they could meet. He didn't even have time to hang up, before he saw Marc with… a girl. His heart started pounding, he lost all power in his feet. He searched for somewhere to sit down. The girl with his brother was Deanna. At least that's what he thought. But they had seen him, so he couldn't run away, like Deanna had done earlier, even though he wanted to.

Somebody else was even more surprised than Victor. Alia couldn't believe her eyes, when she saw a double of Marc standing in front of her. Marc had never told her that he had a twin. Victor mistook her expression of genuine surprise, for guilt and he threw her such a glare of bitter disappointment, that Alia became even more confused.

"Hi Victor," said Marc. "Have you been waiting long?"

"No, I just got here," said Victor, wondering if Deanna would have the courage to admit in front of Marc, that she knew him. But Alia just wanted to leave them alone and look for her sister. It was a fascinating coincidence that Marc had an identical twin, as she did. But she didn't want to intrude. So when she saw that Marc's brother wasn't very happy to see them together, she decided to leave. This guy was a little aggressive and the way he kept staring at her made her decidedly uncomfortable. Then Marc had the brilliant idea to introduce them.

"This is my brother, Victor."

"Hi Victor, I'm-" started Alia.

"Don't play games!" Victor cut her off. "I think my brother has the right to know who you really are."

"I don't understand," said Alia surprised.

"Tell him how we met, how we went horse riding in the forest!" cried Victor, who was so hurt that he felt his heart would burst. It was even worse that it was his brother he was jealous of. She was meant to be with him, not with Marc.

"I'm sorry," said Alia calmly. "I have never seen you before in my life"

"Alia, what is my brother talking about?" said Marc starting to worry, as the atmosphere grew worse by the second. His own feelings started to surface, to see his brother so passionate about Alia.

"Alia? Why do you call her Alia?" asked Victor. "Why don't you tell him your real name?"

"Alia is my real name!" cried Alia. "Who are you to accuse me of lying? Why would I lie about my own name?"

"To make a fool of us both," said Victor trying to get closer to his brother, but Marc was not yet convinced that Alia was the enemy. He still needed to think that Alia was an amazing and honest person, the smartest and funniest girl he had ever met. Alright, for now she only saw him as a friend, but in time he could make her love him as he started to love her.

"So what is her real name?" asked Marc, looking at Victor as if indulging a madman or a child.

"Deanna, of course, or you lied to me too? Of course you did! Why would you play with us like that? What kind of monster are you?" roared Victor.

To the boys' total surprise, Alia started laughing. They both felt a little offended by her lack of feelings, and now they didn't know what to think about her.

"I think that you've made a big mistake." said Alia smiling kindly. Now that she understood Victor's anger, she saw that it came from a much nicer place. She was intuitive enough to see how much Victor loved her twin sister, even if he wasn't willing to admit it. She was disappointed that Deanna had never told her about him. But that explained her strange behaviour of late.

"What are you talking about? And why are you laughing at us?" asked Victor.

"You have fallen in love with my twin sister, Deanna."

"Your what? And who said I'm in love?" he said trying to rearrange his emotions, which were flying up and down like a yo-yo.

"You're not the only one who has a twin. I have a twin sister, Deanna and she did go horse riding yesterday, apparently with you," said Alia, relieved to have solved this weird puzzle.

"You never told me you had a twin sister," said Marc, equally relieved.

"And you never told me you had a twin brother," said Alia.

"He's always been ashamed of me," said Victor. "He thinks he's better looking."

Alia sensed he was relying on jokes, to cover his embarrassment for the outburst, which had made him betray his feelings for Deanna.

The three of them strolled on together, carrying on the conversation, now they had discovered this strange coincidence, of being identical twins. After a while, Alia decided it was time for her to find Deanna. When she arrived home, she wanted to tell Deanna about her discovery, but her sister wouldn't listen. Alia had no idea that Deanna had seen her with Marc, that Deanna was also in love with Victor and that Deanna didn't realise there were two of them. So she couldn't understand Deanna's attitude. She wanted to tell her that Victor was in love with her, but she had no idea what Deanna's feelings were. Alia decided to leave Deanna alone for a few days, to give her time to calm down.

Chapter Thirty-One

BÉA'S MISSION

In the meantime, Béa was searching for a strategy to get close to the girls. She knew it wouldn't be easy, as the two of them were so self-sufficient. That's why they didn't have any close friends. But this misunderstanding between Deanna and Alia had come at the right moment. Deanna had no one to talk to, and Béa was in the right place at the right time.

When Béa arrived on her weekly cleaning day, Deanna was at home still furious about Alia and Victor.

"Hello, Deanna" said Béa smiling as she entered the apartment.

"Hi," muttered Deanna, without so much as a glance at her.

"What's wrong?" asked Béa, not knowing which button she had pushed.

"What's wrong? What's wrong?" cried Deanna. "I'll tell you what's wrong! Everything is wrong! That I have a twin sister is wrong!"

"Why do you have a problem with your sister?"

"She always told me that I can have any boy I want."

"And it's true! Only a fool would not want to be with you!" said Béa, getting an idea of the problem.

"Well, the only boy I want, is the one boy I cannot have," said Deanna and started to cry.

"Why ever not?"

"Because SHE has got her hands on him!"

"Who's she? Alia? I didn't even know she had a boyfriend!" said Béa with genuine surprise.

"Neither did I! What kind of sister is she? A sneaky one, who knows she's guilty."

"Does she know you like the same boy?" asked Béa.

"No."

"Who met him first?"

"I don't know."

"She doesn't even know that you met him too?"

"No… but…"

"Why didn't you tell him about you two?"

"I don't know… Maybe because we're not together yet."

"What? So he's not actually your boyfriend?" asked Béa.

"Not really… no. We just met a couple of times, by accident. But I love being with him."

"So, to summarize, you're angry because your sister didn't guess that you like a boy, who you didn't tell her about and who after all, is not even your boyfriend?"

"Well, yes…" answered Deanna starting to see the flaw in her argument.

"I understand that you are hurt, but I hope you see that is not your sister's fault. On the other hand, that boy is not very nice if he gets your hopes up and then hangs out with your sister."

"I still can't believe that he could do that. Honestly, I can't imagine how can he live with himself."

"He's not worth destroying your relationship with Alia."

"Yes, but I still have to live with that."

"Maybe Alia will see that he's not good for her," said Béa.

"Maybe," said Deanna a little calmer. "Thank you."

"Glad to be of help."

"That doesn't mean that I am ready to make it up with her. Let's not forget, she has hidden her relationship with Victor from me."

"Maybe she was afraid you would steal her thunder. You know very well that everybody is drawn to you."

"Don't try to find excuses for her. And on top of everything, he is not good for her. They have nothing in common!" gasped Deanna.

"Unfortunately, you'll have to wait for her to discover that on her own… Believe me, if you are meant to be together, you will be. If not, you cannot twist their arms to do what you want."

"Maybe, but that doesn't mean that I have to stand there and watch! It would be too painful!" Deanna started to cry again, as she threw her head on Béa's shoulder.

Chapter Thirty-Two

A FENCING LESSON

Deanna started to melt, but the next day, as soon as she set eyes on Alia, all she could see was THEM holding hands. As usual, when an image is so painful, the brain has a tendency to embellish it. By now Deanna could swear that she saw them kissing too.

The girls had to leave together, as they had a fencing lesson in half an hour. They said nothing on the way. They barely looked at each other.

They arrived, changed clothes and they went to join their fencing instructor.

Alia stopped to read the rules up on the wall at the entrance.

RULES ESTABLISHED UNDER LOUIS XIII AND LOUIS XIV
USED IN OUR TIME
When entering the arms room one must uncover himself;
It is forbidden to speak of religion or politics;
One shall not swear;
One shall not use indecent words;
One shall not banter;
One shall not mock another;
One shall not use his sword in the arm's room without a mask and
glove;
One shall not disturb those who fight…

"Don't tell me that you are interested in rules and honour!" Deanna interrupted her reading, in a scornful voice.

"What do you mean? When didn't I play by the rules?" asked Alia who had no idea, what on earth all this was about, and didn't know of course, that Deanna had seen her with Marc.

"Just drop it, let's go, our teacher is waiting," snapped Deanna, turning her back on Alia.

Their teacher's name was Benoit, he was young, very pleasant and had a lot of patience. All the children, his students, loved him and respected him.

When it came time to fight against each other, Deanna couldn't hold her feelings back anymore. She started attacking Alia as if her life depended on it.

"Hey, watch out!" cried Alia.

"Why? What did I do?" asked Deanna attacking once more.

"Why are you being so aggressive with me?"

"I don't understand why you never told me you had a boyfriend!" said Deanna.

"Because I haven't," whispered Alia, not wishing to make a scene.

"And you keep lying to me! Why do you feel the need to hide it?"

"I am not lying."

"Girls, girls!" Benoit interrupted their duel by calling everybody's attention to them. "Today we will work on the defence. Who knows a few techniques? Alia?"

"Yes, I just need someone to attack me," replied Alia.

"I'll do it, with pleasure," said Deanna, immediately. "Sometimes attack is the best form of defence!" And she embarked on a vengeful and highly aggressive attack on her sister. Luckily Alia was wearing her mask, because Deanna showed no mercy.

"Well done, Alia!" said Benoit enthusiastically. "Did you all see how she managed to defend herself, as if her life depended on it?"

"I think it did actually," whispered Alia looking inquiringly at her sister.

"I saw you with him at the cinema yesterday," said Deanna, gasping for air.

"I met this boy, but he's not my boyfriend. We met twice, by accident. We are just friends."

"I saw the way he looked at you," Deanna accused her.

"We just met. Trust me, we're just friends," repeated Alia. She decided not to mention Victor to Deanna. She considered it was not up to her to reveal the secret. Deanna would have to talk to Victor herself.

"If this is true, I'm sorry I reacted that way. Let's finish our lesson and go home," said Deanna. She was relieved to see that Alia was really not in love with Victor. But she couldn't stop thinking about the way Victor had looked at her sister.

"Ok. En garde!" said Alia and they continued with their lesson. Deanna was better at fencing but today she was distracted, so Alia won every time.

Chapter Thirty-Three

THE PRAYER

The girls went home together. When they arrived Béa noticed their mood had improved somewhat and it made her happy to see them getting on. But Deanna was still not herself, she looked worried. But she said nothing, she wanted the girls to come to her. That night turned out to be a very long one for Deanna. She couldn't get to sleep after all these emotions. At least she knew her sister wasn't interested in Victor, but she still didn't know how he felt.

The next day Gloria left earlier than usual. Now that Béa was the new spy in their house, she had to change her routine. Every night they had a long conversation to get the script ready for the next day. Soon Gloria had to take the decision to give a hint to Harcourt, to put him on the wrong track. But she still had no idea how to do that. It had to be perfect, because Harcourt knew enough to suspect a lie.

So by the time Deanna woke up, the girls were at home alone. She slipped out of bed, without waking Alia. She wasn't hungry, so she dressed and left the apartment, to take a walk. She didn't even think where she was going. She just drifted through Paris. At one point she took the bus, but she had no direction. She didn't even realise that instinctively, she was heading for Neuilly, the place where she last saw Victor. As if such a coincidence could be possible again. What was she hoping? He was probably at home dreaming about her sister. They probably had more in common, they liked the same movies obviously. And more importantly, she didn't believe in platonic relationships between a boy and a girl. Alia had always been a dreamer, she was naive enough to think that they could be just friends, but Deanna knew better.

The fresh air of the morning started to erase the effects of a sleepless night. She was thinking straight now. All she had to do was to find Victor and ask him. She was used to being in control, this was the first time she had ever experienced this situation and she wanted it to stop. She couldn't bear another day without knowing where she stood with him. Just as she was about to call Victor's umber, she felt two warm hands cover her eyes. Deanna recognised the irresistible scent of Victor, the same as when they were in the forest and he helped her get back on the horse. She turned around and looked at him. He was breath-taking. He had been running and his hair was a mess, the tee-shirt was sweaty and she could see all his muscles through it. His eyes were literally sparkling, and Deanna immediately believed he must be confusing her with her sister.

"Hi," said Deanna trying to be casual.

"Hello, now I have trouble guessing which is which. I'm sorry, but I still don't know you very well," said Victor blushing.

"Deanna, I'm Deanna," she answered confused. She was surprised to see he didn't even try to hide the fact that he had been flirting with her sister too…

"Ok. I just wanted to see you to talk about something important," he pressed on.

"I think I know what it is," said Deanna feeling she was about to finally find the answers to her questions.

"How can you know?"

"I know that you met my sister."

"I did, but what does this have to do with anything?"

"Don't worry, I won't stand in your way. I'll just need some time to get used to the idea," said Deanna sadly, feeling the tears welling up in her eyes.

"What do you mean?" he said, beginning to be alarmed by her strange conversation.

"I don't know about you, but it doesn't happen to me very often, that I meet somebody, who I have so much in common with. Maybe that's the difference between me and my sister. You have more in common with her."

"Your sister? Why are you even talking to me about her?"

"I was just thinking that you wanted to tell me, how much in love you are with my sister and that the honourable thing to do, would be for you to stop seeing me," sighed Deanna, finding the words painful to articulate. She wanted to leave before he could see her cry, but when she turned away, he took her by the arm and pulled her closer to him.

"Do you think that I am in love with your sister?" he asked gently looking her straight in her eye. "Why?"

"Isn't that what you wanted to tell me?" asked Deanna, trying to avoid his gaze, which seemed to be analysing her every expression.

"No, not at all. I only have one thing in common with your sister and that's you. I only met her yesterday."

"She told me you met a few times before."

"No, she met my brother. But I see she didn't tell you. She's even nicer than I imagined," said Victor, moving even closer to Deanna.

"Your brother?"

"My identical twin brother, Marc."

"*What?*"

"Just like you, I have an identical twin, who I never told you about."

Now they were almost touching.

"Why not?" asked Deanna and realised she had lost all feeling in her legs, as if she was floating on air.

"The same reason you didn't. For once I felt unique. You made me feel that I was enough." Victor was so close now, that he was just whispering in her ear.

"If Alia has known this since yesterday, why didn't she tell me?"

"I guess she wanted you to hear it from me."

"Hear what?" she asked, taking a step back so she could look into his eyes.

"That you are unique, that you are beautiful and fun. And that I couldn't stand to be just a friend, that I want more."

"More?" whispered Deanna, hoping she wasn't imagining all this, hoping that it wasn't just a dream and she would wake up alone.

"I want you to let me love you," said Victor, shyly caressing her hair near her ear.

Now Deanna was sure she was dreaming. Ever since she felt the horrible bout of jealousy, all she could think of was this moment. And now that it was here, she couldn't bring herself to believe it was real. She took another step back to look at Victor. He was serious and he was waiting for an answer.

"Do you have any feelings for me, or should I go and hide in a rat hole somewhere, waiting for you to forget what I just said?"

"How can you even ask that question? I fell in love with you the moment you asked me to go on that ride with you."

Victor took a step towards Deanna, put both his hands on her cheeks and kissed her. She melted in his arms. An hour went by and they couldn't let go of each other's hands. They knew they both had to return home, but decided they would have to meet again later. The sun felt warmer, the colours looked brighter and life felt beautiful again for Deanna. She wanted to go home and ask Alia's forgiveness, for being so unfair to her. She wanted to meet Marc, to see him for herself. She suggested to Victor, that they should all get together and meet each other.

Chapter Thirty-Four

HARCOURT

Maxime Harcourt never imagined he would end up a common spy, following two teenagers throughout Paris. He was born of a noble family. The Harcourt line went way back to 1094 in Normandy. His was one of the last noble families that still had living heirs. They had a branch in England and one in France. Maxime belonged to the French Harcourts. He had received a very good education and his parents were very proud of him. As in every noble family they had high expectations of their son. Where it all went wrong, was when Maxime met a girl, who didn't fit into their exclusive society. He was destined to marry a pleasant, well-educated woman, from his own aristocratic class, who must be prepared to sacrifice her own career, in favour of his. But hearts do not obey reason. Maxime was so much in love with this girl that he decided to elope and he left his deceived parents behind.

The girl he fell in love with was a journalist, called Cynthia. She was stubbornly independent and very curious, with a penchant of transforming everything into a story. She even investigated his family. At first their love was enough to keep them occupied, but after a while she started to show signs of boredom. He was too conformist for her, she was too wild and restless for him. So they decided to go their separate ways. He returned to London, because he didn't have the courage to confront his parents yet. She left for Paris and landed a job as soon as she arrived.

In London, Maxime found himself with a lot of time on his hands and decided to investigate his family line himself. To his surprise, there were many references to the Harcourts in the public archives. He decided to do something more with his life, than just chasing girls and made plans to pursue his investigation in France. However, just as he was about to set off, he met The Peacemaker. He was old enough to be his father. He seduced him with promises of a better life, without obligations, with freedom. All Maxime desired was to choose his own destiny and this man soon became the father he never had. Unfortunately, Maxime failed to understand that his new friend was there for his own reasons.

The Peacemaker was smart enough to hide his own agenda, to give time to earn Maxime's trust. About a year after they met, Cynthia tried to contact Maxime. But the Peacemaker was there to prevent what would have been a catastrophe for his plans. So Maxime never knew that Cynthia had even tried to find him. The Peacemaker wasn't ready to share Maxime with anybody.

But Maxime was happy. He forgot about everything, Cynthia, his parents, everything belonged to a past he wasn't very anxious to return to.

Then one day he saw some disturbing news about his father, splashed across the internet.

"CEO of the most powerful energy company, dying. Their biggest competitor on the market ready to seize the lead."

How come he didn't even know that his father was ill? How was his mother doing? He realised that he had to go home. He had deserted them for far too long. But when he shared that with his friend, all hell broke loose. He had no idea how dangerous the Peacemaker could be, and it terrified him. It hadn't occurred to Maxime that actually he'd been nothing more than a prisoner all this time, now he had to find a way of escape. But the Peacemaker had built his prison well. Maxime was now without money, and completely dependent.

Then, surprisingly. the Peacemaker decided to let Maxime go, on one condition, that he would remain his faithful servant and when the time came, he would return.

Maxime hoped that as soon as he got home, his parents would help him escape the influence of the Peacemaker, that they would provide him with a job and money. But he had arrived in Paris too late. His father had died and when he visited his mother, he found her in a care, and suffering from Alzheimer's disease. In the years Maxime had been absent, the company had been put in the hands of a board of directors, and he had no place there.

So he found himself without parents, without money, without a job. But the Peacemaker waited in the shadows, ready to offer him the means to live as he wanted, with one condition, to be at his service 24/7. For a long time, he didn't understand the Peacemaker's reasons, but he would soon find out why was he such an important piece of the puzzle.

For the time being, he was forced to witness the boring life of two teenagers during the summer holidays. The Peacemaker had explained almost everything to him, but he didn't understand why he couldn't go for the diary himself. Why did they have to wait for the girls to find it? After all these years of waiting, he wanted to see the powers of that famous diary. He knew that The Peacemaker couldn't use it himself, because he wasn't of noble origin. He was using Maxime for that. But it seemed even Maxime wasn't good enough to find it himself. He regretted leaving his peaceful home and loving parents to chase a dream, which was soon to become a nightmare.

Chapter Thirty-Five

THE TREASURE HUNT CONTINUES

It was the best day in Deanna's life. The boy that she was in love with, felt the same about her. Her twin sister was not the backstabbing witch, she had believed and life in Paris was growing more perfect by the day. When she got home, Alia was still in bed. Deanna couldn't wait to tell her sister how it went with Victor, so she woke her up, with the news that she was now the happiest girl on the planet. And Alia was happy for her. So when Deanna proposed to Alia to share the clues they had with the boys, she was relieved to see that they had the same thought. So they got ready and went to meet the boys. Alia had chosen the tea room in the bookshop. They were almost alone and the few people who were there, concentrated only on the books. They chose a table in the back room and ordered some tea and cheesecake.

When the boys arrived, Deanna couldn't believe her eyes, faced with two versions of Victor. The four of them started to laugh at their own situation.

"I never used to believe in coincidences," said Alia.

"It's not a coincidence, it's destiny," said Victor.

"I don't believe in destiny," chipped in Deanna. "Everybody builds his life as he sees fit."

"So you don't find strange that I met you the same moment my brother, my twin brother, met your sister?" asked Marc.

"My twin sister," added Deanna. "Yes, I admit it is pretty incredible."

"And this coincidence led to some problems, I understand?" said Victor smiling.

"How could I imagine that you had a twin brother, who was in love with my sister?" said Deanna blushing.

"Sorry, Deanna, but we are not in love!" laughed Alia. "We are just friends. Right, Marc?"

"Yes… just friends," said Marc lowering his eyes.

Alia was completely oblivious to the pain her words had caused Marc. But Victor sensed it and realised that his brother was not in such a happy situation. But he couldn't say anything and he wasn't sure that there was anything anyone could say to help.

"Ok, my fault," said Deanna, but she could not forget the way that Marc had been looking at her sister.

They abandoned this awkward subject and began talking about each other. After an hour they knew what each one of them was about and all the details of how they had met.

"I wanted to see you so badly, that once I thought I saw you on the road, biking in the forest," said Victor.

"Where?" said Deanna, surprised.

"In the Rambouillet forest, a couple of weeks ago."

"We were in the Rambouillet forest a couple of weeks ago," said Alia, exchanging looks with her sister.

"Really? So I wasn't imagining it. I'm relieved. At least I know I'm not mad."

"But what were you doing there?" asked Alia.

"We went visiting an old convent with a friend and his parents. And you?"

"We were just enjoying a beautiful day out with our grandmother," answered Deanna. And then, as if they were reading each other's minds she continued. "We have a question to ask you."

"What?" asked Marc curious.

"What would you say if we invited you to a treasure hunt?" said Alia.

"Of course," said Marc, his eyes lighting up.

"Then we have one that might interest you," said Deanna.

"As it happens, we have one for you, too," said Marc looking over at Victor. But Victor smiled to show him that he didn't mind sharing their secret.

"Ok, we'll start with ours and then we'll look at yours, if that's all right with you?" said Alia.

"So, what are we looking for?" said Marc.

"A diary. It was our mother's," replied Alia.

"And why is it hidden?"

"We don't know, that's why we want to find it so badly. We have reasons to believe this diary cost our parents their lives," said Deanna.

"What? What could be in a diary that's worth killing for?" asked Victor, astonished.

"We were asking the same questions. Our research brought us to Chateau d'Esclimont, when you saw us in the forest. But we need to find a means of transport to go back there, because we didn't have time to finish our search."

"I understand," said Victor. "Our parents work every day and they wouldn't help us anyway. They see us as kids just playing detective."

"Nanna helped us once but only because we tricked her into doing so. She had no idea why we were really at that castle. So I don't think we can do that again, especially with you," said Deanna.

"What do you think about Béa?" asked Alia.

"Who's Béa?" said Marc.

"Béa is our housekeeper, slash nanny, slash friend, slash spy for Nanna."

"So, can we trust her?" asked Marc.

"We need to make her a double spy, but she seems easy to manipulate. Give me two days and she'll become our best friend. Plus she has a car," said Alia.

"Ok, so if we take Béa on our journey, do we tell her anything or do we hide our true purpose?" asked Victor.

"I think it's best to keep as much of it to ourselves," said Deanna. "And tell her only what she needs to know."

"Won't she talk to your grandmother?" asked Marc.

"I don't think they are that close. But we must give her a story that Nanna would buy. If we work together it shouldn't be too hard. One of us will distract her while the other ones search for the diary."

"Yes, but we still need a pretext to go there," said Victor.

"We can say that we want to throw a surprise party for our parents and we need to recce some locations," said Marc.

"That could work," said Alia. "But we must go slowly. Let's get to know Béa better."

"Great minds think alike," said Marc, grinning at Alia. "We must give her the impression she is our friend, and then ask her for help. We don't want her to think she's being used."

"So, shall we start by suggesting a girls' day out?" said Deanna. "What would we like to do for it, Alia?"

Chapter Thirty-Six

THE BEGINNING OF A BEAUTIFUL FRIENDSHIP

Béa was starting to feel a little worried about the agreement she had struck with Gloria. She had a meeting with Harcourt every day and to date she had failed to give him anything that would satisfy him. She was aware that the girls were leading a relatively normal life, but she didn't want to upset Harcourt who had her destiny in his hands. She was torn between the girls and her own dreams of motherhood. But she was still convinced she was doing the right thing. So when Deanna came to her and asked if they could all visit the Louvre together, she was thrilled. Her enthusiasm should have raised Deanna's suspicions, but the teenager was happy to see her own plan succeeding. They set a day when Béa wasn't working and all three of them turned up to face a Louvre full of tourists.

Luckily, they had thought of buying their tickets on the internet, so they didn't have to wait long, but the crowd was unbearable. They only visited the Roman Empire and Egypt sections. Two hours later they were outside drinking soda on the grass in front of the museum.

"Well, that didn't go too well," said Béa.

"It was terrible. I've never seen so many people per square meter," said Alia lying down on the grass.

"At least we know now that we must visit it in winter, when there are fewer tourists."

"On the other hand, it was very interesting. I loved the temporary exhibit of graphic art," said Alia, which made Béa feel a little more cheerful.

"And the mummy," enthused Deanna.

"I expected to see more of them," said Alia.

"I knew I shouldn't have watched that movie, about the museum, where all the exhibits come back to life in the night," said Béa, laughing.

"Don't worry, the mummy couldn't walk with all that toilet paper wrapped around her," said Alia.

"So what shall we do next? We got our cultural pill, now how about some shopping, or a movie?" said Deanna.

"A movie sounds like a good idea," said Béa, rather enjoying their girls' day out.

After the movie they went home. Béa was happy to see that her plan to get closer to the girls was working. She had double pressure as both Gloria and Harcourt were expecting her to get into the twins' lives. She accompanied them back to their apartment and they decided they should all do something together the next day. The girls planned to introduce Béa to the boys, so that she would agree to drive the four of them to Chateau d'Esclimont.

The next day the boys chose their best clothes, and they looked so smart. The aim was to inspire confidence, so that Béa would approve of them. It was crucial that she didn't suspect any ulterior motive, so they decided not to offer any explanation of why the Chateau in particular. Deanna and Victor were the romantic couple that needed to be left alone from time to time. Alia and Marc would be the good friends that forced the lovebirds to spend some time in the real world. They had everything figured out, but of course, they had no idea that Béa was a spy for Gloria. If they had known, they would never have introduced the boys to her. But now it was too late, if they wanted Béa's help they had to give her some information. A lie is better when it has some truth in it.

The day went very well, the boys were charming as they knew they needed Béa on their side. Béa told them the story of her life including her dream to have a child. Of course, she didn't mention the evil Maxime who threatened her dream, nor the price she had to pay to make it come true.

They decided to wait a little before starting to ask for favours. They didn't want to raise her suspicions. Béa, on the other hand was happy that she had something to tell Harcourt. She didn't understand his interest in the girls, all she knew was that she had to report every move they made. In the meantime, she had a meeting with Gloria.

Chapter Thirty-Seven

THE RESEARCH

Béa was wondering what Gloria did all day long. The girls were alone most days, and she knew Gloria didn't have a job. In fact, Gloria was the heir to her family's fortune. She didn't care to show off her wealth, and she always wanted to teach the girls how to live with less. Even the girls didn't know how much money their grandmother had. She had raised them to respect everyone no matter his or her social status. She had her big house in England, they had the apartment in Paris and a few other estates throughout Europe. The family fortune had been made in the mirror business. Her father, like his father before him, was the largest manufacturer in England. The factory was sold when she was just a child but she still owned shares, which assured her a comfortable income.

But Gloria's attention lay elsewhere, the hunt for the second diary. She knew that it existed, but no-one had seen it for a few centuries. She spent days in the libraries in Paris, trying to find traces of the diary. She didn't know where the first one was but she had some ideas and she knew that she had to keep the girls busy to protect them from it. But the first one couldn't do what the second one could. So when Béa called her to confirm her meeting, she was deeply engrossed in a book on old manuscripts. The biggest mistake she could make was to assume that she knew what she was looking for. She would soon question that, just because she had seen the first diary, did it mean the second one had to be identical? But she had to postpone her research as Béa was on her way. They met in a coffeehouse to give the impression to Harcourt, if he was watching them, that they were two friends meeting to enjoy each other's company over a cup of coffee.

"So, what do you have?" asked Gloria.

"Big news, your Deanna has a boyfriend."

"Deanna? Already? I had hoped that she would give me more time to adjust."

"Adjust to what? You are at home here, now. And she's starting to make friends."

"She told you that?"

"She didn't need to, I met the boy. And Alia has an admirer but she doesn't see it yet."

"You met Deanna's boyfriend? And Alia's friend? You've really succeeded in becoming their confidante."

"Yes, they really like to talk to me and to share with me. They had a difficult moment because of the boys, but everything is fine now."

Béa told Gloria everything, the whole story about the twins, how Deanna had shown her dark side when she was jealous. Gloria was speechless, when she realised how much she was missing out on the girls' lives. She decided to make up to every moment she should have been there. She was happy that Béa had done a good job, but she didn't want Béa to replace their mother. So her next resolution was to be more involved in the girls' lives.

"Ok, I think you're in the perfect position now, all you have to do is not lose their confidence. And if anything unusual happens, come to me as soon as possible."

"For now I think the boys will keep them busy and at least they don't go out all alone. They are in good hands."

"I have one favour to ask you. I need to go to England for a couple of days. Could you stay with the girls? I've been waiting for a while to see if they trust you, so that I can leave them with you."

"No problem, they might even like it, we could do some shopping, have fun."

"Define fun," said Gloria smartly. "You and the girls might not understand the same thing. Deanna might enjoy shopping but Alia you have to let her choose what she wants to do. I'll leave you my credit card and some money so you can entertain them as they wish."

"Ok, but when do you leave and when do you come back?" asked Béa.

"I'll talk to the girls but I'll leave no later than a week from now," said Gloria.

"And about Harcourt, what do I tell him? Where did you go?"

"Tell him that I had to go home to settle a problem with a neighbour, or something. We mustn't lie to him, because I'm sure he'll send somebody with me. We need him to trust you."

"Right, I'll take care of everything. And when do you come back?"

"If all goes well, I'll be back in two or three days."

"And if not?"

"I'll warn the girls if anything changes. One more thing before I forget, don't let them enter my room. And if Harcourt decides to pay a visit, please let him try to find what he is searching for. And let me know as soon as he leaves. Try to convince him to ask you where to look. Tell him we have hidden cameras installed all over the apartment and that it is under surveillance by the police."

"I hope he'll believe me because I can't stop him if he wants to break in."

"I'm sure you'll do your best," said Gloria. Then taking some money from her purse, she paid and left.

Béa waited another five minutes before leaving. She had a difficult mission on her hands and her entire future depended on its success.

Chapter Thirty-Eight

GILBERT FOLLOWS GLORIA

Béa did her job and told Harcourt that Gloria was leaving for England. He did exactly as Gloria predicted, he asked Gilbert to follow her. All he had to do now was to wait for her to leave so he could go after her.

"What do you want me to do while I'm there?" asked Gilbert.

"Just be there in case she finds something," answered Harcourt.

"But how will I know that she found something? I can't see her coming to tell me."

"As a rule, she goes there to sort out a problem with the estate agent, who wants to put her house on the market. You just have to see if that's the real reason. If not, follow her, wherever she goes, you go."

"Excuse me, but what exactly are we searching for?"

"I have an idea, it's a long shot, but I think she's after the Silver One, the second diary. She knows the location of the Golden One. If she has both, nobody can stop her."

"But why doesn't she use the first one to find the second?"

"It's not that easy. There is no way of knowing where the Silver One is. If they were connected, Samantha would have had them together. But she lost her life searching for the second diary."

"And now Gloria is doing the same thing?"

"That's why we'll let her do all the work and at the end, when she succeeds, we'll get it from her," said Harcourt, clenching his fist.

"IF she succeeds. Do you really think she's capable?"

"She must be. She is smarter than her daughter, who found the other one.

But this one seems harder to get. It will come to her… if she's worthy."

"I think you're forgetting something," interrupted Gilbert. "Didn't you tell me that the diary only responds to people who have noble blood?"

"The first one, yes."

"So, is Gloria from a noble family?"

"Well… I never thought of that. You might be right. Even if she is on the right track she could never touch it."

"So she needs the girls to finish the job?"

"Or me," sneered Harcourt. "Depends who gets there first."

"So Gloria is searching knowing that she can't touch it? Why?" said Gilbert.

"Maybe she's planning on involving the girls later, when she gets closer. That's what I would do."

"I feel that you have an agenda with those twins."

"As soon as I find out that Gloria has the Silver One, I shall use the girls as a bargaining chip."

"The diary in exchange for the girls?"

"That's right. Our patience will pay off and they will be of use to us in the end."

"Ok, so you let me know when I'm leaving for England."

"As soon as our spy gives the sign."

"And this woman, do you really trust her?"

"No, but I trust blackmail. I left her no choice."

"Ok. So keep me posted."

"Don't worry, just be prepared," said Harcourt and escorted Gilbert to the door, audience over.

Gilbert went straight home. He thrived on action. Give him a mission and he wouldn't rest until it was accomplished. He packed a bag and waited, ready for the sign from Harcourt. What he wasn't ready for, was the series of surprises this trip had in store for him. He feared he may have to resort to violence at some stage, even though he might not relish it, but nothing could have prepared him for the events which lay ahead.

Chapter Thirty-Nine

A BEAUTIFUL CONCERT

After a few days, Gloria decided that she was ready to leave. She asked the girls if they were happy with Béa staying with them for a few days. As Gloria was out all day long, it wasn't a very big change for the girls. Béa was more present in their lives and anyway, they were keen for her to play her role in their research for the diary. They were looking for an excuse to go to Chateau d'Esclimont. The boys were working on it too, but it was Deanna and Alia that needed to ask Béa to take them there.

A day after Gloria left, Deanna came up with a brilliant solution. She found out there was to be a piano concert at the castle and she bought five tickets as a thank you to Béa for taking care of them. It was the perfect scenario, and the best part was that Béa couldn't refuse without offending the girls. The concert started at eight o'clock so they had to stay the night. It was also the perfect opportunity to search the room, where they suspected the diary had been hidden.

The boys took up their tickets from Deanna, determined to persuade their parents to let them go. When they saw that Béa was ok with everything, they put it to their parents and asked if they could join the girls. As they had a responsible adult with them, they agreed. In fact, the boys' parents were happy to see they had found girlfriends with such a positive influence. They had never dreamed to see Victor so happy to go to a piano concert! Perhaps Deanna had managed to tame him. Marc was a different story. His parents were a little worried about him. Sometimes he was very happy, especially when he was with Alia, but sometimes they caught him just standing and staring into the middle distance, his thoughts elsewhere. They were afraid that he was very much in love, but the feeling wasn't mutual.

Marc hoped that going to that romantic castle with Alia would make her realise that she too had romantic feelings for him. He wasn't sure how much longer he could stand this situation. He wanted to hold her in his arms, to tell her how much he liked her voice, how lovely she looked in blue. He was starting to hate that role of "friend", he was being forced to play. It was a torture for him to see Victor with Deanna, to watch them falling in love, exchanging tender looks, kissing at the end of a date. He was content to see how happy Victor was, but he couldn't understand why he didn't have all that. But the night at the Chateau d'Esclimont could change everything, at least so he hoped.

They made a plan. They would go to the concert together and after a few minutes Victor would fake a stomach ache and have to go to the bathroom. They didn't want to risk Béa searching the lady's room, for one of the girls, so it was better to send Victor to look for the diary. If he had difficulties, Marc was supposed to go and see if he was all right. That way Béa was forced to stay with the girls. They arranged to meet in the lobby, after the concert, to share what they had found with the girls.

They arrived at the hotel. Béa, Alia and Deanna had a room for three and the boys a double. Alia loved the setting, the decorations in classic style, the huge beds, it made her feel like a princess. She couldn't believe she was about to sleep in a real castle. As they arrived very early, they had the right to take a tour. Béa was as impressed as they were. In the afternoon, Victor and Deanna used intimacy as an excuse to split up and go for a romantic walk. This way Deanna showed Victor the statue and the direction it seemed to indicate. Victor took a pink chewing gum and threw it on the window.

"What are you doing?" asked Deanna panicking.

"I'm leaving a marker. Have you seen how many windows this castle has? How will I know which room it is?"

"You're right, James Bond," said Deanna with admiration. "As long as nobody comes to clean it before the concert."

"Let's hope they don't. They have to be very busy with the artists' arrival. Have you seen all the bodyguards?"

"Yes, I didn't even know the pianist was so famous. I hope he'll be good enough to keep Béa's attention, while we're searching the room."

"If Béa gets bored, you will try to entertain her until I come back?" he said looking concerned.

"Don't worry, Alia and I will think of something if the situation gets out of control. But keep your phone close. I've even got a Bluetooth to keep in touch."

"Me too. But we'd better use phone messages to communicate. If you're at the concert you can't talk, but you can write."

"Ok. Come on, let's get ready for the concert. The others will be thinking we got lost on the estate," said Deanna, taking Victor's hand.

On the way back, Victor stopped to admire the balcony that the Rochefoucauld family had added to the classical pediment.

"Wow, what a self-centered lot they were" he said, looking at the carving that represented the family's motto: 'IT IS MY PLEASURE!'"

"No, you misinterpret it. As a lot of people do," explained Deanna. "It comes from a more complex phrase: 'We do what we have to do, but our duty is not a load. It is our pleasure!' Sounds a bit more noble now, doesn't it?"

"If you say so," said Victor loudly, as she opened her mouth to argue some more. For once she agreed with him.

And so they got back to Alia and Marc, who were in their respective rooms, showering and getting ready. Béa was completely ready and waiting impatiently for Deanna to come back. She felt responsible for the girls and she didn't want anything wrong to happen to them. Especially since she knew that Harcourt would almost certainly be at the concert. He hadn't told her he would come, but she knew he didn't trust her enough to leave her alone with the girls. So when she saw Deanna entering the room she was so relieved, she didn't bother to ask her where she'd been. With a casual greeting, Deanna headed for the shower and started to prepare herself.

Chapter Forty

STILL BEFORE THE CONCERT

A few hours earlier, when Deanna and Victor left for their walk, Alia and Marc found themselves alone with Béa. Normally, that wouldn't have bothered them, but they still had some details to clear before the concert. Without looking at each other, they both thought at the same thing.

"Alia, would you like me to show you the pool?"

"Of course," answered Alia understanding what Marc was trying to do. "Béa, would you like to come with us?"

"No, I don't like the pool. I don't know how to swim and I didn't bring my swimsuit."

"Ok, then we'll see you later, we shan't be long" said Alia quickly before Béa could change her mind.

Alia and Marc left in a hurry. Béa thought that they really wanted to go to the pool, as all teenagers do. So she went back to the room and got herself ready for the evening.

Marc was excited to spend some time alone with Alia. Ever since the four of them met, they hadn't had the chance to speak in private. As they set out, along a beautiful, perfectly aligned path in the park, he started to ask her questions.

"So, what do you think we should be looking for? A vault, a bookshelf?"

"I have no idea," admitted Alia. "Whatever looks out of place."

"And if we don't find anything?"

"Then we must search elsewhere. The compass and the map couldn't have been there by accident. There is just one thing more thing," said Alia.

"What?"

"In the same room where we found the map, there was a piano sheet that seemed as old as the map and the same kind of paper."

"Have you got it?" asked Marc.

"It never left me. I put it in my wallet between two photos."

"Can I see it?"

"Of course," said Alia and took out a piece of paper, with writing on both sides. It just looked like an ordinary piano sheet. "Do you play the piano?"

"No, do you?"

"Not at this level," she said. "It looks hard. But I'm sure it has something to do with the map. There's only one way to find out. We must find someone who can play it for us."

"Maybe when we get back. I'll ask my parents to find us a piano teacher, I'll take two lessons and I'll get bored. But at least we can find out who the composer is," said Marc.

"Genius! And if the teacher asks you where you got it, just say it was in a book you found at the flea market," said Alia, beaming at him.

"Good idea," said Marc blushing with pleasure to see Alia admiring his ingenious ideas. "Keep it for now, I'll take it when I go to my first lesson."

"Ok. Do you think we're crazy to chase a dream like this?" asked Alia starting to have doubts about their plans.

"No, I think it's ador… a normal thing to do, especially if you think it will give you information about your parents' death," said Marc taking a step towards Alia.

"I think you don't want to hurt my feelings, but I 'm starting to see how insane we are to think that four teenagers can find something, that some pretty smart adults tried so hard to hide."

"I really think that if there is something out there, we can find it. But I don't want you to be disappointed if there is nothing," said Marc getting a little closer. "I know that for you it's not just a treasure hunt. I see how much it means to you And so it's important for me too," Marc persisted, gently.

"Why?" asked Alia, ruining the moment that Marc was trying to create.

"Well… because… I have always dreamed of living such an adventure. I grew up with these kinds of books. I just hope this is the real thing."

"Me too," said Alia and just for a second she put her head on Marc's shoulder. And just for a second, Marc stopped breathing. His cheek touched her perfumed hair and as he instinctively raised his hand to caress her face, that second became shorter than he expected, Alia had already resumed her normal position.

"Now, let's go and get dressed," she said. "I hope Deanna and Victor have finished their job."

"Oh, I'm sure they have," he said sadly.

They both went to their respective rooms. After a while, the five of them met in the lobby.

Chapter Forty-One

THE CONCERT

Deanna realised they had very good seats. The room was not huge but it was very beautiful and it gave her the impression of being at a private concert. She sat next to Victor, while Marc sat next to Alia and Béa. Alia started to worry. She had put all her hopes in this plan and as far as she knew, there was no plan B.

The concert started, the solo pianist was a young prodigy, about 25 years old, very passionate and captivating. As planned, after a few minutes, Victor whispered something to Marc, got up discreetly and left. Béa looked at Marc, who mimed the stomach ache. Béa returned her attention at the concert. After two minutes Marc got up too and left. This time Alia whispered to Béa that he had left to see if his brother was all right. Béa smiled and continued enjoying the music.

But there was someone else in the room who had noticed the boys' behaviour. Harcourt left too, believing they had been to the bathroom to escape from the concert. He was convinced the boys were only there to impress their girlfriends. But he still wanted to know what they were doing. The girls were now stuck for another hour and a half, with Béa watching them anyway. So he decided to follow the boys. However, by the time he got out, they had disappeared. Then he heard some voices in the corridor. The fact they were whispering aroused his suspicions. He followed the voices and he found the boys, counting doors.

"Which one do you think it is?" asked Marc.

"I counted the fifth from the left, but I could be wrong. But I did leave a 'souvenir' on the window," said Victor smiling.

"What?"

"Pink chewing gum."

"This door is locked," said Marc trying the handle. "What if the room is locked too? We can't go breaking and entering."

"I don't think we have to," said Victor, pushing the door with his shoulder.

The boys got inside the room with the pink chewing gum on the window. When Harcourt arrived, he saw an empty corridor so had no idea where the boys had gone. He knew they must be in one of the rooms, so he decided to wait for them to come out and he had a plan.

Marc's excitement level had soared when they managed to open the door, but it soon wore off, when they found themselves in a storage room, full of cleaning stuff and a few old paintings, which must have once been used to decorate the hotel rooms. At first glance they weren't originals so they didn't seem interesting. They started their search. They turned every painting, they looked for a secret vault but there was nothing. Victor found a few shelves containing books about the castle. They didn't seem very interesting except for one about symbols. He decided to take it just in case.

Meanwhile, the concert was keeping everybody in the audience on their toes. The artist, as soon as he had finished a piano sheet, he threw the pages to the public. At the end he asked if somebody in the audience played the piano. A girl stood up and the pianist asked her to join him on the stage. He asked if she was capable of playing something from his repertoire. She said yes and she asked for a piano sheet from the public.

Alia had an idea. She gave her the paper from her wallet. It was a perfect opportunity to have someone play it. The girl took it and started playing. The artist soon realised that it wasn't his, but it was so beautiful, he didn't want to interrupt. It only lasted about two minutes but when she finished everyone had tears in their eyes.

Béa and the girls went back to their room as soon as the concert was over. They were hoping to find the boys, but their room was empty. Béa asked Deanna to call Victor, she was starting to worry.

When Deanna made the call, Victor answered, but she couldn't hear his voice very well. She asked Alia to come and listen with her. They both tried to understand what was going on. They could hear a male voice, but it wasn't either of the boys. Then they heard Marc talking but it wasn't clear, it sounded as if the phone was in his pocket. The girls soon realised that the boys had got into trouble. They told Béa that they had to go, that the boys had decided to go for a walk to get some air. Béa agreed but insisted they didn't stay long.

Alia and Deanna knew exactly where to look for the boys, but they were anxious about what had happened. When they got closer, the voices became clearer with every step they took. And then they saw Marc and Victor in the corridor. Marc had a book in his hand and a man was threatening to take them to the police for theft.

"Listen, boys, you don't realise how lucky you are that I'm prepared to give you a second chance!" said the man getting closer. "If my boss finds out that I let you get away with this, I would be fired on the spot."

"But sir, we didn't want to steal anything, we were just looking for the bathroom and we ended up in this storage room by accident," said Marc sweating.

"And what is this book you are holding? Where did you find that?"

"Inside, on a forgotten bookshelf, between brooms and vacuum cleaners."

"So you were trying to steal it!"

"No sir, I just found it interesting and I would have read it tonight and put it back by tomorrow," said Marc.

"And I am supposed to believe you? You are taking me for a fool. I am the security officer, responsible for this castle. I can't let thieves run around without punishing them. But I think I can let you off, just this once if you return the book to me," said Maxime d'Harcourt.

"Of course sir, I'm sorry," said Marc and handed the book to Harcourt, whose only desire was to see what was in it.

As soon as he got his hands on the book, Harcourt let them go. He was afraid that a real employee from the castle would overhear them and come to check what was going on.

Marc and Victor hurried to get back to their room, and ran straight into the girls, who had been hiding just round the corner and had witnessed the whole scene. They headed back to the girls' room together, so Béa could see all was well. They had decided to wait for Béa to go to sleep and then meet to discuss what had happened.

Béa was relieved to see them safe and sound, and took herself off to bed. The girls waited for her to fall asleep, then sneaked into the boys' room. Victor was on the bed and Marc sat at the table, with a lamp focused on something.

"So, what happened?" asked Alia. "How did you get into trouble?"

"I don't know. I'm pretty sure that nobody saw us when we got inside. So unless he was following us, I have no other explanation," said Victor.

"Why would he follow you? Do either of you know him?" said Alia.

"No," said Victor. "He told us he was from the castle security, but that's all."

"He can't be," said Deanna. "Alia, do you remember during the concert, the guy responsible for security was sitting right next to the stage. He couldn't have been with you."

"But why would this guy lie about who he was?" said Victor.

"To get his hands on what you found," said Alia.

"But, how could he know what we found?" asked Victor.

"He didn't, said Marc, swivelling round to face them. "That book was only a backup plan. If we got caught, we had this excuse. The book doesn't have any value, at all. But this does," he said, showing the objects he had been studying under the lamp, to the girls.

"What is that?" asked Alia, looking over Marc's shoulder. He had a shiver when he felt her breath on his ear.

"I think it's a bracelet," said Marc. "But it's not made of gold."

"And this?" said Alia, taking the box in both hands.

"Well, as you can see it's a box of some kind. But I don't know how to open it," said Marc.

"We'll try to open it, but first tell us how you found it?" said Deanna. "Was that all there was, or did your stalker interrupt the search?"

"There was nothing left. But let's start from the beginning," said Marc. "As soon as I left the concert, we found the room that we were looking for. At first, we were really disappointed to see that it was just an ordinary storage room, but we started looking. And that's when I saw the book, that I gave to that stranger. We found nothing interesting. Meanwhile we were listening to the concert downstairs. We heard all the applause, and thought it was all over, so we started to leave the room. And then we heard another song, completely different from the rest of the music at the concert."

"It was my piano sheet, the one that I showed you before," said Alia. "I gave it to… but finish your story, it's more important."

"What piano sheet?" asked Deanna. "Why don't I know about it?"

"I found it on the table near the map, the day before we left. I didn't think it was interesting and we had more important things to worry about."

"Ok, we'll talk about it later," said Deanna, slightly annoyed at being left out.

"So, the moment the song started," continued Marc. "The bookshelf began to move and it opened into a vault, the size of a small room."

"Do you think it was the song that opened the vault?" asked Deanna.

"It would be quite a coincidence, don't you think? If the song and the vault were not related?" asked Marc. "Especially since you found the piano sheet in the same place as the map, that indicated this castle."

"So the vault was programmed to open, when that piano played that special song?" said Alia. "In that case we were REALLY lucky. Do you realise the odds of that happening?"

"I think that's the whole point, it means nobody could open the vault by accident, only the person who had all the elements," said Marc. "But don't you want to know what we found in the vault?"

"Of course, we're dying to see!" said Alia getting close enough to touch his arm.

"Well, first of all we found this," said Marc, holding up a bracelet, in the form of a bronze serpent, biting its tail and on its body an engraving: 'En to pan.'

"I know this one," said Alia. "It is the snake Ouroboros. And this means 'The one, everything'."

"Ouro… what?" asked Marc, impressed by how smart she was.

"Ouroboros, the Serpent King, the symbol of eternity. It can be seen in a lot of paintings throughout the ages, even though it's a pagan symbol. It shows the time that will come to the starting point again, every time the stars come back to the same position. It was the Christians who changed this vision of time, into one that had to be a straight line, with a beginning, the birth, and an end, the judgment day."

"But why do you think it was hidden in a vault? It doesn't seem very valuable," said Marc, studying it again.

"Maybe it is, depends on how old it is," said Deanna.

"So you think somebody stole it? Then we should give it back. Maybe the person that hid it there will come and look for it?" said Alia.

"I don't think anyone will come looking for it any day soon," said Marc. "By the look of it nobody has touched the vault in a decade. I'm sure that even the owner is not aware of that vault. It's hardly a Las Vegas kind of security."

"Let's get back to our little treasure. What else did you find?" asked Deanna.

"We found these two parchments. But they're written in Latin. Do you speak Latin?" asked Marc.

"I understand Latin, but I don't speak it," said Deanna.

This time it was Victor's turn to be impressed.

"Let me see it," she said, taking it from Marc's hand. "It's a poem." She read it out for them:

"Very dulci mendiante,
Non in maio, paulo ante,
Luce solis radiante,
Virgo vultu élégante
Fronde stabat sub vernante,
Canens cum cicuta.
Illuc veni fato dante,
Nimpha non est forme tante,
Equi pollens eius plante,
Que me viso festinante
Grege fugit cum balante
Metu dissoluta..."

"What does it mean?" asked Victor as soon as she finished reading.

"Wait, I can't translate directly," said Deanna, taking up the hotel's complimentary pen and notepaper.

She started writing. The others maintained a tense silence, while she worked. Finally, after a little help from her phone, Deanna was ready to read, to see if it made sense:

"In the middle of sweet springtime,
Not in May, but a little before
As the bright sun shone
A maiden with a pretty face,
Stood under the green foliage
Playing a pipe
I came there assigned by fate
No nymph has such Beauty
Or is worth the equal of her barefoot.
When she saw me hurrying
She fled with her bleating flock
Overcome by fear."

"This is Carmina Burana," said Marc in a moment of inspiration.

"It can't be. Carl Orff wrote that in 1935," said Victor. "This must be much older than that."

"Not Orff 's Carmina Burana, but the poems that inspired Orff. It's a collection of 24 poems on different subjects," said Marc.

"Why would somebody steal such a poem?" asked his brother.

"Again, I don't think it was stolen. The original is in Bayerische Staatsbibliothek in Munich," said Marc. "But why would somebody go through all this trouble to hide a fake manuscript?"

"Maybe it's not the manuscript that matters, but what is written on it. Maybe the poem is the clue?" said Alia.

"Ok, then. What does it mean? And where does it lead us?" asked Victor.

"I don't know. But maybe we should see the other one," said Alia.

Deanna took the second parchment and started writing. This one was shorter so she finished faster:

"Mec feoda sum
Feore besnypede
Woruld-strenga binom
Waette sipping, dyfde on waerte…

"What is this?" asked Victor.

"I don't know," said Deanna. "I'm reading as best I can. And it goes on, but it's useless to continue. There's no way we can do this without the help of an expert. I think I know who could help us. But you have to give me at least two or three days."

"Ok. So, I think we've done enough for one day," said Marc. "Let's sleep on it and we'll try to figure things out when our brains are less tired. I don't know about you, but I'm exhausted from all this excitement. Maybe tomorrow we'll find out who our mysterious stalker is."

"Yes, one more mystery to solve," said Alia. "Good night, then."

"Good night!" said the guys in unison.

The girls returned to their room, where they found Béa sleeping like a baby, completely unaware of the girls' – and the boys' - adventures. If she had any idea just how furious Harcourt was with her, she would not have been sleeping so well.

Chapter Forty-Two

HARCOURT

After the incident with the boys, Harcourt headed for his room, to study this book they had found. He was convinced it was the diary and they had been about to give it to the girls. He couldn't look at it, while he was with them. He had to give the impression it was his job just to recover anything that had been stolen from the castle. But as soon as he was safely inside, he opened the book, only to discover that it was …just a book. Instantly furious, he tore the book apart without thinking that it wasn't his to destroy. He had been so sure that he was on the right track, because he could see no other reason for them to sneak around like that. It hadn't occurred to him to search the boys. He saw the old book in the boy's hand, took it and he left.

At least he knew the girls didn't have the diary yet. Now all he could do was to lie low and let Béa do her work. Oh, Béa… where was she? If the girls were still at the concert, it meant that either they didn't trust Béa yet, or the boys were acting alone, behind the girls' backs. In both cases Béa had been useless. She had to get closer, if not he, Harcourt would get rid of her.

He decided to give her a chance to make up for the bad job she was doing. At least she drove Alia and Deanna to wherever they wanted to go. But now the boys posed another problem. When he saw how they all met up in the first place, he would have never guessed how close they would become, and so quickly. Now he needed them to be followed too, because they might have precious information. Right now, though, he knew he must leave the castle immediately. The risk of bumping into the teenagers in the morning was too great. He hoped and prayed they would forget all about him.

When Harcourt arrived home, he received another message from Gilbert. They had waited such a long time to witness anybody getting closer to the object of their searches, the diary, and just as things were moving, something completely unexpected happened. Gilbert's message troubled him even more than the huge tactical error he had just made at the castle. It concerned Gloria. Her trip had taken a turn nobody could have predicted.

Chapter Forty-Three

GLORIA GOES BEHIND BARS

As soon as Gloria arrived at her old home, she realised something was wrong. The front door stood wide open and there was mud all over the floor.

She needed to keep a low profile, so she decided to try to find out what had happened, by herself. She couldn't ask her neighbours, because once they knew she was back, they would never leave her alone.

She thought maybe she'd been robbed and started searching the house for missing objects. She was not overly concerned, because she had prepared for this, by leaving a few valuable items around the place, to keep any would-be burglars happy. But nothing was missing, and yet everything had been turned upside down. She went upstairs and started looking in every room that she had closed before leaving.

Now all the doors were open and so were the closets. Still nothing had been taken. She started looking between the papers she had left in a mess, to give the impression that there was nothing important amongst them. That's when she noticed fingerprints in the dust. She didn't know that the girls had taken the quill and the map, so she assumed the intruder had gone off with them. When she realised that somebody had also entered the ballroom, she started to sweat. There were too many things related to the diary for all this to be a coincidence. She followed the footprints in the dust, only to see that they led to one of the mirrors. And then they stopped.

What puzzled her even more, was that there were two or three sets of footprints in the other rooms and only one set in the ballroom. She tried to figure out what had gone on here, but there were too many possibilities. She returned downstairs and made herself a cup of coffee. Then she stood, looking out of the window, only to see that nothing had changed in her old village.

She felt nostalgic about the quiet times she had lived there with Deanna and Alia, after the loss of their parents. She was fully aware she was being followed by Harcourt's spy. She knew that the girls were being watched by Harcourt himself. So freedom was just a distant memory. And as long as she didn't find that diary, Maxime wouldn't leave them alone. The only thing that kept them safe was the fact that Harcourt could not use the diary without the girls. And Gloria knew that she had to find the second diary, before anybody else. That was the most difficult part, because it hadn't been seen in over a few hundred years and she had no hard and fast clues to work on. She only had a few vague details, which had led her back to England. She couldn't stay here in the village for long, she needed to get to London to continue her research.

Gloria was sure that nobody knew she was back, but as soon as she finished her coffee, there was a loud knock at the door. She didn't even have time to open it, before a man pushed his way in, looking very threatening, followed by another, who was equally aggressive.

Across the street, Gilbert had been staking out the house, waiting to see if Gloria decided to leave. It was pretty late and he imagined that she was at least as tired as he was after the trip. So he assumed that she would go to bed. As he prepared to leave his hideout, he saw two men entering Gloria's house, with force. He didn't know what to do. Was he supposed to let her deal with them or was she in real danger and needed his help? If he went in, she would realise he'd been following her, and his cover would be blown. On the other hand, if the two men killed Gloria, for sure Harcourt would kill him too. He edged closer to hear what was going on in there and try to discover why those two men had entered her house like that.

When he got as close to the window as he dared, he heard three voices. One was obviously Gloria's, the other two had to be the two men.

"But officer, I don't understand," said Gloria with a faint voice.

"The neighbours saw Lydia Reynolds enter your house," barked one of the men. "And that was the last time she was seen. We have been looking for her ever since!"

"But you do realise that I don't live here anymore. Since June."

"I know that you left without a word. You took the girls and you didn't even warn the school."

"I had to leave, there was an emergency. It's still legal to decide to live somewhere else," she protested.

"But what was the rush?" chipped in the second man's voice, higher and more shrill. "Nobody knew why or where you went."

"It's nobody's business!" Gloria came back a little too vehemently. She knew she had to show good intentions in finding Lydia.

"And where are the girls?" said the first man.

"At our new home. I just came to pick up some things I had forgotten. So tell me, what happened to Lydia?"

"We don't know. One day she was seen walking down this road, your neighbour, Mrs Lane saw her come in this house, but she never came out. And nobody has seen her since."

"Maybe she went out the back door," said Gloria, trying to be helpful. "I have one that leads to the back garden. I don't use it very often, but it's a possibility."

"Yes, except she never showed up at home either," said the high-pitched voice.

"So it was you who searched my house?" asked Gloria with relief.

"Yes, we came a few times and we tried to get in touch with you, but the only person who had any idea where you were, was Lydia's grandfather, the postman. He thought you were in Paris. How insane was that?"

"Yes… insane," said Gloria trying to smile.

"Well, at least you had an alibi, because Lydia's mother wanted to accuse you of kidnapping her daughter," said the first man, who seemed to be in charge.

"What? Why would I do that?"

"I don't know. And then, she wanted to accuse your friend."

"Which friend?"

"The man who arrived after you left and started asking around the village about you. He said he was a friend of yours and he wanted to surprise you."

"I don't know anything about that. Did he tell you a name?"

"Not to me. But if you don't know him, why would he say he's your friend?"

"I have no idea. I would like to understand some of this myself," said Gloria. She started to think that the police officers were not the only people to have entered her house, which could explain why those items were missing.

"So Lydia goes missing," said the reedy-voiced officer. "A stranger appears in our village, asking strange questions about you and you left without a word. You can understand our dilemma?"

"Yes, I'd like to help you more but I don't have any answers."

"I'm sorry," said the boss man. "But you have to understand that you are our main suspect. She was last seen at your house."

"But I wasn't here. I can prove it. I have the train tickets for me and the girls. And why would I do anything to harm Lydia?"

"As yet, I don't know, but as she was at your house and you are somehow related to a stranger that talked to her mother just two days before her disappearance, you shall be held in custody."

And so Gilbert saw the two police officers take Gloria out and head to the local police station. He couldn't believe his eyes. Things couldn't be worse. He had no idea what to do next, and that was when he sent Harcourt the message, which shocked him to the core.

Chapter Forty-Four

THE PEACEMAKER GETS ANGRY

As soon as he got Gilbert's message, Harcourt realised that they needed help from someone more powerful, someone capable of tracing that girl, so Gloria could be released. He knew she had nothing to do with it, not just because she had no reason to, but because she had never been out of his sight, since she arrived in Paris. He called the only person he knew with the power to locate the missing girl. Before speaking, he took a deep breath, it would take all his courage to explain what had happened.

"I know why you're calling," said the Peacemaker, tersely, without even waiting to hear "hello".

"Then you'll know we need you to have Gloria released," answered Harcourt a little confused.

"What's happened to Gloria? I thought you were talking about your pathetic failure at Esclimont!" cried the Peacemaker, sending shivers up Maxime's spine. "Have you managed to do anything right? I thought you sent your friend after her."

"I did… but the police…"

"What about the police? Are you telling me that your servant wasn't able to get her out of trouble?"

"We could never have seen that coming," grovelled Harcourt, mightily relieved that his boss was at the other end of the phone and not standing in front of him. "Some village girl's gone missing, last seen at Gloria's house, of course the police are going to arrest her, what else would they do? It's not our fault, how could we have known?"

"You should have. How many mistakes do you think I am willing to tolerate? If things continue to go this way, your services will no longer be required," said the Peacemaker with barely concealed menace.

Harcourt knew what would happen to him if his "friend" would suddenly find him useless, and he started to sweat.

"Wait a minute," he tried to defend himself. "This whole kidnapping problem was nothing to do with us. Can you can help us get Gloria out?"

The Peacemaker was not very happy about Harcourt's failure with the boys, but he agreed to help with Gloria. Maxime wondered how the Peacemaker could possibly know what had happened at the castle. He was hoping to avoid that conversation, but it seemed his boss was very well informed. From now on all they had to think about was how to get Gloria out of prison.

The Peacemaker told him that he would contact him, as soon as he had some information about the missing girl. But according to him, and he had to agree with the Peacemaker, the girl had probably just eloped with some older guy, who promised her a life of adventure. She was probably off somewhere, trying to show the world that she was a grownup and as soon as she realised that the man was just a conman, she would return home. She wouldn't be the first teenager to rebel against her parents.

A few days later the Peacemaker called. He had found no trace of Lydia and he had a hard time admitting it. However, he already had another plan, which would solve the problem of Gloria once and for all. Gilbert was instructed to find somebody desperate enough to lie to the police for money. He found a homeless man, cleaned him up and dressed him in smart clothes. Then they dropped him off near the police station. He played his part well and did as he was told. He went in and reported to the police that he had seen the girl they were looking for a few days ago. She was riding on the back of a motorcycle, with her arms wrapped round an older guy, dressed in black leather.

As soon as the police had his declaration, they decided to release Gloria, who would never find out what had happened. In her eyes, Lydia had really run away from home with some boy. Honestly, she didn't care very much about Lydia, she was just relieved to go home. There was little enough time to complete her research as it was, this incident had been a serious interruption. The moment she got home she called Béa to see how the girls were doing. She told her that if they were all right, she would stay a little longer. Béa encouraged Gloria to stay as long as she needed.

The Peacemaker told Harcourt to keep an eye on the boys to prevent another incident like the one at the castle. Meanwhile he was in charge of searching for that missing girl. He was sure that one day the police would figure out, that the homeless guy had been sent as a decoy, to make them release Gloria. But at least Gloria was now free and focused. Gilbert continued to watch her every move. She left her house a day after her release from the police. He followed her to London, where she spent most of her time in libraries.

One day Gloria decided to go to dinner at an unusual place, a church in Trafalgar Square, called St Martin-in-the Fields. When Gloria found herself before the magnificent Corinthian portico, with its eight massive columns, she couldn't help but admire the wonderful work of James Gibbs. As she stepped inside, she noticed the intricate plasterwork decorations on the barrel-vaulted ceiling, the work of Giovanni Battista Bagutti and Chrysostom Wilkins.

After a brief tour round, she decided to visit the crypt, not normally known as the liveliest part of any church. However, the crypt underneath St Martin-in-the-Fields is quite different. It has a thriving restaurant called the "Cafe in the Crypt" and a souvenir shop. She went downstairs and ordered some food. Whilst waiting for it to arrive, she amused herself by looking at the hundreds of photos on the walls. It was a crypt so the lighting wasn't brilliant, and she had to peer at the images. After a few moments, she stopped in front of a particular picture and suddenly froze to the spot. Next to a boy with long hair, she saw her own daughter Samantha, staring back at her from the photograph. There she was, young and smiling at the camera, looking exactly as Gloria remembered her. She even had a tag with "Employee of the month". Gloria was shocked to realise that she never knew her daughter had worked here, of all places. And in the picture, the other person was her husband. This was even more incredible, because as far as Gloria knew him, he would never have worked in such a place, a café beneath a church in the centre of London.

She sat down and started eating and about an hour later she understood. Samantha had to be looking for the Silver One and the clues had led her here. But maybe it was a dead end or they just couldn't go any further. Working there must have made her task easier. She could walk around without being searched every ten seconds. So there had to be something there.

While Gloria was starting to feel rising excitement at the progress of her research, Gilbert was growing increasingly frustrated, not knowing what on earth they were doing there. He had been following Gloria for days now and she didn't seem to have a clue about that diary. As he stood spying on her, a group of tourists came by, led by a tour guide, giving them chapter and verse at the top of his voice:

"As you will know by now, crypts of churches like this were used to bury famous people," he said and then started to reel off a few names of people, who had played a role in the history of England.

What draw Gloria's attention was the name of Thomas Chippendale, the famous furniture maker. She knew she had seen his name somewhere else recently, and needed to remember where. But she knew she was being followed, so she decided to stop right there. As soon as she could find a way to get rid of her follower, she would come back to continue her research.

Gilbert felt exhausted. He had been following Gloria, till eventually he seemed more tired than she was. Ever since they left France, he hadn't had a proper night's sleep and he couldn't see any logic in Gloria's actions. So when he saw her heading for the hotel, he was relieved. Finally, he could go to bed too. He waited about 15 minutes outside the hotel, until he was sure that Gloria was not going to emerge again that night, then he left. Gloria waited to see him enter his own hotel, not very far from hers. When she saw his lights go out she took her backpack and left. This time she didn't want to share her amazing discovery with anybody.

Chapter Forty-Five

BÉA

The morning after the concert, Béa woke up without any idea of what had happened while she had been sleeping. She would soon find out, but not from the girls.

Harcourt was furious because he had been forced to show himself to the teenagers. Luckily the girls weren't there, at least that's what he thought. If he had known that the four of them had figured out that he wasn't who he said he was, he would have killed Béa. He left before breakfast planning to see Béa as soon as she got back to Paris.

When she woke up, she saw the girls who were too excited to oversleep and they all got ready for breakfast. The boys were already waiting for them downstairs, sitting at a table and drinking hot chocolate. Victor stood up and took Deanna's hand, to lead her to sit next to him. Marc got up too and stepped shyly towards Alia, who smiled at him and gave him a short "Good morning". He thought it would have been a better morning, if he could kiss her, and hold her hand and get her breakfast for her.

They talked only about the concert during breakfast. Béa wanted to know what had happened during the concert, and the boys made Béa talk about the show. While they were eating, the piano player came in to have his breakfast. As he sat down, a man in a suit approached him and asked him a question.

"That is the security guy," Deanna whispered in Victor's ear.

"Him? Ok, so it's definitely not our guy."

"Obviously not," she replied. "But then who was the other one? And why would he lie about his identity?"

"I don't know," said Victor in a low voice. "But I don't think it's the last time we'll see him.

"Mm, but next time we'll be ready for him," she said.

Béa sat down next to them, so they had to change the subject. When they finished breakfast, they went to their rooms to pack and get ready for the journey home.

When they arrived back in Paris, Béa dropped the boys off at their home and the girls at the apartment. She told them she had had to go home for a few hours. But as soon as she left, she called Harcourt and they met five minutes later in the garden of Tuileries.

"Where were you last night?" asked Harcourt as soon as he saw her.

"At the concert with the girls," answered Béa, not understanding Maxime's tone of voice.

"And the boys, where were they?"

"Well, one of them was sick and the other one went to see if he was Ok."

"What if I told you that while you were enjoying the piano concert, the boys broke into a room of the castle looking for something."

"What? What did they take?" she said, horrified by this news.

"Nothing. I was there to prevent that. I don't think they found anything."

"Do you know what they were looking for?"

"No, it's your job to find out. It seems the girls have started the search for the diary."

"Do you really think that it is the diary they were looking for?"

"What else?"

"But who told them about it? I don't think it was Gloria because she seems determined to keep this a secret."

"Who else then?" said Harcourt, becoming more and more agitated.

"What if they have it and now they're looking for the second one?

"We would have found out if they had it." he said.

"One day you'll have to explain to me why everybody is so crazy about that diary," said Béa, exhausted by the activities of the past couple of days.

"If you're lucky, you'll never know," he said tersely.

"Why, is it so awful?" she said. "Why does Gloria want to keep it hidden and everybody else wants it out in the open?"

"Because it is like a very powerful weapon, if somebody else has it you are frightened, if you have it, you can rule the world."

"Do you think the girls are aware of what they are doing?" she asked.

"I don't know, that is why it is so important to prevent them from using it. But they have to find it."

"Why them?" said Béa. "Why not you?"

"Because the diary only answers to the person closest to its last owner. And the last owner was Samantha, their mother."

"Maybe the girls are just trying to find some answers about their parents? Maybe they think they will find it in the diary?" said Béa, hoping to convince Maxime not to kill the girls.

"But I can't have the diary while the girls are alive," said Harcourt, in such a matter of fact way, it was chilling.

"What shall I do next?" she said, trying hard not to react.

"You need to see if the girls have found something at the castle, or at least what they were looking for. And you need to be more persuasive, so they don't sneak around the next time they plan something, let them know you are on their side."

With that, Maxime left Béa alone in the park, more worried than before, not only about her future but that of the girls too. Maxime seemed determined to get rid of them, as soon as they served his main purpose. She couldn't wait to see Gloria come back. She wasn't capable of making all these decisions by herself. What neither Béa nor Harcourt thought of, was that the park was in full view from the girls' windows and Alia in particular spent a lot of time at the window, fascinated by the view.

Chapter Forty-Six

ALIA IS ALL ALONE

As soon as Béa left, Deanna left too. She couldn't wait to meet Victor for a real date. Of course, their main subject was still the treasure hunt but they needed to be alone to enjoy each other's company. With Béa around, they felt chaperoned. The difference between Alia and her sister was that Deanna never felt the need to be alone, to spend some time with her thoughts. So when Deanna left Alia alone at home, it didn't bother her, because that gave her some time to think, a welcome moment of solitude. By the time she got to the window with a cup of tea in her hand, Béa had just met Harcourt in the park. She was surprised to see that Béa was not heading home, but she was shocked when she saw who she was talking to. She recognised the man that had verbally attacked the boys at the castle. Why was Béa talking to him? Was it Béa he was following? But then why had he taken the book from Marc? Alia realised that she could never answer all those questions by herself. So the first thing she could think of was to call Marc.

When he saw her message on the phone: 'Come to the bookshop ASAP' he was so excited that he forgot to change his slippers.

Alia didn't leave the window until both Maxime and Béa had gone their separate ways. Only when she was sure there was nothing more to be seen, did she go downstairs to meet Marc, who was already waiting at a table.

"Long time, no see," said Alia, sitting down opposite him.

"Yes, very long time since this morning," he smiled.

"You're probably wondering what could be so important to make me want to see you so soon?"

"I don't mind," he said. "I wasn't doing anything." Then regretted saying something that made him sound like a loser.

"Neither was I," she said. "Deanna left on a date, so I was alone at home. And guess what I have just seen through the window?"

"What?" said Marc, leaning forward.

"Our guy from the castle."

"What? How can it be him? Do you think he followed you home? Because if so, you are in danger and we should call the police. He may be a stalker."

"Yes, but if we call the police, we'll never know what he really wants from us," she said emphatically.

"You're right, but he may turn dangerous. I don't want you exposed to that, just to find out who he is."

"You're nice to worry, but I don't think he's after me. It was Béa he met with in the park."

"Béa? Isn't she married? Do you think she's having an affair with this creep?"

"No, there was nothing romantic about their meeting. There was no physical contact, just a lot of aggression from him. He doesn't seem to appreciate Béa a lot."

"Then what do you think they were doing there together?"

"Honestly, as paranoid as it may seem, I think they are both here to spy on us."

"But why?" said Marc. "What did we do to make them follow us?"

"Well," said Alia. "The only explanation is that they want the diary too." She stared back at Marc, as if reading the expression on his face.

"I thought that too, but why would they want your mother's old diary?"

"Because I am starting to think that it was no ordinary diary. My parents died because of it and even though we haven't got it, yet, it seems to be putting us in danger already."

"If it is not so ordinary, what's so special about it?"

"The only way to know is to find it. And as you can see it has been far too well hidden to be 'just a diary'."

"They'll never let us get our hands on it," said Marc, sitting back in his chair. "As soon as we get close, they'll steal it from us. The way he tried at the castle."

"Not if we can stop them from following us," said Alia, the beginning of a plan forming in her mind.

"What are you thinking?" asked Marc. She was so beautiful lost in her thoughts, he could have looked at her for hours. But he wasn't allowed, because she was really not interested in him like that. It was very obvious that he didn't stand a chance and it was tearing him apart. He had to find another girl to try to forget about Alia. He was intoxicated with her presence in his heart and his mind. Sometimes thinking about her was so overwhelming that he couldn't sleep, or eat or even breathe.

"I think that it would be enough, for us to act as if we had no idea we were being followed and so get them on the wrong track."

"I see what you mean. There are two of them and four of us."

"That's right. Two will mislead them and the other two will continue the research."

"Genius! You're a genius!" said Marc and hugged Alia in the enthusiasm of the moment. As soon as he realised what he was doing, he was so embarrassed, he wanted to step back. But Alia saw him blush so she kept him close long enough to let him know that she didn't mind and so the difficult moment passed.

"We'll see about that," she said smiling at him. "First we need to come up with an idea, that would make them believe in it."

"But we need Deanna to give the second text to that person who can help us," said Marc remembering their talk at the castle.

"I have the first one with me," said Alia. "Do you feel like studying it with me?"

"Of course. I'm dying to find out where it leads us."

"I wouldn't use that expression if I were you," said Alia and started laughing.

"Right. Ok," he said, with a wry smile. "Come on then, let's see it."

"It talks about a beautiful girl with her sheep," said Alia.

"And then the boy comes and she runs away. She runs away from love."

"She is afraid of love. She has never known love."

"How can you tell that the boy is in love?" asked Marc.

"He had never seen such beauty as hers before. He must be in love."

"So everything revolves around the idea of love. Maybe we must search the…"

"Goddess of love!" they said in unison.

"Aphrodite," said Marc. "And the most famous sculpture…"

"Venus de Milo," said Alia. "Do you think my mother could have hidden her diary in the sculpture? In the most guarded sculpture in the world?"

"It was just an idea. What if we went and took a look at it?"

"What, now?" she said.

"Yes, now. We'll be there in five minutes, we look at her and we'll be back in no time."

"Ok, let's go," said Alia, fired by his enthusiasm.

When they arrived at the Louvre, they went in like regular tourists, the only difference being, they didn't pause to look at any of the famous exhibits until they reached the statue of Venus.

"So, what now?" asked Alia smiling and out of breath.

"Let's see if there isn't a place, where your mother could have had access to the sculpture," said Marc and then turned to one of the guards. "Excuse me, why is there a hole below her right breast?"

"Because," answered the man. "It is the original place of a metal tenon, which supported the right arm that was carved separately."

"Ok, thank you. Did the statue leave this room in the last ten years?"

"Of course. We took it to the restoring room. She stayed there for six months. They even found a small piece of paper in that hole."

"What?" said Marc.

"Yes, from 1936," said the man, warming to this conversation. "Exciting, right?"

"Yes, very," said Alia. "Thank you for all that information, it was fascinating."

"Happy to be of help. Enjoy your visit and Paris, the city of love," said the guard winking.

"Thank you," said Marc, suddenly leading Alia over to a corner and taking her in his arms.

"What are you doing?" asked Alia, surprised.

"I think we have company," whispered Marc in her ear, trying to control his heart. Having her in his arms was like a dream come true even if it was just a pretence. She was there, so warm and surprisingly not repulsed. She hadn't pushed him away and her cheek was touching his.

"Where?" she said.

"At the other side of the room. How did our stalker find us?"

"That's what stalkers do, they follow you everywhere you go."

"Ok, in that case, shall we go back to the bookshop, now we have some information?"

"Absolutely," she said, smiling. "But for that I need you to let go of me first."

"Oh, sorry!" said Marc embarrassed again, as he let go of her and they both went out, as if nothing had happened.

Maxime was very happy to see that the twins were searching actively for the diary. But by the looks of it, they had hit a dead end. When he saw them go back to their tea, he decided to leave them alone and he went home.

Alia started to look around, to see if they were still being followed. In the bookshop it was easier to be on their own. There were just the two of them. The other tables were empty and they felt extremely grateful for it. They knew that from now on, they couldn't speak freely, even at home. They had to find a place where the four of them could gather and talk. And they had to find a way to get rid of their spy. They were afraid that not only would he steal their discovery, but he was a serious threat to their lives.

Marc told Alia that he had an idea, but first they had to determine the next clue to finding the diary. Alia decided it was time for her to go home, in case Béa was back. She didn't trust Béa now that she had seen her with Harcourt. She was even angry at herself for having trusted her. At least Béa had helped them find the manuscripts at the castle. Luckily she had no idea what they had found there. But Alia could hardly believe that Béa would want to put their lives in danger.

Chapter Forty-Seven

REVEALING THE SECRET

Béa got back as fast as she could and found Alia at home sleeping. She was relieved to see that at least one of them had not gone out. She imagined that Deanna was out with Victor and when Alia woke up, she had this confirmed.

Béa was starting to feel guilty for allowing Harcourt into their lives. At first she thought that if she helped him to get the diary, he would leave everybody alone and they would all live happily ever after. But now she realised that at some point she would have to sacrifice something. And it had to be her dream, or she would become an accomplice to murder. There was no doubt that Harcourt was capable of killing the girls just to get his hands on the diary.

Deanna was flying on the wings of love. Finally, she found a moment of solitude with Victor. And after all the excitement of their night at the castle, she wanted to talk about something else. But of course, as soon as the usual romantic conversation started, that every new couple enjoys, their thoughts turned to the one thing that obsessed the four of them.

"You're still thinking about that parchment, aren't you?" asked Victor.

"Aren't you? I have to talk to that one guy who can help us, if not I'll go crazy!"

"Who is he?" asked Victor feeling a little jealous.

"He's my fencing teacher. He's obsessed with ancient languages. He could at least tell us which language it is, or if we're lucky he could even translate it for us. Why don't we ask him right now?"

She took out her phone and called Benoit, her fencing instructor. Twenty minutes later, they were on their way to meet him.

"Do you have the text?" asked Victor.

"Of course, I took a photo on my phone."

"Smart," said Victor and kissed Deanna on her cheek. He was still a little shy so he wouldn't dare go further.

"Thanks. Now, let's find out if that manuscript tells us where to look for that diary. I still can't believe that our mother would go to all that trouble to hide her diary from the world."

"Maybe she was hiding it from the world but not from you?"

"Then she should have left it in England, with Nanna," said Deanna.

"Maybe she didn't want your Nanna to have it. Or maybe she didn't have time to show it to you before she…" he stopped, suddenly aware of what he was about to say.

"Before she died?" said Deanna, finishing the sentence for him.

"Sorry, I didn't mean to hurt you."

"You didn't, I've made my peace with it. That doesn't mean that I wouldn't do anything to have her here with me. But I feel that if I had her diary, I could get closer to her."

"We'll find it, don't worry," said Victor caressing Deanna's hair.

"Here's Benoit. Hello!" she called out, stepping away from Victor.

"Hello Deanna, so what can I do for you?"

"I need to know if you can translate this for us," said Deanna straight away, showing him the text on her telephone.

"Ok, wait a second. It is ancient English…" started Benoit.

"That is English? Are you sure? Because I don't recognise a word of it," she said surprised.

"Yes, I'm sure. Do you want to write down what it means?"

"Of course. Go ahead," said Victor taking out his own phone, as Benoit dictated.

"Some fiend took away my life and worldly strength too, wetted afterwards, dipped in water."

"What is that? What does it even mean?" asked Deanna, fearing they might never find the answer.

"It is a riddle," said Benoit. "I have already read something like that. When I was studying ancient English, I went on a course at Oxford University library.

"And so you did," said Deanna smiling.

"And there they had an ancient manuscript called Hugo Pictor. But we didn't have the whole text. And I don't remember the rest of it."

"You know more than enough. Let's see if we can't find the second part of this riddle," said Deanna starting to look on the internet. After a few minutes scrolling the results, she came cross the entire text so Benoit was able to keep going.

"The riddle continues, a bird's delight races across the surface, leaving dark tracks and dyes from trees, and the whole is covered with boards and skin, and it becomes a help for great men and itself is holy. Another riddle is: 'I saw four things in beautiful fashion…, journeying rapidly in the company of three fingers, leaving dark and vivid footsteps as they all travel across the parchment together.'

"So it is about a parchment, as it describes the process of fabrication," said Deanna.

"Exactly. Where did you find this? You know it can't be an original. The original is in a box at Oxford."

"I know. We found it in a book and it didn't explain the meaning so we were just curious," she said, feeling a little guilty at lying to him.

"Ok, now you know. But you see, you need the end of the manuscript. What you had was not the entire text."

"That's right! That's exactly what we need!" Deanna almost yelled in excitement.

"Deanna, what happened?" asked Victor a little worried.

"Nothing," she said, then turned to Benoit. "Thank you, you've been such a great help."

"You're welcome," he said looking a bit bemused. "Bye Deanna. Nice to meet you, Victor."

"Nice to meet you too," said Victor eager to leave so he could talk to Deanna in private.

As they left and Deanna started to look in her phone again.

"What are you looking for?" asked Victor.

"Well, if this text had a part missing, all we have to do is to look at the Carmina Burana to see how it goes on. We focused on the one part that we have, and didn't consider that it is not meant to be seen in isolation. There's a huge manuscript in that library."

"I'm sure we can find the whole manuscript on the internet," he said.

"Ok, let's see. It has to be the next poem," and she quoted the Latin she had just found:

"Dum Diane vitrea
Sero lampa oritur
Et a fratris rosea
Luce dum succenditur,
Dulcis aura Zephiri
Spiras omnes etheri
Nubes tollit, sic emollit

Vi chordarum pectora
Et immutat cor quod nutat
Ad amoris pignora…

"Do you understand it?" asked Victor.

"I'll try to translate something. 'When the crystal lamp of Diana rises late and when it is ignited by the rose-coloured light of her brother, the sweet blowing breath of the west carries all clouds from heavens, and so too it softens souls by the power of its musical strings and transforms the heart faltering from the efforts of love'"

"Do you think that's it? That we should stop here?"

"I don't know," replied Deanna. "We should ask my sister's and your brother's opinion."

"Ok, let's see if they are willing to get together to talk. Maybe we should leave it until tomorrow. And we have to find somewhere to meet, without Béa or our stalker being able to eavesdrop."

"Ok, in that case, do you mind accompanying me home?" she asked.

"Of course not, at least I can make sure that nothing happens to you."

"With you around Victor, nothing can harm me, I'm sure," she said leaning towards him.

"I wouldn't let anyone get to you," said Victor and he straightened his back, which made him look taller and even more handsome. Deanna agreed that a boy in love is irresistible. She melted like an ice cream in the sun.

And so they went home with the plan to meet the next morning for a jogging session, in the hope that no stalker would be able to keep up with the four of them.

Chapter Forty-Eight

GLORIA

Gloria left Gilbert to sleep away the time in his hotel room. She was happy to see that she was more resilient than him. She wondered if he wasn't at the heart of her police problems. But would he be capable of kidnapping a girl just to get her into trouble? And why would he? She thought that he wanted her to find the diary. But on the other hand, if he wasn't involved, what had happened to Lydia? In the end she set aside all these questions and started to focus on the main event, trying to pick up where her daughter left off, in the quest for the whereabouts of the Silver One.

She went back to the church where she had seen Samantha in a picture. She took the photo down and started to examine it for clues. After a few minutes she spotted something. She couldn't believe that she had missed it before. Just behind Samantha, there was something that she seemed to be trying to point out. It was a picture, a sketch of the church. She looked on the other walls and she found it. There were photos of St Martin-in-the-Fields in the 18th century. And the one behind Samantha was the one with the burial ground.

Gloria decided to ask somebody who worked there who was buried there. The employee gave her a few names, but the one that got her attention was Thomas Chippendale. She had heard of him, he was a famous cabinetmaker. His work was highly valued. She decided to go further and asked if there was any piece of furniture which bore his signature in the church.

Apparently, there was one chair that his family offered to the church on the day of his burial. She asked to see it. The employee told her that she could see it but not too close because it was considered to be very fragile. Nobody had touched it in 400 years. He showed her where it was and he left Gloria alone.

Now Gloria started to feel the excitement of hope. She sensed she was coming closer to the end of the journey. There was only one person missing, her daughter who lost her life before getting to the end. She would have liked to share that with her, but now it was too late. She asked herself why Samantha didn't go forward. Why did she give up everything and move to Paris?

What Gloria didn't know was that the Peacemaker had already started haunting her family and that Samantha got scared under his threats. It was the Peacemaker that convinced Samantha to leave all her research behind and get far away from the second diary. Maybe the Peacemaker knew that he couldn't get his hands on the Golden One, the one Samantha already owned and he couldn't allow her to have them both.

Gloria knew nothing of Samantha's life in London and now she was starting to discover how close her daughter had come to finding the Silver One.

She started to look around. There were no surveillance cameras, no guards, nobody to stop her from studying the chair.

It was an extraordinary piece of furniture, in mahogany. She searched gently all round it and then ran her hands underneath. Suddenly she felt the shape of a small box, sewn into the chair's blue fabric. She took out the penknife she always carried and slit the material. The box fell easily into her hand. It seemed as if someone had hidden the box in such a way as to cause the least possible damage to the chair.

With the box safely in her bag, she quickly left the church trying to think of a safe place to study her discovery. Finally, she went to her hotel room, afraid that Gilbert would notice her absence and realise that she had escaped his surveillance. She knew she was safe as long as Gilbert thought she didn't have the diary. So she had to give him the impression that he was in control and that she had found nothing. But when she got to her room and opened the box her whole world collapsed around her. In that box, despite everything Gloria had been hoping, lay not diary but a large key, one designed to open a very large door, as in a medieval prison.

Gloria realised she was getting closer but she was tired of all these adventures. She had risked everything to come back to England, only because the clues had led her there. She had lived the humiliation of being arrested by the police in her own home. She had agreed to be followed by a strange man. She had almost destroyed a piece of history. And now it seemed that it wasn't enough. She had to go further, to find the lock for her key.

Her next thought was for the girls. She had left them with a person who was supposed to spy on them. They were now surrounded by people who had every reason to harm them. She had to protect the twins. She started to doubt Béa's loyalty. After all she really wanted a child and apparently Harcourt had the means to give her that. So she decided to go home to Alia and Deanna. She missed them and now she didn't have any clue to continue her search. It seemed endless, hopeless. The next morning Gilbert followed her on her way to Paris. He was relieved that he didn't have to do anything, but he was also afraid of Harcourt's reaction, when he found out that they had gone to England for nothing.

Chapter Forty-Nine

THE TWINS

The next morning the four teenagers got together in the gardens of Neuilly, after running swiftly through the forest on their "jogging" exercise. It was far enough to leave Béa behind. She wasn't even up when the girls left. Harcourt was able to follow them but only to the edge of the forest. He realised that he needed a bike to keep up with them.

The four of them joined in with the other early morning joggers. They managed to lose themselves from sight very quickly on the narrow pathways. When they were sure that nobody was following them, they stopped and took out all the pieces of parchment they had. Deanna had done her homework. She had made four copies of all the translations she possessed. Now they were all holding the same cryptic message in their hands.

"Where do we start?" asked Alia to break the ice.

"Let's sum up," said Victor. "We have a poem that talks about love, another about a quill, one about..."

"Sorry to interrupt you, Victor, but I see a clue in the last poem I translated," said Deanna. "Maybe we should start there?"

"No problem, what did you discover?"

"It talks about Diana, the goddess. Maybe there is a lamp with a crystal Diana somewhere?" said Deanna.

"If that's true, we're doomed," said Alia. "There are so many of those lamps, you can even get them on the internet." She started searching on her phone.

"Not necessarily," said Deanna smiling. "Don't you remember where we saw a lamp like that? It might even be the original."

"It does look familiar" agreed Alia. "But I can't put my finger on it."

"It was hard for me too, but it finally hit me around midnight. It was at the concert at the castle of Esclimont."

"Of course!" said Alia. "I can't believe I didn't remember."

"Well, we did have other things on our minds at that time. But that it is a very good clue. The problem is how can we go back there without being followed?" said Deanna.

"Well, I think we have a solution," said Marc looking at Alia.

"We?" asked Alia, surprised.

"What if we send our spy on another lead?" said Marc, trying to prompt her.

"I didn't know we had another lead," said Alia, and then she started to understand, where he was leading.

"What are you two talking about?" asked Deanna.

"When you went on your date," said Marc. "We got back together to try to untangle those poems. And we went to the Louvre to see the statue of Venus de Milo, because we thought that the poem was about the goddess of love. But now that you've gone even further there are more odds of finding something at Esclimont, than in the famous statue of Venus."

"But our stalker doesn't know that we found the poems. So we can just give him the information we want him to have," said Alia.

"Exactly. But do you think he will bite the bait? He seems quite smart," said Victor.

"Smart or not, he seems to want that diary very much. I think he will do everything to get it," said Alia.

"So we need to convince Béa to convince the stalker?" asked Victor.

"That shouldn't be too difficult," said Deanna. "Leave that to me and Alia. Let's move on. The other poem, about that parchment?"

"It is a riddle about a parchment, that part we understood and then it talks about three fingers…" said Victor.

"And something that leaves footsteps on it. Who can leave footsteps on a parchment?" asked Marc. "In the company of three fingers."

"It's a pen!" cried Alia, suddenly.

"Maybe a quill pen, as at that time they didn't have pens as we know them now," said Deanna.

"Yes, a quill pen, like the one we found at home," said Alia not realising that the boys had no idea what she was talking about.

"Do you think the poem talks about OUR quill?" asked Deanna, also not aware of the surprised looks on the boys' faces.

"Erm excuse me, but what are you talking about?" asked Marc trying to get their attention.

"Sorry, you don't know," said Alia. "But before we left, we found the map that led us to the castle, a quill and a backpack. Until now, the quill didn't seem to be all that important."

"Well, at least we don't have to look for it, we have it in our room," said Deanna.

"You keep it in your room?" asked Victor. "What if Béa goes in there and takes it?"

"I put it in a safe place, that not even Nanna knows about," said Alia proudly.

"Ok, but it doesn't hurt to check," said Marc. "But the quill is useless without the diary. So we still have to look for it. I don't even know what the importance of the quill is."

"We'll see as soon as we have the diary," said Alia. "And I think we're getting closer. All we have to do now is to get rid of the stalker."

As they all left at the run, they could see him getting closer, riding a bicycle down the forest track behind them.

Chapter Fifty

THE DOUBLE AGENT

By the time all four of them arrived back at the apartment, to have lunch with Béa as arranged, Alia and Deanna had devised a plan about how to use her as a middle man, between them and their stalker. They had no idea who he was or why he didn't go after the diary himself. But as long as they had him breathing down their necks, they couldn't get on with what they wanted to do. They were sure that as soon as they found the diary, he would take it from them. So he had to disappear from their lives, at least until they got the diary and read it.

Deanna made a copy of the love poem and put it on her bedside table, for Béa to find. Later, as they were all sitting at the table together eating, and Béa was attending to the next course, they started an argument that she couldn't fail to overhear.

"Wait! What are you saying? That the only possibility is Venus? Like in… Venus de Milo?" asked Alia loudly.

"Have you got a better idea? If you have, please do share it with us!" added Deanna, sneaking a look at Béa, to see if she was paying attention.

"Let's assume that it is Venus that the poem is talking about," interrupted Marc. "How could your mother have hidden the diary inside?"

"Don't you remember what the guy at the museum told us? The statue was taken to the restoration room a few years ago. It would have been the perfect opportunity for our mother to do it," answered Alia a little less loudly. She was afraid that Béa would see through their strange show.

"And how could she have hidden it inside? That would definitely have left some sort of mark, which would be plain to see," said Deanna.

"Well, it does have a little scar, under the left breast. They say it is the hole made at the creation of the statue, so nobody is surprised to see it," explained Marc.

"It makes sense," said Victor. But that leaves us with another problem…

"How to get it out!" said Deanna, finishing his sentence for him.

"It will be impossible," said Alia. "Digging in an abandoned courtyard is one thing, but destroying the most highly guarded work of art, in the most renowned museum in the world, is another. We are too young to finish our life in prison just for the sake of a clue."

They finished eating and the boys gave a polite thank you to Bea for such a delicious meal, then left the apartment, having made arrangements to consult with the girls later. Deanna and Alia took themselves off to their room, still discussing the issue.

"What are we supposed to do, give up?" asked Deanna as they had finished eating and they were heading to their room.

Béa had listened to their conversation with a lot of interest and was about to arrange a meeting with Harcourt, when Gloria unexpectedly walked through the door. Béa was taken by surprise but she was relieved to know that she was no longer responsible for looking out for the girls on her own.

After giving Gloria all the information, Béa said she should call a meeting with Harcourt. He was bound be very pleased with what the girls had found out. Gloria agreed to let him know but not right away. She asked for a day to talk to the girls. She was ready to share what she knew with them. She had tried to keep them away from the diary, but apparently it was too late. They had started without her and she wanted to be involved. When Samantha found it, Gloria had turned her back on her daughter, now she wanted to help. She knew now that there was no way to fight it. The diary had a will of its own and people felt the need to own it, in order to taste its power. Now, all that she had to do was to help the girls find it.

Two days later, she told Béa that she could share the great discovery with Harcourt. So when Béa went to see him, he saw her arrive with big a smile on her face.

"I hope it is worth it. I had tickets to the opera," said Harcourt, belligerently.

"Oh, it's definitely worth it," she said. "I have news, important news."

"You'd better. Because the other day the girls left the apartment without you noticing it. You are not a very good guardian."

"However, I am a very good listener."

"Go ahead. Tell me what is so important?"

"The girls know where the diary is."

"Are you sure?"

"At the castle," she continued, knowing she had finally got his attention.

"While we were at the concert, the boys found a parchment."

"A parchment? When?"

"When you stopped them and accused them of theft."

"But they gave me an old book," he said with growing sense of unease.

"Yes, but they had something else in their pockets."

"They are smarter than I thought. They fooled me," said Harcourt, almost to himself.

"They are even smarter than that. The four of them succeeded in solving the mystery behind the message in the parchment," said Béa.

"So they must have the diary by now?"

"Not yet. There seems to be a problem. The diary is untouchable."

"There is no such thing! If it is on this planet nothing is impossible," said Harcourt, thinking of the immense power that the Peacemaker possessed.

"Well, according to the manuscript, the diary was hidden in the statue of Venus de Milo."

"The one at the Louvre?"

"The one and only. Samantha had access to it when it was taken for some plastic surgery. And it has a small hole on the left."

"Yes, I know, I saw it recently," said Harcourt, remembering following Alia and Marc straight to the statue. Now he was sure they had tried to see if there was a way to take the diary out. But the statue was far too well-guarded for that.

"It is way too complicated and risky for them. So they stopped there," said Béa.

"Are you sure that they are not trying to find a way to steal it?"

"Don't forget, for them it is just an ordinary diary. It belonged to their mother, but it's not worth it. They would end up with a criminal record and all their future would be destroyed."

"You're right," he said. "It is not a mission for teenagers. Finally you proved yourself useful. Leave now, and don't talk to anyone."

Béa left Maxime to dream about a way to extract the diary from one of the most secure works of art that ever existed. At least he didn't doubt her. But still she wasn't sure she had been convincing enough. All their plan depended on that. She was starting to feel tired. She wanted all this to be over and to get back to her ordinary life. But it was far from over.

Chapter Fifty-One

MAXIME

"I know sir, I know it sounds crazy," said Maxime on the phone. He was pacing round the room in circles, and sweating heavily. "I wouldn't tell you that if I didn't think it was a viable option. Samantha worked on the statue, when they took it in the basement of the Louvre to clean it."

"And are you sure that the girls won't try to get it?" asked the Peacemaker at the other end of the line.

"How could they? Even for us it might prove impossible."

"Nothing is impossible. We will find a way. If Samantha was able to hide it inside the statue, we will be able to retrieve it."

"This might be the best idea. If Samantha used the opportunity to put it inside, we just need a new reason to take it to the restoration room," said Harcourt.

"I can help you with that but you'll have to do it yourself. Do you think you can handle that?"

"Of course. Give me a few days and I'll tear the statue inside out!" said Maxime with conviction.

"I can give you one day," offered the Peacemaker, with a sense of finality.

"I'll try."

"You'll have to do more than that. It is our only chance and I'm not ready to give up on that diary."

"Very well. Just let me know so I can prepare the intervention."

"Tomorrow," said the Peacemaker. "Venus de Milo will go to the restoration room tomorrow. And you will get me the diary, tomorrow."

"Send the details to my phone."

"Agreed. And Maxime?"

"Yes?"

"Don't screw it up. This might be our last chance. Let's put it this way, your last chance."

"I'll do my best, sir," said Maxime and realised that the Peacemaker had already hung up the phone.

He had less than 24 hours to prepare the intrusion into the Louvre and an attack on one of the world's masterpieces. He knew he wouldn't sleep that night.

The next day he had a message from the Peacemaker on his phone. It instructed him to be near the statue at 10 o'clock that morning. He didn't even know what to expect. He had his tools ready and he went to the museum as soon as it opened. He didn't want to risk getting delayed by bus loads of tourists and miss the deadline.

As soon as he arrived, he saw a large number of children gathered around the statue. Amongst them one that seemed particularly interested in it. The others were talking and laughing. This one was focused only on Venus. Maxime saw him take a small object from his pocket. From where he was standing, he couldn't see what it was but as he got closer, he realised it was a small can of coloured hairspray. Suddenly, the little boy started to spray pink dye on the statue. By the time a guard saw what was happening, the front of Venus de Milo was completely covered in pink.

The teacher who was in charge of the children and the guard started screaming at him in panic, to make him stop. They pulled him out of the group. He was surely in a lot of trouble but Harcourt seized the opportunity. A few minutes later a group of Louvre employees came to secure the room, and to guide everyone outside, while the statue was taken down an emergency staircase. As the Peacemaker had instructed, Maxime was wearing a white coat, hidden beneath his raincoat. He saw that the other employees were dressed just like him. The only thing he had to do was to get rid of the raincoat. So he stuffed it into a garbage bin and followed the others down into a deserted workshop, where he managed to conceal himself at the back, while the rest of the men returned to the scene of the crime to find the aerosol can and determine what exactly had been used to desecrate the famous statue. Once they had analysed it, they might know how to clean the statue without causing it more harm. He heard them discussing whether it wasn't already too late to save this iconic masterpiece.

All he needed was the few minutes they had given him to be alone with the Venus de Milo. He made a small hole at the exact place of the first one. He figured it would be less obvious if the hole was already there. He took a tiny fibre optic camera from his pocket and inserted it through the hole in the statue. He watched intently through the viewfinder, as the camera's light illuminated the interior of the famous statue. Nothing. There was nothing there. He checked again and again, but there was no sign of the diary.

He whipped the camera out and fixed the hole with a small tube of liquid plaster, to disguise the defect he had created in the statue. Before he could finish, one of the museum staff came in looking for something. As soon as he saw Maxime, he realised that something was wrong so he left without a word and called the police.

When it comes to great treasures, such as the Venus the Milo, the French police are nothing if not efficient. Maxime didn't even have time to hide his toolkit, before the police appeared at the door of the lab. He realised that for him, the chase was over.

Chapter Fifty-Two

ONE OUT, ONE TO GO

Gloria watched the news on TV. She was stunned to see that their plan had worked so well. But the man they had caught, Harcourt, was not the one who had been following her in London. So they weren't completely free. But at least one of them was out of the picture, for a while. The other man was easier to get away from anyway. She had avoided telling the girls how dangerous Harcourt was. They obviously thought of him more as a competitor for the diary, than a threat. As long as he stayed in prison the girls were safe.

Alia and Deanna came into the kitchen, just as Gloria had finished her coffee and was about to go in search of them. They had a lot to talk about.

"You read my mind," said Gloria. "I was just coming to see if you were awake."

"How could we sleep when things are starting to get interesting?" said Alia.

"Not that we were bored," added Deanna. "That is the last thing that we can say about our life in Paris!"

"I can't sleep either," said Gloria. "Thinking about how close we are to our goal."

"So what did you want to talk to us about?" asked Deanna.

"You will be pleased to know that our plan worked perfectly and our spy is behind bars for attempting to destroy Venus de Milo."

"So Béa was convincing enough. Now all we have to do is to continue our search," said Deanna.

"What do you have in mind?" asked Gloria. She had no idea how far the girls had gone with their research.

"Well now that you know everything, you can help us," said Alia. "We need to get to the castle of Esclimont."

"Why there?"

"Because we have reason to believe that the last clue we found leads us there," replied Alia.

The girls explained all the details to Gloria. A couple of hours later they were on their way to the castle. They picked the boys up from their house on the way. Gloria couldn't hide her emotions. She was aware that she was tracing her daughter's last steps. She hoped that along with the diary, she would find an explanation to her disappearance, or maybe a clue to the whereabouts of the second diary that Samantha was looking for.

She knew that the girls were not even aware of the existence of a second diary. She was ready to talk to them about it, but only if it was necessary. For now she kept the key she had found in London with her. She didn't know how much she could really trust Béa in her house. Now that Harcourt was in prison, Béa was more unpredictable, because she was afraid that he would blame her for his situation. After all, she was the one who suggested that the diary was in the statue.

The moment they arrived at the castle, the four teenagers ran towards the entrance. But they didn't know that the concert room was open only during the concerts. Luckily that night there was a harp concert and they still had tickets. The only problem was that the mission to steal the lamp became more difficult with a whole audience present.

They had no choice but to wait until eight o'clock. Until then they had to think of a way to either steal, or to break a lamp in order to extract the diary. Gloria offered to do it herself, but Victor had a good point, if they were caught in the act they didn't risk much because they were under 18. At least if they broke it. That way they could say it was an unfortunate accident.

But the problem was how to break a mural lamp "by accident". Alia had another idea and in the end they all agreed, it was the best one. Marc was falling deeper and deeper in love with her. Her idea was bold and he didn't like the thought of putting her in harm's way, so he proposed to exchange places with her. Putting together a plan took about two hours. But they were all satisfied at the end. Alia was aware that it took a great deal of courage for Marc to do what he did. But she was so absorbed with their plan that she didn't give it a second thought.

One hour before the concert started the five of them sat drinking hot chocolate on the great terrace of the castle. The moment the concert started, they entered the room and prepared to do what they would soon find out was not such a good idea after all.

Chapter Fifty-Three

JAIL TIME

At the same moment the police arrested Harcourt, the Peacemaker received a panicked phone call from Gilbert. The Peacemaker was not very eager to meet Gilbert but he and Maxime had organized an automatic call in case something happened to one of them. So when he saw that Harcourt's mission had failed, Gilbert took out his phone and tapped the number, forbidden to him in any other circumstances.

The Peacemaker had already received the information that Gilbert wanted to give him, because he had more than one informer.

"What really happened?" asked the Peacemaker, just so he could have a second opinion on the latest event.

"I don't know," said Gilbert. "The statue was being taken to the restoration room. Mr Harcourt followed them and as he was trying to do what he had to do, the police arrived. It was really, really fast."

"One might say that they knew what was about to happen?" said the Peacemaker.

"I thought so too. It was as if somebody had warned them in advance."

"The only people who about it, were me and you and…"

"But we had no interest in sabotaging his actions!" said Gilbert quickly.

"Don't worry, Gilbert. I'm not accusing you. The other person who knew was Béa, but she depends on the success of his mission too. So I don't understand why she would betray us."

"Maybe she got too attached to the girls," offered Gilbert. "And knowing Mr Harcourt, he might have told Béa that once the girls had the diary, he would kill them."

"I hope he wasn't so reckless. But you are right, Béa is no longer useful. I'll decide later what to do with her. Now we have to focus on getting Harcourt out of prison."

"How can we do that? He was caught in the act. It is impossible to deny what he was doing. He was there to break the statue."

"It might seem impossible to you, but for me it's only a question of time. In the meantime, I need you to take Harcourt's place and keep an eye on the girls."

"Of course. Don't worry, they won't make a move without my knowing it," said Gilbert trying to sound confident.

"I hope so, for your sake," said the Peacemaker and hung up the phone.

The next morning Gilbert went directly to Rue de Rivoli, but after a few hours he realised that the girls were not at home. He was worried and he had every reason to be, since the girls were at the castle. He didn't know what the Peacemaker could do to get Harcourt released, but he was happy that he didn't have to finish this mission all by himself. He was frightened of the Peacemaker, but he knew that Gloria was smarter. And he was frustrated at not being allowed to use force to get information from the girls. He was sure that Harcourt was planning to kill the twins but for now he needed them alive, but Gilbert didn't understand why.

He decided to approach Béa to see what she knew. It wasn't very hard to find her as she had a very predictable schedule and he had seen her many times, when he watched her apartment. Now the only thing that concerned him was that she might recognise him from the visit that he had paid them, when they lived in Gloria's apartment. But it was such a short encounter and she had been very scared at the time, so he doubted she would remember him. Just to be sure, he cut his hair, dyed it and shaved off his stubble. Now he looked like a young designer, searching for new talent. He even adopted a different accent to deceive her.

"Sorry Miss, I think you lost something," shouted Gilbert behind Béa.

"Oh, what?" she said.

"Sorry to startle you, but I saw this wonderful scarf on the ground behind you."

"It's not mine but it is very beautiful," said Béa looking at the scarf, which Gilbert had brought along with him.

"I wonder who lost it?" said Gilbert. "I would really like to meet the lady, and where she bought it. It would be perfect for my next fashion show, at the Prix de Diane Longines."

"Oh, you're in fashion business?" said Béa, unable to hide her excitement.

"Yes, I create hats and other accessories," he said, smiling.

"I love hats! I even have some personal creations," said Béa starting to hope that somebody might be interested in her hobby.

"Would you like to show me? I am always in search of new talents and new ideas."

"Of course, I have everything at home. I could show you."

"Now? Do you have the time?"

"I just have to go and water the plants for a friend. You can come with me and we can go to my place from there. I'll show you what I have."

"Ok. Is it far?"

"No, we are here," said Béa without even thinking for one second that she was being manipulated.

Gilbert followed her upstairs. At first, he was afraid that Gloria might be there, but then he thought that Béa would not be watering the plants if she was at home. So when they got into the apartment he tried not to look too inquisitive. But as soon as Béa disappeared into the living room, he went straight into Gloria's bedroom. He noticed that the room looked like she had been gone for a week. He wondered how he could get information from Béa.

"Whose apartment is it?" he asked casually, as if he didn't care.

"A friend. She is away for a few days, so I come to do her cleaning and take her mail."

"It is a very nice apartment. I have never seen one like this. When I come to Paris I always stay in a hotel."

"Do you visit Paris often?" asked Béa.

"Every time I have a new show. Next week I'll be in Milan."

"Milan? I've never been to Italy," said Béa, wistfully.

"If I like your work, I'll take you with me next time."

"I don't think my husband would approve," said Béa blushing and regretting having said that.

"Oh, you're married. Then we will have to take him with us," said Gilbert smiling. "Is your husband also working for your friend?"

"Yes, he used to. But now she doesn't need him so he works elsewhere."

They continued their small talk. Gilbert was happy with what he had achieved. At least now he had a connection with Béa. He couldn't find out where Gloria had gone, but Béa didn't know either. He went to her place and saw an impressive collection of hats. Gilbert had seen her a few times at Gloria's and every time Béa had been wearing a different hat. So he assumed they were her weakness.

When he left, she was convinced she had hit the jackpot. She never thought she could make a career out of her passion, but why not? She was so happy that she didn't even stop to think that it was all too good to be true. And she didn't feel the need to talk to Gloria about Gilbert either. So for now, Gloria and the girls were keeping secrets from Béa and in return Béa was keeping her encounter with Gilbert from them.

Chapter Fifty-Four

JUSTICE IS BLIND

In the meantime, Harcourt was living a nightmare. He was put in a prison cell and allowed no contact with the outside world. But he knew the Peacemaker would waste no time in getting him out of there. But the days went by and he had no news, no visitors, no phone calls. He was just starting to panic that he had been abandoned, when a man in a suit came to his cell door and presented himself as his lawyer. He had been sent by the Peacemaker and he had only one purpose, to free him as soon as possible. The Peacemaker needed him more than ever and apparently he had enough influence to get him released.

However, during those few days that he had spent in prison, he had gained another 'friend', the police officer in charge of the Venus de Milo case. His name was Jean Bruneau, he was young and extremely ambitious. There was nothing to investigate about this incident. A boy put some paint on a statue and this man was found in the restoration room trying to make things even worse. End of story. But when the police officer witnessed the early release of Harcourt, he realised there must be more to it than that. It was impossible for anyone to be freed in such a short time, for this type of offence. So the day that Harcourt left the prison, Bruneau decided to follow him to get to know him better.

He didn't know anything initially about the situation, but he soon gained an impression from his own private, undercover investigation of Harcourt. He watched as the twin girls, living at Rue de Rivoli came under threat from Harcourt. Then there was a man who met with Harcourt in clandestine destinations, Gilbert. This man seemed to be changing his identity, every time he visited a woman who worked at the apartment Rue de Rivoli. He soon detected that Gilbert was not Béa's friend, even though she firmly believed that he was.

So Jean Bruneau decided to step in and try to help these women, who seemed to be at risk from two obvious criminals. It was his job and besides the girls seemed really nice. He had observed that they both had boyfriends, although the situation was a little weird being two twin couples. Jean wasn't aware of the trouble he was getting the girls into by meddling. The Peacemaker was not someone to mess around with and he was already very angry with the girls, who had outsmarted him on several occasions. The presence of the young policeman was about to become a declaration of war for the Peacemaker.

While the Peacemaker was using his well-connected friends to get Harcourt out of prison, the girls, helped by Gloria, were getting closer to their target. Alia had the feeling that they were really close, that this one was the last clue. She and her sister could not take any more disappointments. Deanna on the other hand was more pragmatic. She merely prepared herself for the next step.

"The concert will begin any minute now. Is everybody ready?" asked Gloria, looking worried. She was the adult and she was responsible for the four teenagers. They had planned it, they had switched roles so that she would be the most exposed in case of real danger, but she was still not at ease with the plan. However, since they didn't have a better one, their only hope was to try their best to make it succeed.

"Let's go," said Alia, taking Marc by his hand. Marc felt a shiver at Alia's touch. Then he realised that Alia too was a little afraid and she was looking for encouragement.

"Let's," said Deanna, getting up and taking Victor's hand.

The five of them went to the concert room and found their seats, which had been deliberately chosen to be closer to the lamps. Alia and Marc on the left and Deanna and Victor on the right. Gloria was in the middle keeping her purse really close. There were two identical lamps, so they couldn't be sure which one to take. They decided to take both. As soon as the concert started Gloria took out a few smoke capsules from her purse and activated them. Ten seconds later it was impossible to see in the room. The smoke was so thick that everybody was stepping on everybody, trying to leave the room.

The security guard took control and in a few minutes everybody was evacuated from the room. Gloria was the last one to leave as she had to be the distraction for the guard and was supposed to pretend to faint. The boys were able to retrieve the lamps and the girls put them in their purses. The four of them made it to the car, where the instruction was to wait for Gloria. But after ten minutes, they began to realise that something was wrong. Gloria should have been there by now. But instead an ambulance arrived at the scene and Gloria was taken off to hospital before their eyes. Unbeknownst to them, Gloria had genuinely lost consciousness from breathing the thick smoke.

Alia considered trying to drive, but Marc calmed her down. It was really not a good time to attract the attention of the police. Not after what they had done. Just when they were discussing getting someone from the hotel to call them a taxi, a strange man jumped into the driving seat and drove them away in their own car. They didn't even have to time to act. The four of them were in the car with a strange man, who was obviously abducting them.

"I know you," said Alia after a few moments. "You're the man that was following us. I've seen you before. You… and the other one."

"You know nothing, young lady. You should keep your mouth shut and you might get out of this alive," said Gilbert.

After a few hours with Béa he had succeeded in obtaining the information he needed. He came as soon as he could, trying to compensate for Harcourt's absence.

"Leave us alone," demanded Marc, who was in the front passenger seat. He felt like attacking their kidnapper, but he didn't want to put the others in danger. They were travelling quite fast and he had no idea what Gilbert's intentions were.

"I'll leave you alone as soon as you give me what I came here for!" shouted Gilbert.

"And what is that?" asked Deanna, starting to believe they might survive this.

"Don't act like you don't know."

"We honestly have no idea what you want from us," said Alia and put her hand in her purse, where she had the Diana lamp. She was trying to feel something that might show her if the diary was there.

Deanna was doing the same. But she had more luck, because after a few minutes she felt the head of the statue turning. She undid it and she put her finger inside. Her heart started to beat faster as she felt a piece of paper inside. She succeeded in taking it out without a sound. Alia saw her but managed to keep a straight face. Deanna put the piece of paper in her bra where she hoped the kidnapper wouldn't search, then she had the good idea of screwing back the statue's head.

"I want that diary!" said Gilbert.

"What? What diary?" asked Alia, aware she was playing a dangerous game. She had no idea why somebody else would want a teenager's diary.

The only thing that she could think of was that her mother may have witnessed a crime, a murder even, and she had written about it and that somehow Gilbert was related to that murder and he wanted to destroy the evidence.

"Your mother's," he demanded. "I need it now. I'm tired of your games. Because of you, my boss is in prison. But don't worry, he'll come out soon enough and he will teach you not to play with grown-ups!" He was trying to scare them. He didn't want to harm them but if he had to, he would.

"Well, you see, we don't have it," said Marc.

"I don't believe you. Then why did you put on that show, at the castle?"

"We never said that we weren't looking, but we don't have it… yet."

"So what did you take?"

"We took the two Diana lamps on the sides," said Alia looking at Deanna. They both understood that it was meaningless to try and hide the statues.

"Why? The clues led to the Venus de Milo," said Gilbert starting to see that those children had been smart enough to send Harcourt on a wild goose chase. The only thing that they forgot was that Harcourt wasn't acting alone.

"Well, we weren't sure. We wanted to take this possibility out of the equation," said Marc. "We had two ideas, Venus or Diana. Now we can see which one is it."

"Give me the lamps, now!" ordered Gilbert.

The girls took them out and handed them to Marc.

"Let me look at them."

Marc gave one to Gilbert, but as he was driving, he wasn't able to study it in any detail. So Gilbert took them both on his lap. A few minutes later they drove into a small village and pulled up outside a cottage. Gilbert had prepared everything for this kidnapping. The only thing that didn't go as planned was Gloria's accident. He had prepared a room for the children and one for Gloria. He didn't want the teenagers to see what he was ready to do to Gloria to extract information from her.

He took them one by one and locked them up in the house. Finally, the four of them were in the same room, where each of them had his own bed. As with many of the houses in the region, each room had its own small bathroom. The window was small, the blinds closed. So, nowhere to run. And anyway, they had no idea where they were. Marc thought of looking for the name of the village but it was dark and for now it was irrelevant. In any case, Gilbert had taken all their phones, so it was impossible for them to communicate with the outside world. And all they wanted for now was to be left alone to study the paper they had found inside the lamp.

Chapter Fifty-Five

ON THE WAY TO THE HOSPITAL

As soon as she was taken in the ambulance, Gloria woke up. She realised she had passed out as a result of breathing in the smoke. Her first thought was for the girls. She had left them alone at the castle. She made a sign to the young male paramedic, who was keeping the oxygen mask on her mouth and nose, to take it away. When she regained her voice she started to talk very fast.

"I'm sorry," he said. "You'll have to speak a little slower. I didn't get that."

"Where are the girls?" asked Gloria with a faint voice.

"Which girls? You were alone in the concert room."

"No, the girls must have got out faster than me."

"There was no one left when we took you. And the concert room was empty, my colleagues checked twice," he assured her, gently.

"I have to call the castle, because I had two girls and two boys with me. And I am responsible for them. And I'm afraid for their safety!"

"Ssh, calm down. I'll call Esclimont to see if they are there. I'm sure they're safe and sound!"

He took out his phone and made the call. At the end of the conversation Gloria understood that there was no sign of the teenagers. Now they decided to call the police to officially report them missing.

"Where are you taking me?" asked Gloria.

"To the hospital. You were unconscious for about ten minutes."

"Yes, but now I'm fine," said Gloria, struggling to sit up. "I want to go home now, in case the police find them."

"We need to keep you under observation for at least a few hours."

"In a few hours they could be a long way away," she pleaded.

"Where? Why? And who are 'they'? Are you saying there is somebody who wants to kidnap them?"

"Not that I can think of, but you never know. Why aren't they at the castle? They don't know how to drive! They are fourteen!" said Gloria beginning to panic.

"I'm sure the police will find them in no time. And they have your phone number to call you."

"I want to make another phone call, please?" said Gloria.

"She took the phone and called Béa. She hoped she would answer even though it was quite late.

"Béa, can you hear me? Thank God you answered!"

"Where are you? What's happened?" said Béa, alarmed by Gloria's tone of voice.

"We have a big problem. Who knew where we were tonight?"

"Nobody, apart from me. Not even Gilles. He is out of town for his job. Why?"

"I'm on the way to the hospital. I'm fine, but we were at the concert and I fainted and now I'm in an ambulance. But the girls are not to be found! They are with the boys. At least they were."

"I'll be right there. When you arrive at the hospital send me a message so I know where you are."

"Thank you. And you let me know as soon as you have some information about the girls? And are you sure you are the only one who knew where we were?"

"Yes! I'll talk to you later."

"Ok, I'm so grateful Béa!" said Gloria.

"Don't worry, we'll find them."

As soon as she hung up the phone, Béa realised that she wasn't the only one who knew. She had told her new friend about Gloria, when they were together at her apartment. But she couldn't see how he might be concerned. And then it hit her. She was so stupid! Of course, he wasn't interested in her hats! He had only been using her to get information about Gloria. He must be working with Harcourt. And as he was in prison, they had to have another approach. She couldn't tell Gloria that it was all her fault, but now she was convinced the girls must have been kidnapped and she had no doubt they were in grave danger. So she took her car keys and left. She didn't go to Esclimont, she took a detour to the prison to talk to Harcourt. When she arrived she discovered he'd been released. Now she knew that, barring a miracle, the girls were as good as dead.

Chapter Fifty-Six

OUTSIDE PRISON

The first thing Harcourt did when he got out of prison, was to call the Peacemaker and thank him. He knew that it was him who got him released. But all the Peacemaker had to say was to call Gilbert.

"What happened while I was away?" he asked as soon as Gilbert answered.

"We have the girls, but we don't have the diary."

"How come? You weren't supposed to harm the girls as long as they didn't have the diary."

"I was so sure that they had found it." And he explained the whole situation to Harcourt.

Maxime drove for an hour to get to the house where the children were being kept. As soon as he arrived, he started to scrutinise the lamps that Gilbert gave him. But a few hours later they both realised that it was useless. The girls must have interpreted the manuscripts wrongly. He unlocked their room and flung the door open.

"You think you're so smart, don't you?" said Maxime, glaring at them.

"We're average teenagers. What do you want from us?" asked Marc, rising to his feet.

"I want the truth! Why did you steal those lamps?"

"We already explained to your friend. We thought we had a lead there," said Alia.

"I thought that your clues led to Venus de Milo?" he sneered, recalling all those hours he spent in the prison and starting to lose his temper.

"It was one possibility. The other one was Esclimont," said Deanna.

"And that miraculously turned out to be wrong too."

"We are not sure that Venus is the wrong one. You never got to search there, am I right?" asked Deanna.

"No," snarled Harcourt. "Because I was caught! Thanks to you!"

"Nobody forced you to break the law," said Victor bravely. He was aware how dangerous it was to talk like that to the man who had their destiny in his hands. But they had to show that they were not afraid. That way he would think that they found nothing.

"Somebody had to look. I need the manuscripts now."

"We don't have them," said Alia.

"Don't imagine for one second that you're smarter than me. I'll kill you first and then go and search your grandmother's apartment. That way as soon as she returns from the hospital, she can join you… in hell!"

"I can give it to you if you let us go. If you have the manuscripts you don't need us anymore, right?" said Deanna starting to see how serious the situation was.

"I haven't decided what to do with you yet. But if you give them to me, the odds of your getting out of here alive become more interesting."

"I have them on my phone," said Deanna. "Your friend took it, he took all our phones. You search in the photos on mine, everything is there."

Harcourt left without saying a word.

"What were you thinking?" said Alia. "If you give him what he wants he won't need us anymore and he'll kill us."

"Maybe, but at least it's given us some time to find a way out and if he uses my phone maybe the police will track the GPS signal."

"It was an excellent idea," said Victor hugging Deanna. "Now all we have to do is to find a way to escape. We can't wait for the police. And Gloria is in the hospital so she can't come and rescue us."

"Yes, I wonder what happened to her?" said Alia. "And Béa, I wonder if she knows about Gloria? She's the only one that could help her."

"I'm as worried about Gloria as you are," said Marc. "But at least she's free and nobody is trying to kill her. We, on the other hand, we have to find a way to survive this."

"Deanna, show me the paper you found in the lamp," said Alia. Maybe if we give our friend what he wants, we can exchange that for our freedom."

"I'm not sure he would be interested," said Deanna, taking out the piece of paper.

"Why not? Isn't what we are all looking for?" asked Alia.

"I'm not sure. I took a look at it when I went to the bathroom, where I was sure he wouldn't come after me. And it is just a blank page. It doesn't look like a diary and there is nothing written on it. I think we made a big mistake when we interpreted the clues."

"Maybe it really is Venus de Milo," said Deanna taking out the piece of parchment that got them in such trouble.

"Let me see it," said Alia, hoping to understand why those men were so interested in this paper.

But there was nothing that could have explained the fascination those men showed. The big problem was, how would they react if they saw that it was just a useless piece of paper?

"They will kill us when they see that all their trouble was for THIS," said Marc.

"My thoughts exactly. We need to give them hope to find the real diary. The only thing that can keep us alive is to become necessary in their quest," said Alia.

"Yes, but for that we need to know where to search," said Victor. "May I remind you that we don't have any more ideas? We were sure that the diary was in one of those lamps. I still can't believe that it's not there."

"Hold it up for a second," said Alia. "I want to put some direct light on it. Maybe it is our next clue. We must be missing something."

So Alia tried to redirect the light from a lamp they had on the nightstand. But the support was hot, she dropped the lamp and the light bulb shattered into pieces. She wanted to clean up to avoid that the others cutting themselves. But she managed to cut herself instead. With bleeding fingers, she tried to save the piece of paper that was now under the lamp. The moment her blood touched the paper, the colour of the parchment started to change.

"Hey, guys, look!" whispered Alia, hardly believing her eyes.

The others were so busy trying to clean up that they didn't hear her whisper.

"Guys! Look! Something is happening."

Marc was the first to notice the shock on Alia's face. And then he looked at the parchment. It had turned snow white, not yellow as before. And some beautiful handwriting appeared on both sides of the paper. The blood stain was in a corner, but it looked as if blood had been used to write all the words, which now appeared in front of their astonished eyes. Alia started to read out loud, what was written in the scarlet letters.

"Dear Alia and Deanna,

If you read this, it means that we are no longer part of your lives, and I am sorry. The quest you started is a very dangerous one, but wonderful. By now you know that there are many people who will be trying to get their hands on this parchment. But you must know that as long as you two live, nobody else can use it, unless you give it to them willingly.

Its power is amazing. As long as you have it nobody can stop you. But you have to use it wisely as it can do you harm, as it did to me and your father. Normally, it answers only to one master, but as you are twins both of you can use it.

It is impossible for me to tell you everything, but know this. Search for the quill and the Ink master will show himself. Without him the parchment can't show its full power, but you can use it if needed. It will take the shape you want. I chose the form of a diary as it was easier to keep it with me at all times without raising suspicions. All you have to do is to write down what you want or need. But be careful what you wish for.

We love you both very much wherever we are.

Mum and Dad."

By the time she had finished reading, Alia had tears in her eyes and she could barely speak. Marc tried to get closer and put his arm around her. Victor had already taken Deanna in his arms. When the girls calmed down Victor was the first one to speak.

"At least now we know that we've found what we were looking for."

"But it still doesn't give us an answer on what happened to your parents," said Marc.

"Didn't you understand?" said Deanna. "It's our way out of here."

"If they don't kill us first," said Alia. "We have the confirmation that in the end, they can't let us live if they want to use the parchment. We are dead either way. So let's try it. We have nothing to lose."

"Has anyone got a pen?" asked Marc.

"I have something better," said Alia and took out her sunglasses.

"Your sunglasses, how could that help?" asked Deanna.

"Not that. Remember when we were in our home in England, I found this quill that seemed useless at the time. But I kept it and I always hide it with my sunglasses. I'm starting to think that this must be the quill Mum talks about in the letter."

"But we don't have any ink," said Deanna.

"Yes, we do," said Alia.

"They took everything from us," said Victor. "Unless you have that in your magic handbag as well?"

"No, but we can write with our blood," said Alia. "The difficult part is to find the right words."

"Do you still think that this parchment is magic and that it will take us out of here?" said Victor.

"It is our only hope. What shall we write?"

"Let's keep it simple," suggested Marc. "How about, I wish we were at home with Gloria?"

"Ok," said Alia getting ready to get some blood from her finger.

"Wait!" yelled Marc. "I'll do it."

"I think it has to be me or Deanna. The parchment reacted to my blood. It's fine, I can do this."

The moment the quill touched the surface of the parchment, Alia felt a weird connection with it, as if the quill could read her mind. It was more difficult than she had imagined, but as soon as she wrote down the last word, they all lost consciousness.

When Harcourt entered the room, all he saw were four empty beds. The surprise made him drop the gun he had in his right hand.

Chapter Fifty-Seven

BÉA PANICS

Béa had no idea what to do. With Harcourt out of prison, she knew everybody was in danger, including her. She couldn't afford to panic. Gloria trusted her. She tried to call him, but he didn't answer. Knowing that Gloria was heading for the hospital in the ambulance, she tried to find out which one. Before she realised she was already outside their apartment. When she got closer she heard voices. Nobody was supposed to be in there. Her heart pounding, she crept quietly into the apartment, expecting to see armed men, burglars anything but the scene which faced her. Alia, Deanna, Marc, Victor and Gloria were all sitting around the kitchen table, eating and talking.

"Béa, come in!" said Gloria.

"You found them!" said Béa hardly able to believe her eyes.

"Actually, they found me."

"How did you get out of the hospital?"

"Well," Gloria hesitated. "I felt better and they decided to let me go with a prescription." She didn't want to tell Béa everything. The girls intrinsically understood what she was doing.

"Great! So everything is back to normal. I was so worried!" said Béa relieved.

"Yes, back to normal. Do you want to stay and eat with us?" asked Alia, trying to act natural.

"No. It's very kind of you but I have to go home. See you tomorrow."

As soon as Béa had closed the door everybody exhaled in relief. They were still trying to come to terms with what had happened, themselves. Gloria had been in an ambulance, on her way to hospital. She remembered blacking out, then waking up in the apartment. And the same had happened to the four teenagers. The last thing they remembered was being in the room where they were being held hostage. They didn't even dare think that it was the power of the parchment, which had brought them safely home. Even if it had been their wish. All of the events of the past 24 hours seemed like a dream, in fact a nightmare.

They were experiencing the same sensation, as when you go through a terrifying dream all night, and wake up in the morning happy to be in your own bed and able to go on with your life. But they knew that it wasn't over. They had succeeded in escaping from Harcourt, but he would be back, even angrier and more murderous than before. One thing they were certain of, he intended to kill them.

It was crucial for them to discover all the powers of the parchment. And the only way to do that was to find the Ink master, as Samantha had called him. Maybe he could explain to them what was happening. But to find him was a completely different problem. They had no clue where to start. They had the poem, but it wasn't leading anywhere. The only way to find him was to search every shop in Paris, which would be ludicrous. And what if he wasn't in Paris? What if he was in London? He could be anywhere.

In the end, the boys decided they had to go home, their poor parents would be worried sick. Tomorrow was another day. The girls went to bed, exhausted. Gloria decided to wait a little longer before going to sleep. She was still feeling the effects of the medication she had received in the ambulance. But soon enough she followed the others and collapsed gratefully into bed.

Béa was incapable of putting together the loose ends. She was thrilled to know the girls were safe. She had been terrified that Harcourt might have been holding them, or worse still, that he had killed them already. Maybe Harcourt wasn't as lethal as she thought. At least she hoped so. But when she checked her phone, she saw seven missed calls from him. Not a good sign. She decided to call him back as soon as possible. She didn't want to anger him more. And she knew that in order to regain his trust, she had to show that she was still loyal and available.

"Hello?" said Béa, when Maxime answered.

"Where are you?" he asked directly.

"On my way home. Where are you?"

"It's none of your business. Do you know where Gloria and the girls are?"

"Yes, I've just seen them. They're at home."

"*What?* What do you mean, at home?"

"Why do you sound so surprised?" asked Béa.

Harcourt made an effort to calm down. Béa didn't have to know everything. He realised he still needed her help.

"Do you need something?" said Béa, hearing only silence at the other end. "Or can I go home to get some rest? I've had a long night."

"You can go," he said brusquely. "I'll talk to you in the morning, as soon as I get to Paris."

Béa had no idea how much harm she had done. She had put them in danger without knowing. Now that Harcourt had just witnessed its power, he was more determined than ever to get his hands on that diary.

Chapter Fifty-Eight

WHEN THE POLICE OFFICER GETS INVOLVED

The young man, who thought justice had not been served by the early release of Harcourt, was only 19 years old. He was just an apprentice but first in his class. He had been given the opportunity to work with the grownups to get some experience in the field. He was grateful. But he was disappointed to see that none of his colleagues had shared his reaction to Harcourt being set free like that. He had joined the police because he believed in justice and quite simply, the thought bad people should be behind bars. He idolized his superiors, but he could see they were obviously used to corruption. He wasn't. And he wanted to know why somebody would try to destroy the Venus de Milo. Being young and naïve, he didn't stop to think of the consequences of his actions. In his wildest dreams, he wouldn't conceive that someone as powerful as the Peacemaker existed, who could crush him like a fly if he dared interfere with his plans. The day he decided to follow Harcourt and enter into the girls' life was the day he showed up on the Peacemaker's radar. And that was never a good thing.

One day after the mysterious evasion of the girls, he went to their house to ask them some questions. He rang, and introduced himself to Gloria, who decided to let him in. She was curious to find out what he wanted.

"Hello. My name is Jean Bruneau. I am a police officer and I would like to ask you some questions about a man, who has been seen spying on you and your granddaughters."

"I didn't know we were being spied on. Why would anyone be interested in us? Do you think that it's serious?" asked Gloria, as innocently as she could.

"I don't know. But you have to be careful. I saw that you have two girls about fifteen years old?"

"Fourteen. And why would he follow them?"

"Maybe for human trafficking… I don't know. If I show you a picture of him would you tell me if you recognise him?"

"Of course, I would do anything to help you find out who he is and what he wants from us."

"That's him," said Bruneau, showing her a photograph of Harcourt on his phone. "Do you know him?"

"No, I've never seen this man before in my life," lied Gloria, hoping her poker face was convincing enough.

"Are you sure? And this one?" asked Bruneau, showing a photo of Gilbert.

"No, I don't know him either," she said, shaking her head.

"It's weird, because he seems to be a good friend of your cleaning lady."

"She has the right to have friends that I don't know about."

"Of course, but I was hoping you might help me. Anyway, if you see either of these men, or if something happens, or they threaten you in any way, call me?" said Bruneau, handing her his card.

Just then, Alia walked in.

"Nanna, I think I found our ink store- oh, hello!" she said, looking at Bruneau.

"Hello! Excuse me, I was just leaving."

"Don't leave on my behalf," said Alia, smiling. He was the cutest boy she had ever seen, especially in that uniform.

"Oh no," he said. "I'm not, it's just I have to go back to work. My number is the second one on the left," he said pointing to the card. "The other one is my superior's. Call me if you see anything?" said Jean and walked out of the door.

"Who was that?" asked Alia, looking out of the window, hoping to get a last glimpse of the young man.

"Just a police officer, who's noticed our friends' increased interest in us."

"Maybe we should tell him what's going on and how we were kidnapped."

"Do you think that involving the police is smart?" said Gloria, sharply. "How do you explain how you escaped from your kidnappers?"

"Isn't he too young to work in the police?"

"He's not a police officer yet. You seem quite interested in him?"

"No, it's just that I wasn't expecting to find a police officer in our kitchen," said Alia, trying to explain herself. She was really interested in the young man. She had a feeling that she could trust him… and more. But their life was too out of the ordinary to involve someone else in it. The boys were already collateral damage, so for them in was too late. And Victor was in love with Deanna so it made sense to share their secret with them.

"When you came in, you were saying something about the ink store?" said Gloria, returning to the main event.

"Well we searched a list with all the stores that could sell that kind of ink."

"What makes you think you found the right one?"

"The boys found the poems that led us to the parchment and they also found also a bracelet, which represented Ouroboros," replied Alia.

"Who?"

"The serpent that represents time."

"And?"

"Well… look at the photo on the web site."

Gloria looked at the photo that Alia was showing her on her phone. It showed a middle-aged man, standing in front of a shop and on the window, the image of a large snake, biting its tail.

"Maybe you're right. It's too strange to be a coincidence," admitted Gloria. But you must go with Deanna, not with me.

"Why?"

"Because I don't think that the Ink master is too friendly and we want him to help us. So for him to trust you, you should go without me."

"Maybe I should go alone?" said Alia.

"I think he'll know that you have a twin."

"How can he know?"

"Go with Deanna. Don't try to hide anything from him. Be honest, be polite and patient. He'll appreciate that."

"You seem to know him. What do you think will happen when we arrive?"

"I don't know him and I don't know what could happen. All I know is that you catch more flies with honey than vinegar," said Gloria.

Chapter Fifty-Nine

THE INK MASTER

His shop could have been a little improved, but it had its charm. Outside the sun was shining, but inside all remained dark and gloomy. The girls had no idea how an average man could live in such a strange place. They would soon find out that there was nothing average about the owner. As they entered, a doorbell announced their arrival. The shop appeared deserted, no-one stood at the counter. The girls walked further in and started to look around. Alia was sure that if she touched anything, the owner would appear and tap her on her fingers. So she kept her hands in her pockets. Deanna was more daring, so when she saw an amazing pen, she touched it. Nothing happened, so they continued to look around.

"Just because I let you touch one of the most expensive pens I have in my store, doesn't mean that I appreciate your doing that to all my merchandise," said a man coming out a storage room, giving them quite a fright.

"Sorry sir. I just like nice pens," stammered Deanna. "And you have the nicest pens I have ever seen."

"Thank you. You don't often see kids that appreciate things that don't start with an I."

"Well, I do," said Deanna trying to butter him up.

"So, what can I do for you, girls?"

"We are here to talk to you about something," said Alia, finally daring to speak.

"And what is that?" said the owner, becoming even more curious about the twins.

"My name is Deanna and this is my sister is Alia. We received a message from our mother, from beyond the grave."

"And what does it have to do with me?"

"Maybe if you hear the message, you'll understand," said Deanna taking out her phone. She starting reading the riddle that talked about the parchment and the quill.

"I see," said the man as soon as she had finished reading.

"You do?" asked Alia, starting to believe they might be in the right place.

"Well, I need to see something else, to be sure that this is not a mistake."

"What?" asked Deanna.

"Do you have the thing the riddle talks about?" said the man, hesitating.

"What, this?" asked Deanna, taking out the quill.

"Yes, yes… yes," said the Ink master getting closer, like a child towards a lollipop. "Where did you get this?"

"I told you. Our mother left it to us. But we think that it is useless without your help. Can you tell us more?" asked Alia.

"I've been waiting all my life for someone to come to ask me that. Your mother must have been an accident in the parchment's destiny."

"What do you mean?" said Deanna.

"Well I think that The Golden One was supposed to enter in the hands of somebody else. But it got lost on the way."

"The Golden One? You mean the parchment we found?" said Alia.

"Yes. It is called The Golden One as at the beginning it was a golden tablet found on an Egyptian archeological site. Nobody took care of it. It was taken along with other artefacts to the British Museum. As the time passed, other objects more interesting took its place so it was put in the storage room. One day a cleaning lady stole it. She took it home where, to her disappointment, it changed its shape and became a scroll. She realised she couldn't sell it anymore so she left it by accident in the house of one of her clients. They happened to be an old English family with noble blood. When the parchment was touched by that noble blood, it started to show inexplicable messages. At first they were in languages that only specialists understood. The girl that found it didn't know how to use it at first. She learned its power only after it was too late. But she left it to her daughter. Maybe she was a member of your family?"

"But in that case why didn't our grandmother have it before our mother?" asked Alia.

"I don't know. Or maybe The Golden One lost its original master on the way. But the twins had to arrive later. You were not supposed to find it this century."

"What? But when were we supposed to find it? When we were a hundred years old?"

"The problem is, that if you are twins, you need to find The Silver One."

"What Silver One? Are you trying to tell us that there is another one?" asked Deanna.

"Yes, the Golden One has a twin. The legend says that they were part of the same tablet and they were separated, the Silver One was taken to France, where it was never seen again."

"Ok, and why do we need to find it?" asked Deanna.

"Because the Golden One will never obey one of you completely. And trust me, with the enemies that you must have by now, you need all the power you can get."

"What is its power?" asked Alia.

"You haven't understood by now?" asked the weird man, smiling. "All that you write down turns into reality. You can't wish for somebody to die, but you can wish to… let's see, for instance, to be somewhere else. And you can't play with the free will. Do you understand?"

"Yes," they both answered, nodding.

"Exactly. I never saw it so I can't tell you everything. My information comes from what the others have told me," he continued.

"The others?" asked Deanna.

"The other Ink masters. I am not the only one," said the man.

"So what can you do for us?" asked Deanna.

"I can do something for your quill."

"What?" asked Alia.

"I can bring it to life."

Chapter Sixty

HARCOURT

The Peacemaker had never heard Maxime so furious over the phone. He knew that he was feared, so he never felt the need to ask for respect. Harcourt was aware that he had failed. Completely. He didn't get the diary. He hadn't stopped the teenagers from getting it. Now they were invincible.

"Not yet," said the Peacemaker. "There is still one missing piece."

"Yes, the second diary. Why are you so sure that it exists?" asked Maxime.

"It exists all right. But we have no clues for this one. I believe Gloria was onto something when she got caught by the police in England."

"And are you sure she didn't find it there?"

"If she had found it, we would have known. But Gloria can't get it. Now that the girls have found the first one, it is the girls who must find the second one too," said the Peacemaker.

"Why not us?" asked Harcourt.

"Because if you find it now, it would be useless to you, even dangerous, take my word for it. If the girls find it and we take both of them at the same time, we will have complete control."

"Ok, I understand. But how will the girls find the second diary without somewhere to start?"

"They will, don't worry. Don't underestimate them again. If my calculations are correct, they have already met the Ink master who has told them about it."

"The Ink master?"

"The one person in Europe, who can give them the ink they need to write in the diary. Apparently they already have the quill."

"How can you be so sure?" asked Maxime starting to realise how little he knew.

"If they only had the diary, without the quill they would have never been able to escape the other night."

"But we searched them."

"Apparently not well enough. I told you, they are smarter than you want to believe," said the Peacemaker. "Now let's see what we can do to keep an eye on them. It will be a lot harder than before, because now they have the diary to help them. I think the most important element now is Béa. Do you think Gloria still trusts her?"

"Maybe, but I don't think Béa trusts us. Now that Gilbert and I used her, she might not want to serve us anymore."

"But you still have the upper hand with the adoption agency."

"Well, not so much. Because now she knows that we are ready to kill the girls if needed. She is starting to have doubts. Maybe we should look for somebody else?" said Harcourt.

"You mean the boys? Forget it. I saw the way they are looking at the girls. There is nothing that could make them betray their pretty girlfriends."

"I'll think of something. Trust me. I won't let you down again," said Harcourt with conviction.

"You'd better not," said the Peacemaker with a barely concealed threat.

Chapter Sixty-One

LOVE HURTS

Now that they had the diary and a few answers, the girls felt as if they owned the world. They didn't care anymore about their stalkers, all they wanted now was to discover all the powers of the parchment. But now they knew that their mission wasn't over. They also had to find the Silver One. They went straight home, to find Gloria and the boys. Maybe they would be able to help them.

Gloria was happy that at least half of the way was over. But the other one was a lot more difficult. She thought that if she had been a better mother she could have helped Samantha and she would have been here with them. She realised that she had shut down her daughter, the day that she had touched that parchment. She couldn't understand it and nor could her daughter. The Golden One had changed Samantha. She had become independent and strong and confident. She hadn't understood its full power but even if Gloria would never admit it, she was afraid of Samantha and what she had been turning into.

So now that they were on the verge of finding the Silver One, she wanted to be there for her granddaughters. She wanted them to trust her, to involve her in their lives. And the only way to protect them was to help them find it. She had the key that she had found in England, but she had no idea what to do with it. She would know when the time came.

While the girls were relaying the story the Ink master had told them, the doorbell rang. Alia went to the door. When she returned, she was blushing and smiling all over her face. Following her into the room came the police officer, who had been investigating Harcourt's early release.

"Sorry to interrupt," said Jean. "But I wanted to let you know that the man that I am watching has been seen outside your apartment all day long."

"It's Ok, officer Bruneau. You can come in," said Gloria. "Boys, this is the police officer who caught the man, who wanted to destroy the Venus de Milo at the Louvre."

"Oh, did you find out why was he trying to do that?" asked Marc faking surprise.

"No, but what worries me most was that he was set free way too early. And he seems very interested in your family."

"And what do you intend to do?" asked Alia. "You can't protect us forever."

Marc saw the sparkle in Alia's eyes when she was talking to the young officer. He had to admit that he was handsome and strong and he looked perfect in his uniform. He had been dreaming about getting that kind of response from Alia himself, but he was starting to lose hope. Every time he saw Deanna and Victor together, he felt a little jealous of his brother. But until now he had no competition. He knew that nothing could happen between them but it didn't hurt less to see a perfect stranger come and steal Alia's heart. He had tried to forget her, to accept the idea of just being friends. But the last few weeks and all that they had gone through together, just made him love her even more. And love for a teenager is a hundred times more intense. And so is disappointment. And now he was afraid that Alia would use the parchment to try to make the officer fall in love with her. After all it was capable of making their wish come true. He wished he had a diary too. He would have made Alia his girlfriend in a second. That gave him an idea. But for that he had to wait until Bruneau left. A few minutes later the officer decided he had to go.

"What does he want? He's creepy," said Marc as soon as they were left alone.

Gloria closed the door behind him and she left the teenagers alone for a while to take care of some things that needed her attention.

"Not as creepy as the guy who is stalking us!" answered Alia. "He's just doing his job. He is a good policeman who trusts his instincts."

"He has no answers and no solution to our problems. So he is no good," concluded Marc.

"He took from his personal time to come and warn us. What more do you want from him?"

"Answers. To put our stalker back in jail! There are a lot of things that he can do," replied Marc angrily.

"Children! Let him be," said Deanna. "We have other things to worry about." She was keen to stop this conversation. She knew that Marc was just being jealous. But Alia's new feelings for Bruneau were troubling her. Her sister could only get hurt.

"Yes! She's right! I almost forgot," said Marc. "I have an idea how to find the Silver One."

"Ok, we're listening," said Deanna happy that they had changed the subject.

"This parchment does whatever you want, right?"

"Right," said Alia starting to see where he was going with this.

"Then we should try to ask it to tell us where the Silver One is," said Marc triumphantly.

"It makes sense," said Alia. "But I don't think it would work because I am sure that my mother had the same idea. Still, we have nothing to lose."

"Ok. You have the ink, let's do it," said Deanna.

Alia took the quill, she put it in the ink and started writing their wish. As soon as she finished the last word, the parchment turned blank again. They were so disappointed that for a few seconds they were silent. Then they started breathing again. A few lines appeared on the paper. Deanna started to read and she didn't pay any attention to the boys. As she continued they started to exchange looks. They were shocked and the girls didn't even notice.

"What do you think it means?" asked Alia.

"It means that we know where to search the Silver One," said Marc.

Chapter Sixty-Two

DESPAIR TURNS INTO HOPE

Béa was sure now that Gloria and the girls had lost all faith in her. She became even more desperate, because she was felt trapped between the two sides. Harcourt was not pleased because she had failed him and Gloria, who was like a mother to her, had started hiding things from her. She was sure that Maxime wouldn't help her and her husband with the adoption agency. So all the damage she had done was for nothing. But as far as she knew the twins had not found the diary, so there was still a faint hope to get things right.

The next day she saw Bruneau coming out of Gloria's house. She didn't know who he was, but a police officer didn't bode well. And then she saw Harcourt watching from the other side of the road. He was dressed like a biker, who had just stopped to get some rest and a drink of water. But he was resting for far too long and he was very unhappy to see that officer.

"Do you know him?" asked Béa trying to get closer to Maxime without looking suspicious.

"Of course I do. It's the officer who arrested me at the Louvre. I don't like what I am seeing at all."

"What do you think he wants? You were released, you didn't escape. He has no reason to search for you," asked Béa.

"I don't know, but you can find out. You have to ask Gloria what is going on. We both know that I got released because I am lucky enough to know the right people, not because the judge was on my side."

"Well I can try…"

"No, it's not enough! Until now all you did was try! You have to start working for me! I'll meet you in two hours and you'd better have some information for me!" shouted Harcourt.

Béa felt scared. She knew that Maxime was very dangerous and the last thing she wanted was to upset him. So she went upstairs, where she found Gloria alone. It was perfect.

"How are you doing?" asked Gloria smiling.

"I've been better. Gilles is still away with his job. I spend more time alone than with my husband."

"But at least he likes his job. That is very important. What about you?"

"I like working for you. You're like family to me," answered Béa. "It doesn't even feel like a job."

"I'm glad. What news do you have about our 'friend'?" asked Gloria.

"Well, he's always around. He will never give up. He is very upset about the Louvre incident. You know that he got out?"

"Yes, I know. You have just missed the officer who arrested him."

"Why was he here?"

"He's not happy with the early release of our friend. So he's investigating a little further to try to know more about him. And he noticed that he spends a lot of time outside our building. So he came to see if we knew him."

"Did you tell him anything?"

"Of course not. He would think we are all crazy in our chase for a diary."

"You're right. By the way, did you find anything new?"

"No, we are at a dead end," lied Gloria. She didn't trust Béa anymore. After the night she spent in the ambulance, she realised that the people she was playing with were very dangerous. Now, she felt the need to protect the girls every way she could.

"I'm sure that everything will end well," said Béa. "And you will find out what really happened to Samantha."

"Maybe, or maybe not. But as long as the girls are happy, I'm happy."

"Yes, they do seem to be enjoying themselves, with their new friends."

"Alia still pretends not to be in love with Marc. But he is head over heels with her. I don't know how much longer he can go on like that. And now it seems that Alia has a crush on the young police officer!" said Gloria.

"Oh, poor Marc!" said Béa. "He will have to be patient until Alia realises that a relationship with the officer is impossible and illegal."

"Yes, and he has already been patient enough. And he loves her so much… But at least they made some friends here. When we first arrived, the girls were not very happy with the change. I thought that it would take much longer to get close to somebody."

"Yes. But you have to admit that it is a big coincidence how they found each other," said Béa.

"Or fate. Either way I consider myself lucky. At least when they are all together, I'm not so worried."

"And now you have a police officer to protect you."

"I wouldn't say that. He doesn't try to protect us, only to find out what happened with our stalker. Has Harcourt contacted you lately?"

"Yes. He wanted to know if you found the diary, while he was in prison. But I told him that I had no news from you, and that you would tell me if you did."

"Of course. I'll let you know and we'll make a plan accordingly," said Gloria wanting to end this conversation.

"Ok, so I'll start cleaning. There is a lot of work and I want to get back home before Gilles arrives. I want to make a coq au vin for him."

"Wonderful. I need to go out anyway."

Gloria left the apartment and when Béa finished her work, she left too. As soon as she went out she saw Harcourt now dressed like a tourist with a selfie stick and a backpack. She told him everything that Gloria told her. As Harcourt knew that the girls had the diary, he realised that either Béa was telling lies, or Gloria had lost all confidence in her. In both cases Béa had become useless. And useless people are dispensable. She knew too much. He decided to talk to the Peacemaker and ask his opinion, but he was pretty certain that they would both agree to get rid of her. The idea of having Bruneau on his back didn't make him any happier. But that was something that the Peacemaker had to handle.

In the meantime, Gilbert was at Neuilly watching the boys' apartment. He saw their parents go inside and he saw them leave. He wanted to get into their house to see if they had hidden anything. He was amused to see that the boys didn't get their looks from their father. Their mother was very beautiful and seemed younger than she really was. But the twins looked nothing like their father. It was pure coincidence that Gilbert was there and not Harcourt. If it had been the other way around Maxime would have had the surprise of his life.

Chapter Sixty-Three

AT VAUX DE CERNAY

Deanna was reading the same words on the parchment, that the boys had found at the monastery. They had completely forgotten about that.

"I can't believe that there is a link!" said Marc.

"A link? With what?" asked Deanna as she finished reading.

"Do you remember when we decided to start looking for your mother's diary?" asked Victor.

"Yes…"

"And that we told you we had a treasure hunt too?"

"Yes…"

"Well, the day you went biking at Esclimont, we were on a trip with a friend and his parents. And when we arrived, we found this parchment in a bottle."

"What a cliché," said Deanna ironically.

"Maybe, but in the bottle, we found the same apparently meaningless message that you have just read."

"What?" asked Deanna. "This can't be a coincidence. So it means that if you hadn't found your parchment, we would never have known where to look?"

"That's right," said Marc. "And I think that this is what stopped your mother from finding it."

"Possibly. But what do we do now? If we went to Vaux de Cernay what would we be looking for?" asked Alia.

"I don't know, but I bet if we went there it would help us think. We should go home to stay a day or two with our parents and then organize a few days' trip there," said Marc.

"OK. We will inform Gloria about our discovery. I'm sure she will want to bring us," said Alia.

"Are you sure?" asked Deanna. "After what happened at the concert?"

"Yes, because now we have the Golden One to protect us," said Alia.

"We don't even know how to use it properly," said Deanna. "We only tried when we were desperate."

"We should sleep on it," said Marc.

"You're right," said Alia. "We're all exhausted and not thinking straight."

As soon as the boys left, the girls went to see Gloria who was in her bedroom, talking on the phone. She looked quite angry, but the girls were very anxious to tell her the news. When she hung up she looked at the girls. They told her everything they knew. Gloria agreed to take them to Vaux de Cernay as soon as they felt ready.

For two straight days the four teenagers slept. They were so shaken up by the latest events that even the excitement of a new discovery was not strong enough to get them back on their feet. They talked on the phone, but the boys decided to stay with their parents as long as they could. Alia learned everything there was to learn about the monastery. Deanna started to learn how to use the parchment for simple tasks. She asked for small objects, then she asked for sunshine when the sky was cloudy. They were very surprised to see that the parchment was really answering all their wishes.

Alia tried to get Bruneau to come to their home, but as they already knew, they couldn't play with free will. She could have asked to be where he was but that would have only made things worse. They didn't dare ask to go somewhere, because they remembered their blackout the first time they travelled.

They kept an eye on Harcourt who didn't leave their sight. Now that he was convinced that Gloria was lying to Béa, he was determined to watch them nonstop. The girls asked Gloria what information they could offer to Béa without her knowing that they had the parchment. Gloria had an idea that seemed crazy at the time, but the more they talked about it, the more it made sense.

Two days later they decided that they were ready to stop lying around and sleeping in late. They felt stronger and ready to face the new challenges the Silver One had in store for them, at least they thought they were. They prepared for the trip. The boys told their parents that they were going on a few days camping by a lake, with their girlfriends. They gave them Gloria's phone number, took only a backpack each and left.

Gloria took the key she had found in England, the girls took the Golden One, the quill and the old backpack, whose useful purpose was still unknown.

When they arrived, they started to visit the abbey. But they soon realised that there was not much to visit. Almost all of it had been restored and turned into a hotel, so there were many rooms. The staff were busy organizing a wedding, so all in all they were rather disappointed with their research. Then Alia had the idea to ask the parchment to make them invisible, so they could search in restricted areas. Almost immediately, unseen, the two girls found themselves inside the office, where they overheard two men having a heated argument.

"What do you mean you don't want to do it?"

"I think that is a crazy idea to want to get married by an old fountain after all the flooding we had this week."

"Crazy or not they are our customers and they are paying for it. I know it is very difficult to put the red carpet on the wet grass, but they said they were taking full responsibility for the result."

"But why is it so important to get married by a fountain?"

"Because it is a fountain which was famous to help women be fertile. And apparently our bride is not capable of having children. So they are ready to try everything. Crazy as it may sound."

"Ok. But they must be warned that there will be a lot of mud on the carpet and a lot of high heels stuck in it. And the fountain is full of water, you can't even get close. They are really unlucky because when it is dry is a very nice place to visit."

"I will let them know, but they don't want to give up. Their wedding is in three days. Maybe it will dry up a little before then."

And so the two men left the office and the girls rushed back to the hotel room Gloria had booked for them, to tell the others what they had heard. They were beginning to enjoy having this parchment. What they didn't know was that every time they used it, the Peacemaker was able to locate them. So while they hoped that nobody had followed them, the Peacemaker was on their tracks. And Gloria started to see the changes the use of the parchment brought with it. She had witnessed it once with Samantha. Now she hoped she could prevent the horrible destiny that awaited the owner of the parchment. She was convinced that Samantha had paid the price for using the Golden One.

"I know where to look," said Alia. "At least I have an idea. The monk talks about the lack of water during the siege."

"Yes," said Deanna.

"Well it could point to a fountain," continued Alia.

"It could, but we didn't see one," said Victor.

"There is one, and kind of famous too. But with all the rain they don't let the tourists get close. I don't know why I didn't think about it before, I have read about it. But for now there is too much water around it," said Alia.

"I bet we can also help that poor couple that wants to get married there in three days," added Deanna.

"We have to wait until tomorrow, so they don't get suspicious. But we need to dry the surroundings so that we have access," said Alia.

"Tomorrow will be a very, very sunny and warm day," concluded Gloria.

They decided to enjoy the rest of the day and take a walk in the forest. The following day promised to be full of excitement.

Chapter Sixty-Four

THE PEACEMAKER

The parchment was not in his possession. Just now he still had no clue about the Silver One. Harcourt didn't seem to be as useful as he should have been. Béa was more useless than a piece of furniture. And Gloria was aware that she was being followed. Things couldn't have gone worse for the Peacemaker. And yet he didn't feel angry. He felt sure that he needed to take Béa and his husband out of the picture. Harcourt was already dealt with. He was so terrified by the situation that he needed no other punishment. And the girls were doing a great job in finding the Silver One. All he had to do was find a way to kill them. He expected that to be difficult as they had the parchment. But he had no choice, he had to find a way of outsmarting them.

The Peacemaker was connected to the parchment. He didn't know how or why, but every time it was being used, he knew it. And he knew where. That's why he hadn't been able to find it himself. He was wondering if he had the same connection with the Silver One, that he now feared. He knew that it was a lot more dangerous than the Golden One, but more powerful too. And now he knew that the girls had used the Golden One at the abbey, he wondered if they were on the track of the Silver One. They must be. What else would they be doing there? So he asked Harcourt to follow them. By the time he got there the girls could have achieved a lot.

When Harcourt received the Peacemaker's order to get to the abbey, he packed a few clothes, enough for a couple of days, jumped into the car and left. He didn't expect to find anything because the girls now had the parchment. All they needed to do was ask it to let them know, whenever somebody got close to them. He had to find another approach.

The next day couldn't come soon enough for the four teenagers. None of them got much sleep, they were too excited about whether Alia's idea would work or not. The sky was blue and the sun shone brighter than ever. It was almost unnatural. But most importantly, the flooding which had made the land around the abbey inaccessible, had mysteriously vanished. The young couple came out of the hotel and went for a walk in the park. They were amazed to see how everything had fallen into place for them. Thanks to a secret parchment they knew nothing about, they would have their dream wedding.

The girls had to wait for the couple to leave. It took an hour, so they decided to have breakfast while the two lovebirds were planning their ceremony. After breakfast, Gloria went out to see if the couple were still by the fountain. She was happy to see that they had left to check the rooms for their guests.

"It's all clear," said Gloria. "Let's go."

"OK, let's see if we can find something," said Alia putting all her hopes in this quest.

"If we don't, I'm sure we'll find something else soon enough," said Deanna, trying to reassure her.

They left the restaurant and went straight out. They were almost running in their impatience. Deanna and Victor were holding hands. For the first time Alia wished she could hold Marc's hand just to feel his support. They were so close to the end of this journey that she was almost afraid. She was holding the parchment tight. She had asked for the quill to be just drawn on the Golden One and that all she had to do was to touch the drawing. That way it was easier and didn't risk losing or breaking it. And to anyone who didn't know its secret, it looked just like a scrap of paper with a feather drawn on it.

Gloria was only there to help the teenagers. She couldn't do anything. As far as she was concerned, the boys had no part either. But she didn't want to disappoint them. And she couldn't even imagine how important the twins were for the destiny of the Silver One.

"The legend has it," said Alia as they set off, "that Saint Louis made Margaret of Provence drink miracle water from the Saint Thibault fountain and it made her fertile, and the mother of eleven children!"

"Eleven children? It is more like a punishment than a wish come true!" said Deanna.

As soon as they reached the fountain, a car appeared on the road. Alia recognised the driver, it was Bruneau staring at them. He stopped the car but he realised it was too late to do anything. Alia thought he must have come to try to stop her doing what she was doing. She didn't understand. How could he have known anything? Even they had no idea what was about to happen. Then she realised he was not looking at them but behind them. And the look on his face scared her. She took a glance over her shoulder, to see Harcourt standing so close, she could almost feel his breath on her ear. She reached out to Marc, but it was too late. Harcourt pulled him roughly to one side and held a gun to his neck. He had an insane smile on his face.

She looked at Gloria but she couldn't move either, too afraid that Maxime would kill Marc. She looked at Bruneau, but he was frozen to the spot too.

"Don't let me interrupt your plan," said Harcourt.

"Leave my brother alone!" shouted Victor, letting go of Deanna's hand, and trying to get closer.

"If you take another step, it will be the last time you see your brother alive," hissed Harcourt.

"Let's be reasonable," said Gloria trying to calm things down. "What do you want from us?"

"You know," sighed Harcourt. "I'm tired of answering this question. We all know what we are doing here."

"I don't," said Bruneau, who had managed to get in close to the teenagers and now took his gun from under his jacket.

"What are you doing here? This is none of your concern," Harcourt became angry.

"You are my only business now. I knew there was something very wrong with you," said Bruneau.

"Don't force me to make you my first victim. You have no idea who are you dealing with."

"Oh, I can imagine that you are just a puppet in a much larger show. I think you are nobody!" said the young policeman.

"I'll show you what I am," grinned Harcourt and changed the direction of his gun towards Bruneau.

A second later Alia saw the young police officer on the ground with a hole in his chest. Her heart stopped. She thought she was going to faint, then she heard Gloria and Deanna screaming in terror. She saw Harcourt taking back his position near Marc. And then she realised that she had to ensure that her friend didn't suffer the same fate. She stretched her right hand towards Harcourt and opened her palm to reveal the scrunched up parchment in her sweaty hand.

"Take it and let us go," she said full of despair. "I don't want it that much. But you must know that it can't do evil things so it is useless to a monster like you."

"I'll be the judge of that," said Maxime and snatched the parchment out of Alia's hand. But he didn't let go of Marc shoulder. "And I'll take him with me in case I need your services in the next few days."

"No! you don't need him!" cried Alia. "You have the parchment. Let him go!"

"Shut up! Now let's see if you can find the Silver One for me. Play nice and you will all get to leave unharmed."

"I don't believe you!" said Deanna.

"Do as he says!" said Gloria who was sitting beside Bruneau's motionless body.

"All right, Nanna," said Deanna.

"Good girls. Now, what were you doing here?" asked Harcourt.

"The parchment showed us a piece of a letter written by a Cistercian monk, that talked about water so we thought of a fountain," said Alia. "And it is the most important fountain in the area."

"Ok, so let's go and see if you're right," said Harcourt and pushed Alia towards the fountain.

Alia, along with Deanna and Victor got closer to the four pillars that supported the wooden roof. They started looking around, touching every engraving, every minute hole in the stone. Just near the water source there was a little stone bench. The three of them sat down to look up and study the ceiling. As soon as they touched the old stone, they felt the earth moving and everything went dark.

Chapter Sixty-Five

THE DAY THAT EVERYTHING CHANGED

No one could have foreseen what happened. Gloria couldn't believe her eyes.

She saw her granddaughters and Victor sitting down on the bench and all of them suddenly disappeared. She heard Marc's cry and then nothing. She was too strong to abandon herself to fear. She had to get closer to the fountain to try to understand what had happened. But Harcourt wouldn't let her. He had witnessed the same thing and although he was as surprised as Marc and Gloria, he knew that the Peacemaker would be able to explain what had just happened. But he had got what he had come for. So with the parchment in his pocket he let Marc go and he ran to his car.

To Gloria's surprise, as soon as Harcourt reached the car park, Bruneau leapt up and ran to his own car, jumped in and ducked down behind the steering wheel. When Harcourt drove past and out onto the main road, he didn't notice that Bruneau's body was missing. He drove by and a few seconds later the young man left without a word. Gloria and Marc were left alone to try to find the three teenagers who had disappeared as if by magic.

As Harcourt arrived at the road to Paris, he managed to call the Peacemaker, despite his shock and excitement. He had learned a long time ago that he had to prepare for whenever he talked to his boss. He was not somebody who would tolerate babbling or senseless sentences. So he took a few long breaths and he heard the Peacemaker's voice on the speaker.

"I hope you have good news!"

"I do! I have the Golden One. It's ours!" said Harcourt with victory in his voice.

"What? Are you sure?" asked the Peacemaker incredulously.

"I am looking at it.

"And the quill? Do you have the quill?"

220

"No, but there is a drawing of one on the parchment."

"Yes, they must have put it there. Good, good. We must check now that it accepts our ownership."

"What? You told me that it would listen to the person who took it directly from the previous owner."

"Yes, but it is not as easy as you think. So wait for me to get there. Don't try anything before. And the girls? What did you do with them?"

"Well… nothing," hesitated Maxime.

"What do you mean nothing? You didn't let them leave, did you?"

"No, I didn't, but I don't have them either."

"How is that possible?" asked the Peacemaker with barely restrained anger in his voice.

"I wanted them to find the Silver one for me. They had a theory that it was hidden somewhere around the fountain at Vaux de Cernay. But as they sat down on a bench near the water source, they vanished."

"How? They fell in a well?"

"Not exactly. They just disappeared. I hoped you could explain to me what happened. I didn't want to get caught…"

"By whom?"

"The police officer who arrested me at the Louvre, he arrived and I had to take him down."

"You killed that young officer?" asked the Peacemaker, hiding his rage beneath a veneer of calm.

"He tried to stop me. But there's nothing to link me with the murder. I left Gloria and one of the boys at the scene of the crime. They will be the first suspects."

"And the murder weapon?"

"They'll just assume it was thrown in the lake."

"So let's resume… you killed a police officer, you lost the girls and the Silver One and you left two witnesses on the crime scene! Did I miss something?"

"But I have the Golden One," added Harcourt in his defence.

"That is if it works. We'll see that in a couple of hours when I arrive. Prepare my rooms," said the Peacemaker abruptly and hung up the phone.

Chapter Sixty-Six

AT LEAST SOMEBODY IS HAPPY

Béa hadn't heard from Gloria and the girls for a while. She knew that she couldn't hope to have the same relationship with her as at the beginning. But she started to worry, so she decided to pay them a visit. But on the way to their apartment she felt weak and had to sit down on a bench. She got nauseous. She decided to follow her instincts and crazy though it seemed, she headed for the nearest drugstore and bought herself a pregnancy test.

Gilles was always on the road because of his job. But two days ago he got home and told her that his job didn't require so much traveling anymore.

She thought at the time that it was a little weird but she was too happy to ask any questions. She had felt so lonely the last two months that when she found herself with her husband, she forgot about everything else.

She went into a nearby restaurant and asked to use the bathroom. She took the pregnancy test and couldn't believe her eyes. They had tried for so many years, and she was used to the disappointment of a negative result. But nothing prepared her for a positive one. When she saw the two pink lines she couldn't believe her eyes. She went outside, took a deep breath, put her hand in her bag and checked the result once more in the sunlight. Just to make sure, she decided to go to another drugstore to buy a second one, then go to see Gloria to tell her the good news. She wanted to share this with Gilles but he wasn't answering his phone while he was working so she had to wait for a few hours.

When she arrived at Gloria's door and saw that nobody was home, she knew something was wrong. She tried calling her, but no answer. She used her key and let herself in. There were a few clothes on the girls' beds, their small suitcases were missing so she assumed that they had left on a short journey. But that didn't mean that she was reassured. She tried to call

Gloria again. Then she found her laptop. She tried to guess her password. Like a lot of people who are are not very good with computers, Gloria had put a very predictable password. The first thing she checked was the mail list. There was one mail with a reservation confirmation at the Vaux de Cernay for three nights. So at least now she knew where they were. She decided to try to get in touch with Gloria a couple of times and if she didn't answer, she would go and look for them.

An hour later she was in her car and stuck in a traffic jam on her way out of Paris. She sensed that the girls were in danger. She tried to call Harcourt, but he was not answering either. It was not a good sign.

Two long hours later, she drove through the impressive gates and onto the stone paved forecourt of the abbey. And then in the distance she saw Gloria and either Marc or Victor, she couldn't tell them apart at that distance. She left her car and ran to see what was going on. She wondered where the other three were. When she got closer, she realised something very bad had happened. She drew back and listened to their conversation.

"They disappeared… simply disappeared. In front of my eyes."

"It had to be the Silver One," said Marc who didn't know whose disappearance worried him most, his brother or the love of his life.

"How could that be? We haven't even found it yet. And now the only thing that could have helped us find them is in the hands of a murderer."

"Not really," said Marc and took out a little notebook with a small pencil.

"What do you mean?" asked Gloria with a spark of hope in her eyes.

"This morning Alia had an idea, but she didn't have time to tell you about it," said Marc. "She wrote something on the parchment. She asked for a transfer of power to this little notebook. In case the parchment was stolen or lost, all I have to do is write down the password that she chose and a part of the parchment's magic will be transferred to this."

"Why only a part of it?" asked Gloria.

"Because she thought of the situation that we have just witnessed, and she thought to leave a little something to our enemies to get them off our back for a while. She was afraid that Harcourt might try the powers of the parchment right here. And what do you think he would have done, if he'd seen that the parchment wasn't working? That way they will never know that its power is not complete. We were lucky that he left like that."

"He left like that because your brother and my granddaughters went missing. I wouldn't consider myself lucky."

At this moment Béa decided to announce her presence.

"Béa, what on earth are you doing here?" asked Gloria surprised.

"I came to see if everything was all right. I was worried. What happened? Where are the others?"

"We were on the verge of finding the diary when Harcourt arrived and he forced Alia, Deanna and Victor to search for the parchment and then they disappeared."

"Disappeared? How?"

"Just like that! They didn't even have time to scream. But it's good that you are here, because I want to try to do the same thing and see if I disappear. If I do, please take care of Marc and take him home to his parents and let him tell them the story he wants. Ok, Marc? I'll bring your brother back, and the girls!" said Gloria trying to sound confident.

"I can't let you do it, I should be the one to go!" said Marc taking a step forward.

"Don't be silly, I'll take the notebook and the pencil and I'll go and look for them. Béa, please take him home," said Gloria and sat down on the stone bench waiting to disappear. She even wrote in the notebook 'Bring the girls and Victor here!', but nothing happened. Then, she tried 'Take me to the girls!', but nothing happened. She assumed that the power left on the notebook was not enough for such a difficult task.

"Let me try, maybe it doesn't work for you," said Marc sitting down on the bench. He wrote the same things, but he got the same result.

Disappointed, they both stood up and started to look for something that might indicate a secret entry to a tunnel, or a hole or something. But all they found were old stones, and a lot of water.

"Do you know that this is the fountain of fertility?" said Gloria to Béa. "You should try it too. Apparently, it worked for the Queen of France. Eleven children! Can you imagine?"

"I don't need it anymore," said Béa, remembering her amazing news.

"What do you mean?" asked Gloria raising her eyes from the ground to look at Béa, whose face was now glowing.

"I'm pregnant!" announced Béa, smiling.

"Congratulations! How come? I thought you couldn't have children," said Gloria starting to remember what the girls had asked the parchment, before leaving. She didn't want to tell anything to Béa.

"I don't know, but I don't care. All I care is that I'm going to have a baby. So, let's continue our search."

"Ok. But I am very happy for you. Now you need to take care of yourself."

"I will, I will. Where shall we look next?"

"I've run out of ideas," said Marc. "Maybe we should go and ask the Ink Master what he thinks?"

"You're right. I don't think there is anything else to do. But I can't abandon this place. What if they come back? They'll return here. You should get to Paris, and talk to the Ink master," said Gloria.

"I understand. You don't want to leave, in case they come back," said Marc. "All right, I'll go to Paris, but we'll keep in touch. Promise me you'll call me if they come back!"

"Of course. Béa, call me as soon as you get him home."

Béa and Marc got into the car. Gloria returned to her search so she didn't see the tears in Marc's eyes. He tried to control himself but the day had been too hard for him. To be threatened with a gun by a psychopath, to see his brother and the girl that he loved disappear without explanation was too much for him. So he let go of his emotions in the car, knowing that Béa would understand. She was pretty shaken up herself. Marc told her the entire story. Then he realised that he couldn't go home. There was no lie that could cover the truth. And their parents would never accept the reality. They would go to the police to seek for help, but the police would be useless. The only one that could help him there would be Bruneau, but he didn't want his help. And he was still mad at him for leaving them like that. He knew that he had done it to follow Harcourt. But it was not Harcourt's fault either, he seemed as surprised as them. So he decided to go to Gloria's place. Their parents wouldn't expect them for another two days, so they wouldn't worry.

That gave him some time to figure things out. Maybe in the meantime his brother would appear out of nowhere. He was still hoping in the magic of the parchment. He was holding the little notebook close to his heart, ready to use it if he had an idea. He wasn't even sure that it worked. Alia had the good idea to split its power, but they hadn't thought to try it. Then, it hit him!

Chapter Sixty-Seven

BACK TO BRUNEAU

Bruneau drove hot on the tail of Harcourt. He was angry with himself for allowing Maxime to do all that he did. He was now sure that Harcourt was a wizard and he had made those poor teenagers disappear. Even though he had been flat out on the ground, he had seen everything that happened. Harcourt was sure he had killed him so he didn't give him a second look. Luckily he had his bulletproof vest. He realised that he left so suddenly that the boy and the grandmother might think he was crazy. But he had just one chance to find out where Harcourt was heading. So he tried to clear his head and followed Maxime.

The road was winding so it was easy to follow and not be seen. And Harcourt was a little shaken by what he had done and seen. They both went out of the Rambouillet forest and arrived on the road that led to Paris. But he didn't enter Paris. He went on until he arrived at a small village with a lot of beautiful houses near the Seine. Bruneau was forced to stop as Harcourt entered through an imposing iron gate. He got out of the car and hid himself behind a bush to see how far the house was.

It was not a house but one of the small castles that make the French countryside so attractive. Often they are private property, held by a middle class family who inherited it from a wealthy relative. It seems a nice gift at the beginning but the owner gets buried in debts in no time. So the solution is to sell it or change it into a "chambre d'hôte" that helps pay the bills. That is how Harcourt found this small castle almost in ruins. With the Peacemaker's money, he restored it and every time he came to visit him, Maxime would prepare the three rooms he occupied.

Harcourt was never happy when his protector was there. He couldn't even sleep in the same house. There was something evil about him. He couldn't say what, but he felt it. At the beginning, when he met him he misinterpreted this feeling. He saw him as fabulously rich when he needed money. He was so persuasive when he wanted power. But now Maxime was simply afraid of him. He knew that the Peacemaker needed him, but for how long? Now that he had the Golden One, maybe he was no longer useful. So he was terrified by the imminent arrival of his master. He went inside quickly, not noticing the small car that had stopped outside the castle's gates.

Bruneau watched him go inside and that was all. He went back to the car, trying to think of his next move. He was tired, wet from lying on the ground and his chest was hurting from the shot. He had never tried the bulletproof vest before. It might have saved his life, but it hurt like hell, almost like a real wound. It was the first time that he allowed himself to think about his own person. But the moment was over, when he saw another car passing through the gates. This time it was a big black car with tinted windows. He decided to stick around and see what was going on. He wondered if there was any security. He took his chances and climbed over the high stone wall, surrounding the castle grounds. He saw a small house, which must house members of staff. There was nobody there so he moved on to the big building, where he overheard voices.

There were two men, obviously from the last car and another voice that he recognised as Harcourt's. A few seconds later they went inside and the man who had to be the chauffeur, took himself off to the little house. And then, silence. The castle had very large windows with no curtains. He had to stay close to the walls. It was a sunny day so the two men went out onto the terrace, which had a view of the river. There Bruneau could hear every word.

Harcourt was talking to a man who obviously terrified him. He was older than Maxime. He had long, grey hair in a ponytail. He wore very expensive clothes that seemed weird on him, as if he didn't know how to move in them. He touched nothing, waiting for Harcourt to serve him.

"Give it to me!" said the older man impatiently.

"Ok, but don't you need the ink to try it?" said Harcourt.

"I'll deal with the Ink Master tomorrow. For now, your blood should do it."

"My blood?" said Harcourt, alarmed. "Why do you need my blood?"

"Because you're the one who received the parchment. Don't tell me that you're afraid of a small sacrifice. Don't worry, you will survive."

"You know that I would do anything for you. I think I have already proved myself."

"Then stop asking questions and give me a few drops from your hand."

Harcourt took a knife from the table and made a cut on his palm. The blood dripped onto the parchment and the three men saw the piece of paper change colour. Then Harcourt touched the little quill that was drawn on the parchment and the quill seemed to come to life in Maxime's hand.

"Amazing!" said Harcourt not believing his eyes.

"Exactly as I remembered," said the Peacemaker.

"You've seen this before?"

"A very long time ago, when I was younger."

"How did you lose it? Did you give it to somebody else?"

"No, I never owned the Golden One! I once saw the Silver One, but you have to have noble blood in your veins. And I don't. That's why I asked you to help me. Now let's see what it has to tell us."

"Do you think it has a message for us?" asked Harcourt.

"It always has a message from the previous owner. Let's see."

"But Alia was not expecting to give it to me," said Harcourt. "So I don't think she would have prepared a message for us."

"Just read."

" *I see that you succeeded in stealing it from us. I know that you hate us very much, but I hope you don't mind that the last thing I asked the parchment was not to let you do any harm… to anyone. So if you find it a little less compliant than you would like it to be, don't be mad at it. Enjoy it while you can, because if you haven't killed us already be sure that we shall meet again.'"*

"They are feisty, those girls. It is quite a pity that you destroyed them," said the old man.

"I didn't, I told you, I don't know what happened to them. I was hoping you could explain it to me," answered Harcourt still surprised by the message. It worried him that the girls had anticipated his actions.

"It has to be connected to the Silver One. But I know that it will be easier to look for it now that we have the Golden One."

"You still want to own them both? Isn't this one enough?" asked Harcourt, tired of chasing these parchments. He had hoped that now that they had the Golden One, he would be able to rest a little and enjoy its power. He had already seen himself on a beach in the Dominican Republic with a beautiful girl next to him, serving him a fresh cocktail. Who would want more?

"Of course I do. He who owns them both becomes the master of the world."

"But I don't want to be the master of the world. I only want to be the master of my life," said Harcourt.

"You think too small. But once you taste power, you become addicted."

"You sound as though you have already tasted absolute power."

"Kind of… but you wouldn't understand."

"Try me!"

"Another time. For now, let's try to see how the girls have crippled our parchment."

"Ok, what shall we do?"

Bruneau didn't want to listen any longer. He was afraid that someone might see him, spying on the two men. He left a few minutes later, while they were trying the parchment. He was finally beginning to understand, what all this was about. He felt a little dizzy, like the teenagers when they learned about the magic of the parchment. He drove for about an hour and half to get back home. He needed to take a shower and sleep for a couple of hours. He was happy that at least he found out what was happening. Of course he didn't truly believe in the magical part of the story. How could he? He was a reasonable man with reasonable beliefs, not even religious. He went to church only when it was necessary for an investigation. He was not ready to start a new religion around an old parchment. But he saw that there were people who believed in it so much that they were willing to kill for it. Just like a religion. And to think that there was a second one out there… and those nice girls that disappeared looking for it. Everything seemed unbelievable.

He took a shower, went to bed and for a few hours it was like he was in a coma. Much later that evening, he heard a loud knocking at the door. It sounded urgent. He wondered who could be looking for him. When he opened the door, Marc pushed past him into the room.

"I have been trying to reach you for an hour. Why don't you answer?" asked Marc abruptly.

"I've been sleeping. What do you want? Do you have any news about your brother and your friends?"

"No! But I have an idea."

"And what do you need me for?"

"You have to help me!"

"How?"

"It's very dangerous."

"Do I look scared?"

"I need you to help me steal the Golden One from Harcourt."

––––––––––

About the Author

B.A. Knight was born in Romania, but shortly after finishing her studies in Medicine she moves near Paris where she can pursue her passion for French history, filled with stories about brave and romantic knights.

She spends all her spare time with her husband and two daughters who already share her passion. During one of the visits at the Vaux de Cernay Abbey, she has the idea of a magical parchment which can make all wishes come true.

And so The Secret of the Twin Parchments series is born...deeply marked by the sign of Gemini. It is a series of four volumes which shows the exciting adventure of four teenagers confronted with the moral dilemma of what to do with absolute power, while fighting against an evil enemy and the difficulties of adolescence.

B.A. Knight loves to write about magic, hidden treasures, worlds where courage and imagination are not yet obsolete.